The Widows of Westram

Widowed by war...tempted by new flirtations!

Lady Carrie and her sisters-in-law, Lady Petra and Lady Marguerite, each tragically widowed on the same day by the same battle in Portugal, have had time to come to terms with their circumstances.

Now these three beguiling widows aim to seize the day and build their own destinies—in life, and in the realm of romantic liaisons...!

Find out what happens in Carrie's story:

A Lord for the Wallflower Widow

And in Petra's story:

An Earl for the Shy Widow

Look out for Marguerite's story coming soon!

Author Note

I hope you enjoy this second book in The Widows of Westram miniseries. I am hard at work on number three. In this one, I had fun bringing the characters of the village to life and I hope you enjoy them, too. Bonfire Night, or Guy Fawkes Night, was always a favorite celebration for me as a child. My family had a bonfire in the garden and we let off fireworks and ate potatoes in their jackets cooked in the ashes. Writing that scene was a trip down memory lane and I hope it brings back memories for you, too. I love to hear from readers, so if you would like to get in touch, you can reach me through my website, annlethbridge.com.

ANN LETHBRIDGE

*An Earl for the
Shy Widow*

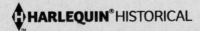

**Recycling programs
for this product may
not exist in your area.**

ISBN-13: 978-1-335-63518-1

An Earl for the Shy Widow

Copyright © 2019 by Michéle Ann Young

Printed in U.S.A.

In her youth, award-winning author **Ann Lethbridge** reimagined the Regency romances she read—and now she loves writing her own. Now living in Canada, Ann visits Britain every year, where family members understand—or so they say—her need to poke around every antiquity within a hundred miles. Learn more about Ann or contact her at annlethbridge.com. She loves hearing from readers.

Books by Ann Lethbridge

Harlequin Historical

It Happened One Christmas
"Wallflower, Widow...Wife!"
Secrets of the Marriage Bed
Rescued by the Earl's Vows

The Widows of Westram

A Lord for the Wallflower Widow
An Earl for the Shy Widow

The Society of Wicked Gentlemen

An Innocent Maid for the Duke

Linked by Character

Haunted by the Earl's Touch
Captured Countess
The Duke's Daring Debutante

Visit the Author Profile page
at Harlequin.com for more titles.

This book is dedicated to you, my good friend and teacher Sandra Atri. Thank you for your patience and understanding and for making me want to go to the gym instead of dragging my feet. It has been a great year and I am looking forward to the next one.

Chapter One

September 1813

Autumn sunlight flooded into the tiny drawing room at Westram Cottage. Lady Petra strode to the window. Beneath a blue sky, a slight breeze stirred the leaves of a nearby oak tree and nodded the heads of the red roses along the path to the front door. A perfect afternoon for a ride, *if* one had a horse.

She sighed and wandered back to her chair. She picked up the embroidery she'd been working on a few moments before. A handkerchief for her brother Red, the Earl of Westram. So boring. She cast it aside and got up to straighten the portrait of her mother on the opposite wall.

'Petra,' her older sister, Lady Marguerite Saxby, said, 'please stop pacing. You are making me dizzy.'

Remorseful, Petra spun around. 'I am sorry. I did not mean to disturb you.'

Auburn haired and green eyed, Marguerite was seated at the table going through her correspondence. As usual, her luxuriant tresses were pinned back severely beneath her widow's cap. Although she returned Petra's smile, there was sadness in her eyes. Marguerite hadn't looked anything but sad since she was widowed.

Did Petra have that same look? She strode to the glass over the mantel and peered at her reflection. Unlike her older siblings, she took after her mother with blonde hair and blue eyes. Did she also look sad?

She closed her eyes against her reflection, unwilling to admit to sadness. Yet perhaps she could acknowledge regret. After all, it was partly her fault that she and Harry had had such a blazing row.

She had been so happy for the first few months of her marriage. It had come as a painful shock to realise that Harry, already bored with his brand-new wife, was seeking his entertainments elsewhere. If she'd been a proper *ton*nish wife and simply ignored his infidelities, brushed it off as something every fashionable husband did, things would have turned out very differently. But it had hurt so much, she could not remain silent. And the more she complained, the worse he behaved until, during their last argument, she'd accused him of not loving her any more. He'd shouted back that he had *never* loved her and had only married her because his father insisted on it.

He'd said she was a stupid little girl who had ruined his life.

The pain had left her speechless.

The next thing she knew he had stormed off to fight the French. Worse yet was him taking her brother and her brother-in-law with him. Not only had Harry broken her heart, but her stupid naivety had cost her sisters their husbands.

She turned away from the glass.

'Do you not have mending to do?' Marguerite asked.
'All done.'

'What about the garden? Doesn't it need attention?'

Petra shook her head. 'Every time I pick up a shovel or pull a weed, Jeb leaps in to take over. Red seems to have given him very definite ideas about what a lady should or should not do. Honestly, I miss making hats.'

'Make one for yourself,' Marguerite suggested.

'It is not the same. Besides, I have more hats than I need. I feel so useless.' Earning an income from their fledgling millinery business had been thrilling, until their brother Red had put a stop to it. He had been horrified to discover his sisters were engaging in trade.

They still received some income from the hats Marguerite designed, but the manufacturing had been handed over to the new owner when they sold the business. Ladies of quality did not enter into the world of commerce.

Marguerite scanned the next letter in her pile. 'Carrie sends her love and says the dog Avery bought her will have a litter of puppies at the end of November, and would we like one?'

'How adorable. Tell her yes.'

Marguerite nodded. 'It would be good for you to have company on your walks. A dog would be just the thing.'

Petra joined her at the table to read over her shoulder. 'She does not say what sort of breed they are? Hopefully, not too large.'

'I will ask her when I reply. You are right. We do not want anything too big.' She set the letter aside and picked up the next one.

Petra wandered over to the sofa and glanced down

at her fingers, rubbing the calluses she'd earned from their millinery efforts. They were already disappearing.

A great many things had changed in the past few months. Their widowed sister-in-law, Carrie, was married, and happily so, while Petra and Marguerite continued to go against their brother's wishes and maintain their independence. Neither of them wanted to marry again. Once was enough for Petra, certainly. In her experience, men promised you the moon to get what they wanted, then did exactly as they pleased. She had been little more than a child with stars in her eyes when she married Harry. How hurt she had been to discover he'd only married her because his father had wanted the connection to nobility. She certainly wasn't going to make that sort of mistake again.

Marguerite gasped, 'The Thrumbys have sold the business.'

'What?' Petra hurried to look over Marguerite's shoulder.

'Avery included a note with Carrie's letter. Here, read it for yourself.'

Petra scanned the note written in a firm male hand. The Thrumbys had received an offer for the business from a Bond Street competitor and had agreed to sell. The new owner created her own hat designs, therefore Marguerite's were no longer needed.

'At least they will continue to employ the ladies in the village to make up the hats,' Marguerite said, her voice full of resignation. 'The quality of their work is exceptional.' She gave Petra a wan smile. 'All due to you, dearest. You taught them well.'

'Dash it all. That is so unfair. We needed that income.' She bit her lip at the pained look on Marguerite's face. 'Now what will we do? Ask Red for help, I suppose.'

Marguerite shook her head. 'No. We will think of something. In the meantime, we will be frugal.'

They were already careful with every penny. 'I wish I could help more.'

Marguerite pursed her lips. 'We will have to cut back on meat... It is so expensive.'

'Well, Red better not hear about that, or it will be all the excuse he needs to put us back on the marriage mart.'

Marguerite paled. 'He is sure to find out eventually. I have to think of some other way to augment our income. Sometimes publishers need illustrators for their books. I will write to them and send some examples of my drawings. Perhaps I can use a nom de plume.'

Petra nodded. 'Good idea.' A recollection of something she'd seen on her way to the village popped into her mind. 'Why don't I see if I can pick some blackberries for jam? We have lots of sugar in the pantry.'

Marguerite gave her a grateful smile. 'Excellent idea. A good supply of preserves will help us through the winter.'

It wouldn't be enough, though. But Petra had an idea about that, too. The countryside was full of free food if one knew where to look. Blackberries were just the start.

Not too many minutes later, Petra had equipped herself with an old straw hat, a large wicker basket and covered her oldest spring muslin with an apron that had seen better days.

Outside, a light breeze cooled the warmth of the sun and she strolled along swinging her basket until she arrived at a blackberry bush hanging over the lane. The last time she noticed it, the brambles had been covered in little white flowers. Now the prickly canes were weighed down with gleaming clusters of black fruit.

Unfortunately, they were on the other side of a ditch and hanging over the top of a dense hedge far too high for her to reach.

Bother. They hadn't looked so high when she was travelling in the trap.

The other side of the bush grew in a field belonging to the Longhurst estate. On that side, the berries were temptingly easy to reach even for a short person such as she. A wooden stile a few feet from where she was standing offered perfect access to the field and the blackberries.

Besides, who would care? No one had lived at Longhurst since she and her sisters had arrived at Westram more than a year ago. According to the locals, the new Earl was away fighting on the Peninsula and cared not a bean for the estate. In consequence, there was no one to care if she trespassed. Besides, it wasn't as if he had planted the brambles. They were part of nature's bounty.

After a quick glance up and down the road, she hiked up the skirts of her old blue gown and climbed over.

Wary of fierce thorns bent on ripping her clothes to shreds, she pushed into the bush using her basket as a shield. Soon it was full of shiny blackberries and becoming quite heavy. A trickle of sweat ran into her eye and she wiped it away on the corner of her apron.

She picked a berry and popped it into her mouth.

Mmm...delicious. And exactly right for jam. She tasted another just to be sure.

The jingle of a bridle and the sound of a horse's heavy breathing had her whipping around.

A tall fair-haired man with an amused expression on his handsome face gazed down at her from the back of a huge brown horse. He leaned forward and let his glance travel down her length. It lingered at her feet.

She glanced down. Heat rushed to her face at the sight of her stockings bared to her garter at the knee because her skirts had tangled with the thorns when she turned. She pulled them free.

When she looked up again, his light blue eyes were twinkling and he wore a charmingly boyish smile. The sort of smile a man knew would cause the nearest female to forgive him.

Her stomach fluttered wildly. She tried to ignore it. Harry had worn the same sort of smile when he sought her forgiveness each time that he had strayed. As an unmarried girl, she had adored that smile. As a wife, she had come to dread it. She'd learned it meant he'd made yet another conquest and was trying to jolly her along as if it meant nothing.

No, a gentleman's smiles and promises, no matter how charming or sincere they seemed, were definitely not to be trusted. She schooled her expression into cool politeness and dipped a curtsy. 'Good afternoon, sir.'

'Good day to you, wench.' His voice was deep and rich and smooth. 'May I ask what you are about?'

Wench? Pinpricks shot across her shoulders. 'What does it look like I am doing? I am picking blackberries.' Dash it. She should not have responded so sharply.

'*My* blackberries,' he said with another smile.

Oh. She winced. 'Then you must be Lord Long-hurst.'

'Indeed.' He inclined his head slightly.

It seemed the wanderer had at last returned. 'Well, sir, this fruit may grow on your property, but since they grew without the aid of any man or woman, it might be argued that they have no particular owner.'

He frowned. 'Are you one of my tenants?'

He thought she was a farm labourer's wife. Dash it all—was she supposed to wear her best gown to go blackberry picking? For a moment she was tempted to play along, but she did not know this man or his character. At first glance, he looked handsome and charming, but she knew better than to judge anyone by appearances. Or at least, she did now. Besides, it would be embarrassing when he later caught her out in her lie. 'No, sir, I am not a tenant of yours. I am Lady Petra Davenport. I reside at Westram Cottage. I am pleased to make your acquaintance, Lord Longhurst.' She bobbed a small curtsy. As a formal introduction, it would have to do.

He removed his hat and gave her another winsome smile. 'So, we are neighbours. Please purloin as many blackberries as you desire.'

Had she not already explained they were not exactly his to offer? She smiled back sweetly. 'As you can see, I have already helped myself to as many as I need.' She frowned. 'Besides, rather than galloping around the countryside and fussing about a few dozen black-berries, I should think you would rather spend your time setting your estate in order.' She gestured to the acres of hay spread out before her.

The amusement in his face faded. Oh, dear. Why

had she let her tongue run away with her when she knew she was in the wrong? If she had known he had finally taken up residence, she really would never have climbed his fence. She opened her mouth to apologise, but he forestalled her with a pleasant smile and a bow.

'As you say, ma'am. I do indeed have a great deal of work requiring my attention. I wish you good day.'

He signalled to his horse to move on and the animal obediently took a short run at the stile. Rider and beast cleared the obstruction in magnificent form. The sound of hoof beats faded into the distance.

A bruising rider herself, she could not help but admire his skill. And he looked so good on a horse. Dashing. Oh, no. She was not going to think of him that way. She shook herself free of such musings. He was simply a new neighbour with whom she had made an acquaintance.

She stomped out of the bushes and heard the sound of tearing. Blast, she'd caught her apron and now she would have to mend it. Well, it would be something to do when she had finished making the jam.

Hopefully she would be busy enough that it would take her mind off his face and that lovely smile. Smiles like that caused nothing but trouble and heartache, yet it seemed that she had still not learned her lesson.

Good Lord, he might even be married. A man didn't stop being charming to ladies, just because he was wed. If anyone knew that, she should.

He'd called her a wench! Mortified heat scalded the back of Ethan's neck. How was he supposed to recognise her as a lady? Not a ribbon or a ruffle to be seen. Tangled up in a blackberry bush, her legs displayed for all to see and with deep red juice staining her full lips, she'd looked like a roundheeled lass ready for a spree.

He was lucky he hadn't given in to the urge to kiss those luscious, ripe lips. Not something he was in the habit of doing or even thinking as a general rule, but in her case, for some reason he could not quite understand, he had been very tempted indeed. Fortunately, the lady's tart remarks had reminded him that no matter how attractively dishevelled a woman might be, he was an officer, a gentleman and an earl with duties and responsibilities to King, country and his family name.

But there really had been something deliciously pretty and alluring about her... He winced. He had thoroughly deserved the sharp edge of her tongue when she caught him ogling the slender legs bared to his gaze. Right now, he did not need the added complication of any sort of lass, common or noble, in his life.

Honestly, though, what sort of lady went about the countryside without even a maid?

Dash it, kissing her wouldn't have crossed his mind under normal circumstances. His army duties had kept him too busy to worry about the ladies, except for the occasional foray when he was on leave, until Sarah had begun to pay him particular attention. Her own husband had been killed, but she had remained on the Peninsula as companion to her sister, the wife of one of his fellow officers. Sarah had stirred up feelings he thought he'd long buried in response to a childhood fraught with drama. A sense that perhaps he did warrant affection from someone. His parents hadn't thought so. They had been far too involved in themselves to pay attention to their only child.

When Sarah had entered his life almost a year ago,

she'd been attentive and, well…loving, if he even understood the meaning of the word. There was no denying he'd been smitten. He should have known better than to believe a woman could actually care for him in the way he had thought Sarah did.

Fortunately for him, a brother officer had heard her talking to her sister about how life as the wife of an earl would suit her very well. How she liked the sound of being called Lady Longhurst and would enjoy the privileges a title brought, even if it did require marriage to him. His friend had teased him about how popular he was among the ladies now he was an earl.

Ethan had come to his senses with a jolt and only just in time, because if their relationship had gone much further, he would have been honour-bound to take Sarah to the altar. A lucky escape indeed.

Bitterness rose in his throat like gall. How had he not seen through Sarah's smiles to the truth beneath? It was the first time any woman had trapped him with her wiles and it would also be the last. But apparently, those few weeks of so-called affection had left him feeling that something serious was lacking in his life and made him vulnerable to the first pretty lady he came across now he was back in England.

Damn it! Didn't he have enough to keep him occupied, adjusting to his new position in life without the sort of distraction a pair of blackberry-stained lips brought? He hadn't even known he was the heir to the Earldom until he received a letter from a lawyer hired by some busybody third cousin twice removed who had searched down every line of the family tree, going back as far as his great-great-grandfather to search him out.

Apparently, it had taken some digging to discover

that his great-grandfather, the fifth son of the Earl, had been bribed to take his wife's name in order to inherit the wealth of an old Cornish mining family. With only daughters to their name, the Trethewys had thought they were getting a nobleman, but instead Great-Grandfather Trethewy had been a ne'er-do-well gambler who had lost most of the family fortune the moment he got his hands on it. As a result, both families had cut the connection. Certainly, if Ethan's father had known he was related to an earl, he would have used it to his advantage in some way.

Even after Ethan learned of the title, he had put off returning to England for as long as possible. The army was his life. All he had known since he was a youth. He hadn't mentioned the inheritance to anyone, but somehow the news must have reached Sarah's ears and she had decided to set her cap at him, and make him think she genuinely cared for him. Not once had she mentioned knowing about the title.

He'd been cut to the quick when he realised that was all she'd really cared about.

Not long after he uncovered her deceit, the same busybody third cousin, Lady Frances, had written to Wellington, asking why the General was keeping the last Longhurst Earl captive on the battlefield when he ought to be taking up his duties at home.

Wellington, damn his eyes, had insisted Ethan return to England and take up the reins of his estate. The moment Ethan had put things in order here, he intended to get back to what really mattered. War with the French.

As he galloped up the drive of Longhurst Park, a grand old house with a winding drive lined with trees, his mood darkened further. The previous Earl had left the estate in a wretched mess, as evidenced by a pile of unpaid bills his man of business had presented to Ethan with the expression of a man who saw disaster looming.

Paperwork. Ethan hated it, but he'd been battling his way through it every day since, determined to bring things into some sort of order.

At the stables, he handed Jack over to O'Cleary. The handsome black-haired Irishman narrowed his gaze on Ethan's face. 'What has you so hot under the collar?'

Ethan didn't get hot under the collar. He never unleashed his temper on anyone. He was a big man and, out of control, could do a lot of damage. It was why he had decided to become a soldier in the first place. He gave O'Cleary a look that ought to make him shrivel in his boots, but only made the fellow glare back.

Ethan didn't know when it had happened, but at some point O'Cleary had become more friend than servant. They were of a similar age and Ethan respected the man's skill with horses, but O'Cleary's perceptiveness and frank speaking had also earned his admiration and, yes, a sort of friendship.

Ethan sighed. 'I met a lady on the way back. I thought she was a dairymaid or some such stealing my blackberries.'

'Your blackberries, is it? Since when do you care about brambles?'

Since a lovely young lady with lips stained red had come to his attention. 'She was trespassing on my land.'

'Ah.' He gave Jack a pat.

'Ah, what?'

'Who is she, then?'

'Lady Petra Davenport. She lives in Westram.'

O'Cleary narrowed his eyes. 'Fancy her, do you?'

Ethan glared at him. Much as he might *fancy* Lady
Petra in passing—what man would not when she was so
excessively pretty?—he certainly had no more interest in
her than that. 'You will not speak of a lady in that manner.'

O'Cleary's black brows climbed into his hairline.
'It is protective of this lady, you are?'

As if. The lady needed no protection from him. 'A
gentleman protects all ladies.'

'Ah.'

Could O'Cleary be any more irritating? Possibly. If
given the chance. 'Are you going to let my horse stand
there all day? Or are you going to see to his needs?'

O'Cleary grinned, his blue eyes full of laughter, saluted and walked Jack off.

Ethan stomped into the house. The memory of a pair
of shapely legs had him smiling, too, until he tripped
over the end of one of several rolled-up rugs. Like the
rest of the house, the study was full of pieces of furniture, chairs upended on chairs, tables and consoles
stacked willy-nilly. There were even stacks of ancient
newspapers and journals on the floor, leaving little
room to walk. The last Earl had been a jackdaw, collecting anything and everything. It was ridiculous.

He groaned. He really hated the business of being
an earl. He took off his coat, rolled up his sleeves and
hefted the rug that had tripped him on to his shoulder
and headed for the barn.

To the devil with the paperwork, this was a task he
could get his teeth into. In a few hours he might actually be able to see the floor.

Sitting in the front pew in St Bartholomew's Church,
Ethan was aware of the many curious gazes landing

on him as the service wore on. As an officer, he was used to being watched by his men, but this was a different kind of observation. The gazes were not only assessing, they were hopeful. No doubt they were all hoping to meet him in the melee outside the church at the end of the service. He braced himself and polished up his most charming smile, despite that he'd prefer to go straight home.

It would not be neighbourly. And while he had no intention of staying any longer than necessary, in the army one learned to adapt to local customs.

Naturally, he'd received a call from the Vicar the day after he had arrived at Longhurst. The worthy fellow had made it very clear it was an earl's duty to set a good example for the villagers by attending church every Sunday. Naturally, Ethan agreed. It had been no different in the army. Officers were required to set a good example in all things.

The Vicar had beamed at his assent and further pronounced that, as Earl, he would, of course, want to subscribe to the front pew that had been a tradition in his family for many years. A not-unreasonable request. Unfortunately, Ethan discovered he not only had to pay this year's subscription but also that of the previous fifteen years, since his dear departed predecessor had refused to have anything to do with St Bartholomew's.

He really did despise the former Earl.

Of course, he'd paid up with as much good grace as he could muster. It was what one did, despite the fact that the payment ate a large chunk of his army pay, making another visit to his man of business in Sevenoaks mandatory. While he had absolutely no hope of discovering a nice little nest egg hidden among the Earl's papers, there were still a few tenants left on the estate and he needed to know what rents had been paid and what required collecting.

The congregation filed out and he followed. Right away, he noticed that women outnumbered the men. He frowned. Why would that be? Naturally, he also spotted one woman immediately, Lady Petra, in a particularly fetching bonnet and a fashionable gown and spencer clearly designed to bring out the blue in her eyes. Strangely, her tiny stature stood out as much as his large one. Or perhaps it was that his gaze had sought her out as one of the few people he recognised, even if theirs had been a rather unconventional meeting. He recalled the neat turn of her ankle and her dainty feet as much as he remembered her face. Would she acknowledge their acquaintance? Likely not, given her unfriendliness at their first meeting.

He waited his turn to speak to the Vicar, who greeted each person with a few brief words as they filed out into the sunshine. The man had the aesthetic look of a monk rather than a Church of England cleric. His sermon had been all fire and brimstone about the evils of drunkenness.

'Good sermon, Vicar,' Ethan said when it was his turn to receive a nod and a handshake.

'It is unfortunate that those who really need to hear the words of the Lord do not open their ears.' Reverend Beckridge smiled thinly. 'But never mind. I am glad to see you here today, my lord. Let me introduce you around.'

'I would particularly like to meet other landowners in these parts,' Ethan said.

Beckridge frowned. 'Unfortunately, the owner of the

largest property, Lord Compton, attends the church in Ightham. While his estate is in this parish, the church there is closer to his abode.' He sighed. 'I do not blame him, I suppose, but St Bartholomew's could use the support.'

'I am looking to hire some farm labourers. Perhaps there is a farmer or two among the congregation?'

'There are indeed. But you will find them also short of men. What with the war and the lure of the better-paying factories in the North... But first let me introduce you to the two widowed ladies, who recently came to Westram. Lady Petra and Lady Marguerite, Lord Westram's sisters. In the past year, they have made quite a stir with their industry.'

Lady Petra was a widow? At such a young age?

Ethan found himself inexorably guided to the small knot of women chattering on the path leading out to the road.

At the centre of the group, Lady Petra's bright smile lit her pretty face as if the sun had deigned to send down a ray of light especially for her, yet it became somewhat brittle as he approached, as if she was steeling herself for their inevitable meeting.

The Vicar introduced everyone, including his wife, a sharp-eyed, round-faced lady who eyed him with speculation in her gaze.

'Lord Longhurst and I are already acquainted,' Lady Petra said with a challenging glance. 'We met over a basket of blackberries.'

Instead of his usual easy conversational gambits—the weather, the news—he found his mind going completely blank while he stared at her luscious mouth. He forced himself to speak. 'We did indeed.' It sounded unfriendly.

Her smile dimmed a little.

Lady Marguerite, a much taller lady, with auburn hair and green eyes and a plain mode of dress, looked puzzled. 'You met over... Why, Petra, you didn't say you had met Lord Longhurst when you went blackberry picking.'

Lady Petra smiled sweetly, too sweetly, perhaps fearing he might reveal the awkwardness of their meeting. 'I must have forgotten.'

He winced. If she had wanted to forget, why had she mentioned it now? Women. There was no understanding them.

'You are welcome to pick my blackberries whenever you wish, Lady Petra.'

Lady Petra raised her eyebrows, reminding him that she did not in fact believe they were his to offer. 'How very kind of you, my lord.' She dipped a curtsy. 'If you will excuse us, Lord Longhurst, Vicar, we don't wish to be late for lunch.'

While her sister looked surprised, she trailed after Lady Petra and both ladies climbed into a waiting pony and trap. He watched them drive away, one blonde, petite and pretty and dressed in flounces and ribbons, the other an elegant redhead and plainly gowned. Both attractive in very different ways.

'Such a shame,' the Vicar's wife said. 'To be widowed at such a young age.'

'This war has taken a great many young men,' the Vicar said.

'I am sorry to hear it.' What else could one say?

'Such pretty ladies will not be single long,' Mrs Beckridge added, somewhat pointedly staring at Ethan.

He smiled pleasantly, ignoring the hint. Sarah had

been another widow left in penury by the death of her husband and looking for a replacement. She hadn't tangled herself up in a blackberry bush in order to meet him; she'd twisted her ankle when leaving the dance floor and stumbled into him.

He wasn't fool enough to be taken in twice by way of a pretty ankle. He would do his own choosing of a bride and Lady Petra seemed far too sharp-tongued to make a man a comfortable wife. Besides, when he married, as he would have to do, he'd choose someone solid and dependable who didn't need him to devote his whole attention to her needs and whims. Someone he could leave in charge of things here in England while he returned to his army career. His real life.

'You *really* think I should take Long Longhurst some of this jam?' Petra looked at the prettily covered pots she and Marguerite had filled a few days before.

'I most certainly do.' Marguerite frowned. 'They were his blackberries after all. It is only polite. Besides, it is not wise to risk upsetting our neighbour needlessly.'

Marguerite had not been happy upon learning the details of her meeting with Lord Longhurst.

Petra did not want to meet him again. While his smile seemed friendly enough, she had the peculiar sensation that it hid his true feelings. It seemed to set her at a distance rather than be truly welcoming. Not to mention that he was just too handsome for any lady's peace of mind. 'You really are making a mountain out of a molehill, Marguerite. They grow wild. He could not have said a word about it if I had picked them from the lane.'

Her sister's eyes widened, probably because Petra had spoken with heat. 'But you did not pick them in the lane. You trespassed on his land in order to gather them.'

Petra huffed out a breath. 'Very well, I'll take him a pot.'

'Two, I think.'

'Two? After we did all the work?'

Marguerite sighed. 'Do as you wish. You will anyway.'

Petra stilled, pained by the accusation. Her siblings often teased her about being the baby of the family and overindulged, but she did not think they truly meant it. 'What is that supposed to mean?'

Marguerite shook her head. 'It means nothing. I am sorry. I am feeling a little out of sorts.'

Petra gave her sister a closer look. Marguerite looked pale and tired. Instantly she regretted their argument. 'Is your head aching, dearest?'

Marguerite rubbed a fingertip against her temple and gave her a wan smile. 'I think there may be a storm brewing.'

Petra glanced out of the kitchen window to where Jeb was doggedly hoeing between the rows of cabbages. The sky was clear, all but a few wispy clouds, but Marguerite had always been prone to headaches before the arrival of a storm, so perhaps the weather was about to change. 'Go and lie down. I will bring you a cold compress.' She grinned. 'And after that I will take Lord Longhurst two pots of our lovely jam. I promise to charm him out of the boughs.'

'Ask him to come for afternoon tea.'

Not likely, when the man was so standoffish, though

it was probably her fault. She had been rather sharp with him. And a bit dismissive at church. So what if he was an attractive man? It meant nothing to her. She could at least be civil to him. Dash it all, she really ought to mend some fences if only to declare a truce. They did not have to like each other, but they ought to be able to manage a polite friendliness.

'Go on upstairs,' she said, shooing her sister out of the kitchen. 'I'll bring you a tisane before I go.'

Marguerite gave her a grateful smile. 'You are a dear.'

Relief filled her. She hated being at odds with Marguerite, particularly when she carried some of the blame for her sister's sorrow. If only she hadn't said those things to Harry and driven him away... Perhaps her family was right in saying she was too used to getting her own way. Well, she had got her own way as far as marrying the man she wanted, and look what a terrible mistake she had made. She would be very careful about what she wished for in future. She delivered Marguerite's tea and set off to walk to Longhurst Park, making sure to take her umbrella.

The crested wrought-iron gates to Longhurst Park were open, not in invitation so much as in careless abandonment, the weeds and vines having grown so high it would take a full day of chopping and pulling to free the gates from captivity and have them working again.

The curving drive, lined by lime trees, fared no better. The gravel sprouted tufts of grass and the lawn looked more like a hayfield. As she rounded the bend, though, she was enchanted by the sight of the house. Lovely old red brick gave the place a warm homely look. As she got closer, however, she was saddened to see that a few of the windows had been boarded up and that some of the tiles on the roof were missing.

What had Longhurst been thinking in letting the house go to rack and ruin these past two years? Perhaps he didn't care because he had estates elsewhere like her brother, who owned more than one property.

She glanced skyward and grimaced. It seemed Marguerite had been right. The clouds that had been fluffy and white when she left home were thicker and showing signs of grey.

When no one opened the front door at her approach, she pounded the knocker against the heavily carved wood and stepped back. This portico could certainly use a coat of paint.

The door swung back.

Petra blinked in surprise at the sight of a dark-haired, sullen-faced young man in his shirtsleeves and riding boots. He looked more like a groom than a footman.

'Good day,' she said briskly. 'Lady Petra Davenport to see Lord Longhurst.'

His eyebrows shot up. He opened the door wider. 'This way, ma'am.' The brogue of Ireland coloured his voice.

He ushered her into a gloomy hall with marble pillars and a grand staircase leading up to the first floor. Footmen's chairs lined the walls as if there ought to be a dozen men waiting to open the door. Tables and chests and cupboards were piled on top of each other in one of the corners. Very odd. The Earl must be moving things around.

Instead of asking her to wait while he enquired if his

master was home, the servant led her down a corridor and to a room she guessed would be an antechamber where visitors would wait.

Only—

'A Lady Petra Davenport to see you, my lord.'

Petra's jaw dropped. There at the desk sat Lord Longhurst, also in his shirtsleeves, his blonde hair tousled as if he had run his fingers through it more than once.

The servant left and closed the door behind him. His footsteps echoed on the floor outside and she could hear him whistling as he walked away. How very peculiar.

After a second's pause, Lord Longhurst shot to his feet, reaching for a jacket slung over the back of his chair. He shrugged into it. 'Lady Petra Davenport? Lady Petra?'

He quickly buttoned the coat. There was nothing he could do about the shirt open at the throat. She tried to keep her gaze focused on his face and not drift down to the strong column of his neck or the intriguing sight of crisply curled golden hair peeking seductively above the stark white linen.

'How may I be of service?' he asked.

Service? An image of a broad naked chest flickered across her mind. Good Lord, had her mind really jumped to those ways in which a man could service a woman? Was that why she missed Harry, not for himself, but for the delights of the marriage bed? Could she really be so wanton? Besides, she wasn't very good at bed sport, as Harry had called it, or he wouldn't have gone seeking his pleasures elsewhere. *Boring*, was what he'd called her. Too innocent, whatever that meant.

Sadness filled her. She should never have confronted him. Should never have expected fidelity from him. She knew better now.

She lifted her chin. 'I brought you some jam.'

He blinked as if her words made no sense. He looked gorgeous, almost vulnerable standing there with a puzzled look on his face and his long, strong fingers covered in ink. Then he smiled and a dimple appeared in a jaw already showing signs of fair stubble. Her heart clenched.

And no wonder. He had looked magnificent up on his horse the first time they met, and like a handsome soldier at church on Sunday, but here, now, he looked like every woman's dream of a man in need of a woman's care.

She could even imagine running her fingers through those wavy locks to bring them to some semblance of order. How would they feel? Silky or coarse? And would he let her help him tie the cravat he had discarded on the corner of the desk? Or better yet, let her help him remove his shirt to reveal the full glory of that wide expanse of chest so tantalisingly covered with billowing linen?

Mind blank, she inhaled a deep breath.

His gaze dropped to her bosom. The room warmed. The air crackled with something that made her skin tingle. For a second, her head seemed too light for her shoulders, as if she might float away.

Would he also find her boring? The thought brought her back to earth with a bump.

Longhurst's forehead furrowed as if he had finally figured out her words, but not their meaning. 'Jam?'

'From the blackberries I picked.' Goodness, her voice sounded so small and weak she scarcely recognised it. She straightened her shoulders. 'We made jam out of the fruit.'

She walked deeper into the room, aware of his gaze tracking her every movement as she skirted a couple of armchairs.

'My word, you have a lot of furniture,' she said in awed tones.

He grimaced. 'You would not believe the half of it. I've moved out most of what was in here. At least now you can actually see some of the floor. The house is stuffed full of furniture and knick-knacks. It seems my predecessor liked to collect things.'

No wonder the entrance hall had been so cluttered. She reached into her basket and, like a magician pulling rabbits from a hat, drew out three jam pots one by one and placed them on the desk. 'Blackberry and apple. The apples picked from *our* tree,' she said pointedly.

He stared at the pots as if he had never seen jam before. He swallowed. 'I see.'

Her heart beat a little faster. Too fast.

'As an apology for purloining your blackberries,' she added, completely unnecessarily, but it filled the silence.

His gaze rose to her face. 'There is no need…' He gestured at the jam.

Why could the man not just say thank you and leave it at that? 'If you do not eat jam, then please feel free to give it to your servant.'

His blue eyes widened and then he smiled. Her stomach did a somersault. 'I do beg your pardon, Lady Petra. Thank you for the gift.'

That smile would be the death of her when she ought

to know better than to be taken in. She dipped a curtsy. 'Then I will bid you good day.'

'No. Wait. I mean— Would you like—'

They gazed at one another in silence for a long second or two. She seemed to have trouble drawing in a breath. 'Would I like…?'

'May I offer you a cup of tea before you leave?' Longhurst finally said. 'I am sure O'Cleary is taking good care of your horses and groom for the nonce.'

'Oh, there are no horses or groom. I walked.'

Astonishment filled his expression. 'You walked from Westram. It must be more than two miles distant.'

'About that, I should think.'

He frowned.

Did he not approve of a lady going for a walk? 'I grew up in the country, my lord. I am quite used to using my legs to get about.'

His gaze shot down her length and back up to her face and she recalled how much he had seen of her legs the last time they met. Heat scalded her cheeks and his eyes filled with awareness. Bother, they were never going to get past their first meeting. Mortified, she prepared to turn away.

'But you will take some refreshment before you set out for home.'

It wasn't expressed as a request, but rather as an order and she felt her hackles rise, but then again, she *was* thirsty after her long walk. And she had promised Marguerite to charm him out of the boughs. 'A cup of tea would be most welcome, my lord. Thank you.'

Strangely, he looked relieved. 'Excellent.' He strode for the door and turned when he reached it. He gestured to a chair beside the desk. 'Please, Lady Petra, be seated. I shall not be more than a moment or two.'

And then he was gone.

More orders. The pile of papers on the desk looked highly intimidating and important. She took a turn about the room. It was indeed full of strange items, from ill-thrown pots to finely blown glass ornaments.

Having established that she was not going to instantly obey any man's order, she dusted off an armchair near the window with her handkerchief and perched on the edge of it.

Perhaps he was so dictatorial because he was a soldier used to commanding men on the battlefield. She sighed. She did not like to think about war and battlefields. She hated the whole thing. Poor Harry. Had she really driven him to take the King's shilling? She still couldn't believe she would never hear his laughter again and never be irritated by his devil-may-care ways. While she hadn't made the wisest choice in a husband, it didn't mean she didn't miss him. After all, she had known him most of her life. Her mistake had been not making sure he loved her as much as she loved him before they wed. To discover he saw it purely as a marriage of convenience had been devastating to say the least. He'd called her a silly romantic, as if it was some sort of flaw.

Well, she was a romantic and not ashamed of it either. She couldn't be happier for Carrie and Avery, who had clearly fallen head over heels in love.

Chapter Two

When Ethan found no sign of O'Cleary in the kitchen, he put the kettle on the hob. Damnation. He'd left his cravat in the study. He dashed upstairs and, well used to dressing in haste, soon had a new cravat tied neatly at his throat.

Returning to the kitchen, he found O'Cleary setting a tray with cups and saucers. 'Where the devil were you?'

'Putting the carriage to. I assumed you wouldn't send her back on Shanks's pony. Er…my lord.'

Mollified by O'Cleary's anticipation of his wishes, he grinned. 'Well done.'

'Hmm. Had you not better get back to your guest?' He ran a discerning eye over Ethan and pulled a comb from his pocket. 'Here. This might help.'

Ethan dragged the comb through his hair. 'Thanks.' He strode back to his study.

Lady Petra was gazing out of the window when he arrived. Despite the dust on her hems and the tendrils of hair escaping from their pins around her face, she looked good enough to eat.

Blast it. He had forgotten to ask O'Cleary to add biscuits to the tray. If indeed they had any. She would think him as even more of an ill-mannered brute than she must do already. Why on earth had he made such a stupid invitation?

'Tea will be along shortly,' he announced.

She jumped as if she had been so far away in her thoughts that she had not heard him enter despite the fact he had not been in the least bit quiet about it. Her blue eyes were filled with sadness.

He stiffened. Was it something he had said? Was she one of those females who needed treating with kid gloves? She seemed so self-sufficient, but perhaps it was all an act intended to keep a man on his toes.

Women did that. Pretended. His mother had always fussed over him, as if she loved him, but only when his father was about, to make him jealous of her attentions. Sarah had pretended she cared about him just to gain his title.

Lady Petra's eyes widened as her gaze took him in, clearly realising he had tidied himself up. What? Did she think he had no manners? If he had been a bit rough around the edges when he first joined the army at the age of fifteen, his fellow officers had soon put him straight.

She smiled and he felt like preening at her obvious approval, when he really didn't care if she approved of him or not. He smiled back, it was the obvious thing to do. When in doubt, smile. He'd learned that from his mother's interactions. She'd always stalked off if he'd shown the least sign of being unhappy. Any upset had always brought heaps of coals down upon his head. His mother had told him quite plainly that she had enough trouble with his father without him adding to it.

However, Lady Petra's smile faltered at the sight of his own. 'I really did not intend to put you to so much trouble.' Her voice was light, nicely modulated, music to the ears of a man mostly used to the coarse words of soldiers. Perhaps that was why he had found Sarah so alluring after twenty years of all-male company.

Twenty years. A long time. And yet he was still in his prime at thirty-five. And lucky to be alive, given how long he'd been fighting for his country. Something he'd sooner do than sit here entertaining a lady in his drawing room.

A lady far too attractive to be a soldier's wife. A man would surely worry about leaving such a lovely woman behind when he went off to war. He forced the wayward thought aside.

'No trouble at all, my lady. You'll find O'Cleary is a dab hand at brewing a pot of tea.'

'O'Cleary?'

'My batman. Well, no longer a batman, more a valet-cum-butler-cum-groom. He let you in.'

Her eyebrows rose. 'A man of all work, then.'

'A good description indeed.' He couldn't hire any proper staff until he knew exactly how the estate stood financially. The account books had been left to keep themselves during the last few years of his cousin's illness, as far as he could tell.

Her brow furrowed. 'I understand you inherited the estate more than two years ago?'

His mouth tightened. 'I did, but other, far more important matters engaged my attention.'

She looked shocked.

Could no one truly understand that he did not want this title? He was an army man through and through and here he was struggling with information about yields and labourers and bushels and baskets and… Bah! It was his duty and he would do it, but that didn't mean he had to like it. Well, he would get it licked into shape, provide it with a countess and an heir and get back to what really mattered in short order.

'The French. The war.'

She coloured. 'Yes, of course.' She did not, however, sound convinced. But then she might not, considering how she had lost her husband.

O'Cleary entered with the tea tray, picked his way around the clutter and set it down on the table in front of Lady Petra with a smile and a wink. 'The short-breads are a bit singed. But I cut off the worst of it.'

Ethan cringed at the sight of jagged edges and burnt crumbs. 'You will have to excuse us, Lady Petra. We are bachelors used to army tack. Take them away, O'Cleary.' O'Cleary was still not used to the new-fangled oven in the kitchen. He was more used to cooking over a campfire.

O'Cleary reached for the plate, but Lady Petra Davenport put out a hand to forestall him. 'Thank you, Mr O'Cleary, I am sure they are fine.'

The smile she gave O'Cleary and the grin he gave her back made Ethan want to grab his batman by the collar and heave him out of the door. He blinked at the odd urge. He didn't have a jealous bone in his body. Deliberately so. He'd learned early that it was a pointless emotion.

'That will be all, O'Cleary,' he said gruffly. 'I think Lady Petra can manage from here.'

O'Cleary walked out whistling. The idiot.

The lady poured out cups of tea and added milk. 'The village will be delighted that you have finally moved in.'

'I am glad *they* are pleased.' He picked up his cup and took a sip. Somehow, she'd got it exactly the right strength.

'You do not like the idea?'

'No.' He squeezed his eyes shut briefly. Why on earth was he telling her this? But now he had said it, he could hardly call a halt to the conversation. Even he knew that was the height of rudeness. 'I know nothing about farming or managing an estate. The army is my life.' He sighed. 'I am not cut out for this.' He made a gesture to encompass the house, the land and the whole of Kent.

He'd also been a fish out of water in his father's house, never knowing how to please the man who had sired him, never knowing whether his mother would react to her husband's rants by blaming Ethan for whatever it was Father had decided was wrong that time. Joining the army at fifteen had been a welcome relief from the mayhem in his home. Since then he'd seen himself as a confirmed bachelor. A free spirit.

Lady Petra offered him the plate of biscuits.

He munched on one absentmindedly until he hit a burnt bit. He grimaced, glad to see she had not taken one.

'A good bailiff should be able to help you,' she said. Was that a note of encouragement in her voice? Surely not. She was simply making conversation.

'Indeed. But how does one tell good from bad? Looking through my cousin's estate diary, I have the feeling the man he employed was a charlatan.' What was it about her that had him revealing his concerns? She would think him a terrible bore. It just wasn't done. Unless she was deliberately trying to lure him in with kindness as Sarah had done. He inspected her expression, but could detect no ulterior motive. But then he wouldn't, would he? Ladies were experts at hiding their real thoughts and feelings.

'Perhaps you could ask around among your fellow peers,' she said.

Fellow peers? Did he know any? There was the chap the Vicar had mentioned, Compton, who also served as the local magistrate living near the next village over. Perhaps he should ride over and introduce himself. Though what they would have in common, he could not imagine. 'Good thought.'

She looked surprised and pleased.

He frowned. Had she not expected him to acknowledge her idea as helpful?

She sipped at her tea. 'If I might offer another suggestion...'

He tensed. No doubt this was where he learned the real purpose for her visit. He did not relish making his lack of interest plain. 'Please do.'

'Well... If I were you, I would mow the field where we met as soon as possible. It is perfect for harvesting and if you cut it right away you may get another crop before the winter.'

Why hadn't he thought of that? Because while his horses ate hay, and he made sure they had enough, he'd never questioned how it arrived in the stable. It was not his concern when he had a war to fight. The commissary looked after those sorts of details. 'I will certainly look into it, thank you.'

She gave him an odd look and finished her tea. 'And now if you will excuse me, I really should be getting home before my sister wonders what has become of me.'

Ethan glanced out of the window. 'My carriage awaits you.' To his surprise, the old coach looked in a lot better shape than it had looked the last time he had inspected it and with Jack between the poles it looked almost lordly.

'Truly, my lord, I am quite happy walking.'

'Nevertheless, Mr O'Cleary will be pleased to drive you since Jack is in need of the exercise. I have not had time to hack him out today.'

'Very well. Since you make it impossible to refuse without seeming disobliging, I will avail myself of your kind offer, my lord.'

He blinked at the forthright speech. No beating around the bush or simpering for this lady. He liked it. He knew where he stood. Unless she was using it as a ploy? Well she would not find him easy to gull, so he would just take her words at face value until he discovered the truth.

And thank heaven she had accepted his offer of the carriage. If she had not, he would have had to walk her all the way home, using up a great deal of time which he really did not have. And yet... He glanced out of the window. A walk with a pretty widowed lady on his arm would be very pleasant indeed.

And just the sort of entanglement in which he would not allow himself to indulge.

He escorted her outside and helped her aboard.

Once he had shut the door he went forward to speak to O'Cleary seated on the box. 'No racing, not on the way there or on the way back.' He glanced up at the sky. The clouds didn't look particularly threatening, but one never knew for certain in England. 'Not even if it rains.'

O'Cleary grinned, touched his hat in acknowledgement of the jibe and set Jack in motion.

Lady Petra lifted her hand in farewell as the coach swept away.

Mow the hay. It was the first helpful suggestion anyone had given him and that it had come from such a pretty lady who looked as if she would be more at home in a London drawing room than in the wilds of Kent was quite a surprise.

Although she had not looked quite so ladylike when she'd been picking his blackberries. He squashed the image that popped into his mind.

Likely someone had encouraged her to make herself useful to a bachelor earl. After all, why would the sister of an earl march about the countryside delivering jars of jam if it wasn't to get his attention?

Two mornings after her visit to the Earl, Petra set out to collect mushrooms for the stewpot before the dew was off the grass. She had noticed a fairy ring of them, as they had called them as children, in the same hedgerow where she'd picked the blackberries. She certainly was not going with the expectation of meeting His Lordship, but if she did, she had her excuse ready. After all, while he hadn't specifically mentioned mushrooms, he had told her to purloin all the blackberries she wanted, so why would he object to her picking mushrooms, as long as she offered him some of her bounty?

A tiny tickle of something pleasant stirred low in her body at the thought of meeting Longhurst again. The same sensation she had felt when he was staring at her bare legs. Never before had the memory of a simple glance caused such feelings.

Nor even Harry had had that sort of visceral effect on her, which was what made it so very strange.

When they first came to Westram, she had suggested to her sisters that as widows they ought to be free to take lovers. It had been her anger at Harry's abandonment, both before and after he died, that had made her suggest such a wicked idea. An anger that had faded into regret over time. And she certainly hadn't actually expected to have an opportunity to put such an idea into practice out here in the depths of Kent. No, the last thing she wanted or needed was more hurt in her life.

Besides, this outing was not about her seeing Lord Longhurst again, it was about providing food for their table.

She climbed the stile into the field. At this time of year, the birds were quieter, though there was still the odd cheep as they darted about, feasting on blackberries and grass seeds. The crisp morning air seemed to predict autumn just around the corner. The dew caught the sun's rays and glinted as if there were diamonds scattered across the top of the grass. It would not remain long; a breeze was already ruffling the long stalks like wind upon water.

She found the mushroom ring she had spotted a few days before, and after carefully bruising one of the caps to ensure it turned pink and not yellow, she cut them off and gently placed them in her basket. The next mushroom she found was a giant puffball hiding in the stinging nettles at the foot of an elm tree. It was large enough to provide both her and Marguerite with an excellent breakfast. Careful to make sure the nettles did not touch her skin, she cut the stalk and soon it was also sitting in the bottom of her basket.

She continued up the rolling stretch of land, making her way to the brow of the low hill which ran through the centre of the field.

Because the grass was so long, most of her harvest grew against the hedge, where the vegetation thinned out. Mushroom picking was easier in woods or a pasture with short grass, but since she had promised Marguerite she would not go into the woods alone, she continued up the hill.

By the time she crested the rise, her basket was brimming with assorted mushrooms and it was time to turn back. She stretched her back and looked about. Two men with their shirts off were hacking at the grass at the far end of the field.

Apparently, Lord Longhurst had taken her advice.

She squinted against the sun's brightness. Oh, goodness. If she was not mistaken, one of those men was His Lordship himself and the other shorter, leaner figure, Mr O'Cleary.

She frowned. With only two of them working, and at the rate they were progressing, it would take ages to mow this field. After that, they would have to pile it into hayricks to dry. It would take days to finish. Why on earth had he not hired any help?

Unable to contain her curiosity, she continued

working her way along the hedgerow, picking one or two mushrooms and then glancing up to see if they had noticed her presence while pretending she had not noticed them. As she drew closer, she could see both men in all their glorious detail, though she really only had eyes for the taller blonde giant of a man.

Lord Longhurst's chest was broad and well muscled, like a statue of a Roman god, and his arms as he swung the scythe were the most enticing sight she had ever seen. Oh, heavens, the way the muscles in his back rippled with his movement made her insides tighten in a most shocking way. She fought the strong desire to run her hands over that back and down his spine and... She could not remember ever seeing a flesh-and-blood man who could serve as a model for a Greek god. Such a gorgeous specimen of the male of the human species.

She fanned her face. What on earth was the matter with her? She could not recall ever having such wayward thoughts before. Not even when Harry was alive and still treating her as if he loved her. With Harry, she realised, she'd been all girlish giggles and eager to do anything to get his attention. With this man, her reactions were far subtler in some ways and earthier in others she simply did not understand.

Good Lord. What would Longhurst think if he knew the direction of her mind? He'd likely be as shocked as she was.

The next glance revealed His Lordship pulling his shirt over his head. A sense of disappointment gave her another shock. No, no, she wasn't disappointed. She was pleased because he must have seen her. Yes, indeed he had because the moment he was decently covered he strode to meet her.

As he drew close she became aware of trickles of moisture working their way down from his hairline to his neck. Oh, and the way his shirt clung to his skin was positively delicious. No, no, she meant indecent.

She mentally shook her finger at this new wanton version of herself and composed her face into an expression of polite surprise. 'Good day, Lord Longhurst. A perfect day for working in the fields, is it not?'

He smiled and her heart gave an odd little clench. Oh, she was a fool for those boyish open smiles. She always had been. But she'd also learned those smiles also hid a good deal of boyish vice. Definitely not to be trusted.

'Yes,' he said. 'Although I have to admit, while the sun is a boon, I am grateful for the breeze.'

As was she, as a gentle waft of air carried his scent towards her, earthy sweat mingled with the fresh scent of soap. She inhaled deeply and caught him looking at her with an odd expression.

Surprised by her inability to control such reactions in herself, she swallowed and was startled to discover her mouth was quite dry. 'I have been mushroom picking,' she said, holding out her basket and sounding more frog-like than she would have preferred. She swallowed again. 'Half of these are yours.'

He looked startled and peered down at the fungus. 'Are you sure they are edible? I have heard there are many poisonous kinds.'

Did he think her an idiot? 'I have been picking mushrooms for almost as long as I could walk. You may trust I know what I am doing.'

She and Marguerite had gone on foraging expeditions with their cook, who had taken pity on their motherless state. She'd been a dear old stick and taught them lots about the bounty to be found in the country. She'd also taught them the rudiments of cooking, never expecting it would come in useful later in their lives.

Petra liked being outdoors. Even in those days Marguerite had preferred standing at her easel creating art to tramping around the countryside in all kinds of weather. Now Petra wished she had spent more time in the kitchen, but fortunately their maid, Becky, wasn't a bad cook and between them all they managed to put decent if simple food on the table.

His Lordship made a wry face. 'I appreciate the offer, but I am not sure O'Cleary knows how to cook much besides boiled beef, turnips and potatoes. He'd likely ruin them.'

The way he'd burned the biscuits. A man in Lord Longhurst's position should be able to hire a proper cook, should he not?

'I apologise if I seem ungrateful,' he added, likely to fill the uncomfortable silence.

She pulled her thoughts together and shook her head. 'Not at all. I was thinking what a shame it is that you do not have a cook, that was all. You might find one at a hiring fair, there are several local ones over the next few weeks.'

'Yes,' he said vaguely. 'Perhaps after we are done here, I will look into it.' He glanced over at where O'Cleary was quenching his thirst using a long-handled dipper in a bucket they must have filled from a stream. He dipped it again and poured the water over his head.

'It is hot, thirsty work,' she said.

'And we have barely made a dint in it.'

'What about hiring some men from the village to help you?'

He shook his head. 'The other landlords are keeping them busy. We will do as much as we can and that will have to do.'

The determination in his voice gave her pause. It seemed he did care something about his property.

The last time Harry had joined her brothers during a harvest, he had tossed the hay about and chased her around the stooks and generally caused much hilarity and disturbance. His carefree ways were what she had loved about him as a girl and what had been so annoying about him when they were wed.

She hesitated. 'Would you mind if I made a suggestion?'

Another suggestion? It had been Lady Petra's idea that he mow this field. Was she now spying on him to see if he had followed her instructions? Or was her motive something different? An excuse for her to meet and flirt with him? Before he'd left the Peninsula, his fellow officers had teased him about all the ladies who would be lying in wait for him in hopes of catching an earl. And Sarah had proved just how right they were. He would do his own choosing, thank you very much. A simple bargain between sensible people was all he needed. No pretence of stronger emotions. The very idea of the sort of destructive passions his parents had engaged in made him feel ill. He was not about to be trapped into such a hideous life by a scheming woman.

Lady Petra's presence out in this particular field so early in the day certainly seemed highly suspect. A lady of her stature would have no need to grovel around in the fields to put food on the table. No, there must surely be some ulterior motive for her appearance today.

He needed to be careful. 'Suggest away.' He braced for what might next come out of her mouth.

'You are chopping at the hay, rather than mowing it. You need to take wider, slower swings. It will go much faster and will be a lot less tiring.'

His mouth dropped open. She was now instructing him on how to use a farm implement? Given her petite form, he doubted she could even lift a scythe, let alone swing it. The damn thing was as heavy as it was awkward.

No doubt she was one of those females who liked to pretend she knew something about everything and hand out orders to large and apparently slow-witted men like himself. 'I see.'

She coloured delightfully and for a moment he forgot his annoyance. Which irritated him even more. 'Perhaps you would like to demonstrate, Lady Petra?' he challenged.

'Yes, that might be of more use than trying to explain.'

He stared at her in astonishment and followed her when she pushed through the long grass to where O'Cleary was back to plying his scythe.

She stood watching him for a moment.

'Have you never seen anyone mow grass?' she asked.

'Of course I have,' Ethan said. He certainly couldn't wait to see what sort of hash she was going to make of this with her tiny arms and hands and in her long skirts and fancy bonnet.

She put her basket aside, lifted her skirts and tucked the hems up at the sides into the waistband of her apron, once more revealing those charming calves and finely turned ankles.

His mouth dried.

O'Cleary turned around and dropped his scythe with a low whistle.

'Don't be ridiculous,' she snapped. 'You've seen lasses working with their skirts hiked up before now.'

O'Cleary turned bright red and Ethan knew exactly what sort of work he was thinking of.

Lady Petra frowned reprovingly. 'Dairymaids and such.'

O'Cleary lowered his gaze. 'Yes, my lady.'

'Give me your scythe.'

O'Cleary handed it over. It was nearly as tall as she was. 'I usually use a smaller one,' she said. 'They make them in various sizes.' She grasped the handles. 'Stand back, please.'

She took a long slow swing at the stems at ankle height and a swathe of hay keeled over. She took a step forward and swung again and another swathe went down in defeat. In two swings she'd cut as much as he had with ten.

Clearly growing up in the city with a customs clerk for a father had not prepared him for the life of an earl with a country estate. Neither had life in the army.

'I see what you mean,' he said, relieving her of the scythe and handing it back to O'Cleary. 'May I try?' He didn't want her exhausting herself.

'Certainly. Before you start always make sure there is no one close by. Swung with force, the blade can do considerable damage to a human limb.'

To his nonsensical male disappointment, she stepped back, untucked her skirts and brushed them down, looking perfectly demure.

'O'Cleary,' Ethan growled, 'stay well back.'

He picked up the scythe he'd been using and swung as she had done. The damn thing nearly flew out of his hands.

'It is more about the swing than the force,' she said.

He tried again, this time achieving a smooth half circle that was not nearly as tiring as what he had been doing before. He tried a few more swings and was surprised by how much progress he made.

'Excellent,' she said. 'Mr O'Cleary, it is your turn to try. Move a little to the right so you are parallel to His Lordship but well clear of his blade.'

O'Cleary touched his forelock and did as instructed. Soon he, too, was swinging in great form and moving forward steadily.

So much for his cynicism. Lady Petra really did know what she was talking about. He leaned on his implement. 'Thank you, Lady Petra. We will have this field done in no time.'

She beamed at him and he grinned at her. Her smile faded. 'With only the two of you it is going to take a few days, even so.'

'It will,' he said, unsure what he had done to wipe the smile from her face. Women, they were all the same. He just did not understand them. Indeed, he had no wish to understand them, even if they were as pretty as a picture. 'I ought to get back to work. Thank you again.'

He hefted the scythe and joined O'Cleary, swinging his scythe in easy arcs. The next time he looked up, she was gone from view.

* * *

Over the next few hours, he and O'Cleary made amazing progress, but every now and then the vision of a tiny lady with her skirts caught up, expertly swinging a scythe, popped into his mind.

He felt like he'd been ambushed and had not yet got his troops back into proper order.

Chapter Three

Perched on an upturned bucket, Petra watch Jeb groom Patch with a critical eye. When she had lived at home, she'd had her own riding horse, Daisy, and had learned how to care for her. She enjoyed working with horses, but this was another thing Jeb had decided was too lowly to be undertaken by a lady. So, having helped Becky make the bread first thing this morning, she'd come out to watch Jeb work, mostly so she would not disturb Marguerite at her drawing.

'How old are you, Jeb?' she asked.

He straightened and turned to face her. 'Sixteen, my lady.'

So young! Yet hadn't she known exactly how her life should be at sixteen? Wife to Harry, whom she'd assumed would become a gentleman farmer.

Why had she not seen that, while Harry had enjoyed his visits to her brothers, he was not the least bit interested in the land? He'd liked the hunting and the rollicking around the neighbouring villages getting up to all sorts of tricks, which she had known nothing about. After their marriage, he had made it perfectly clear that residing in the country would be a sort of living death for him. He declared he belonged in town, where he could continue to enjoy the company of his friends and, as she discovered later, any female who happened to come into his orbit.

A pang seized her. She quelled it. She never allowed herself to think about his unfaithfulness. It was simply too demeaning.

She sighed. Red had been right in cautioning her against setting her sights on Harry, but in those days, she had been so sure of everything. Now she felt as if she knew absolutely nothing, although her stupid body seemed to be attracted to the first handsome man to cross her path since Harry died.

Which was nonsense. She hadn't given a thought to that sort of thing before she married, so why would she need to think it about it now she was a widow? She was a lady after all, not some lowly maiden.

Jeb was staring at her. Oh, yes, he'd told her his age. She frowned. 'That means you started working here when you were fourteen. Isn't that rather young?'

Surprise filled his expression. 'Why, no, my lady. Me da started work up at Longhurst Park when he was nobbut ten. Under-groom he were then. He said we were spoiled going to school and not working till we were fourteen as our ma insisted upon.' He grinned. 'To hear tell, it was a fine life up at the Park till the old lord up and died. The fellow that came after him was sickly and spent most of his time in London, so he had no need of the horses or the staff. I was supposed to train there when I was old enough, but it were not to be.' He went back to currying Patch's flank.

'Where does your father work now?'

Jeb shrugged. 'Died of the lung disease three years ago. Leaving Ma to raise five young 'uns on her own. God's blessing it were when this here job came up or we might have ended up on the parish.'

Guilt assailed. Why had she not known this? But it was Red who had hired Jeb before she and her sisters had arrived in Westram. 'I suppose your mother is helping the other ladies with the millinery now?' She winced, as even that work wasn't certain.

'Nah, my lady. She cooks for a family out beyond Ightham.' His gaze held sadness. 'She gets home one day a month. The little 'uns miss her, but me and my older sister do the best we can with them. Suzy does a bit of lacemaking, but it be hard for her to do much with the baby an' all.'

'Baby?'

'Ah, he be four now. Right little handful.' He grinned fondly. 'The other three help out.'

This vision of Jeb as head of a family was shocking. And for a mother to be separated from her young children! A vision of singed biscuits popped into her head. 'Your mother is a good cook, then?'

'Yes. Trained she did, up at the Park when she were a lass. Had to give it up when she married me da, of course, but he had a good job by then.'

A good cook. Now, that was something. 'When will she be home next?'

Jeb rubbed the back of his neck. 'Next week, I reckon, my lady. Sunday.'

'Do you think she might be willing to cook for us here on that day?'

Jeb turned to look at her. 'What, my lady?'

'I would like to invite a guest for dinner, but we

will need someone to cook for us. Your mother can take home any leftovers, and, of course, we would pay her for her time.'

His eyes lit up. 'I'll have my sister write and ask her, but I am sure as how she would be pleased to help out. A bit of extra never goes amiss.'

Hopefully Marguerite would not object to spending a little bit extra next week. Now if she could convince the Earl to accept her invitation, she might kill two birds with one stone by finding His Lordship a cook as well as help Jeb's family out by having their mother live at home. The thought pleased her inordinately, even if it did mean having to entertain the Earl for dinner.

Ethan tied Jack to the fence in front of Westram Cottage. At first, he'd thought to refuse the ladies' invitation to dine with them, but the thought of a half-decent meal, instead of O'Cleary's stew, was far too tempting for any man, especially one who liked his food as much as Ethan did.

Besides, strangely enough, he was looking forward to seeing Lady Petra again. Which wasn't moving the next project on his list in the right direction.

According to his man of business, who had his office in Sevenoaks, he was not entirely destitute. He'd offered the heartening news that if Ethan was careful in the management of the estate, and if he perhaps found himself a suitably wealthy bride, he should come around very nicely.

The noose tying him to this estate was growing ever tighter, but he still had hopes of returning to his army career. After much discussion, Ethan had reluctantly agreed to the man of business making discreet enquiries regarding the availability of such a bride. He had indicated his preference for a sensible woman who would understand the concept of a marriage of convenience. Preferably one who had some experience of country living and all that it entailed, so he could leave matters in her hands. There were to be no commitments or promises until Ethan had met the lady.

He marched up to the ladies' front door and rapped the knocker. After some discussion with O'Cleary, he'd decided not to wear his uniform. Since a military man had little use for civilian clothes, his wardrobe was limited, but he did have a coat he'd bought from Weston on a whim during one of his visits to London. It wasn't exactly evening wear, but O'Cleary had agreed it would do for dinner in the country. Though why on earth the batman thought himself an expert in the matter Ethan didn't know.

A maid guided him to a small parlour at the front of the cottage.

The two ladies rose to their feet when he entered. He gave them his warmest smile and bowed. 'Good day, ladies.'

They dipped their heads in unison.

'Please be seated, Lord Longhurst,' Lady Marguerite said. She glanced at the servant. 'That will be all, thank you, Becky. May I offer you some sherry, Lord Longhurst?'

'Thank you.'

He took his glass when she poured one for each of them. Both ladies perched on the sofa. He sat opposite in the armchair and raised his glass. 'To your very good health.'

'Your health,' they replied.

He took an appreciative sip of his drink. The sherry was of excellent quality.

A silence descended. Ethan dragged out his party manners. 'What a snug house you ladies have.'

'Thank you,' Lady Petra said. 'We like it very much.'

'There is one thing I do not quite understand,' he said, recalling some earlier musings. 'The village has your family name and yet your family does not own any property in these parts, apart from this cottage.'

'It is quite a long story,' Lady Marguerite said. 'But it is not an unusual one. It dates back to Oliver Cromwell's rule.'

'Do not tell me your family once owned Longhurst Park?' Blast, he had not anticipated that when he asked the question, though he should have. He really ought to find out more about this branch of his family's history. He just hadn't thought it important before now.

'Oh, no,' Lady Petra said. She chuckled. 'Actually, it is Lord Compton who is the usurper.' Her amusement lit her blue eyes like sunlight dancing on water. He found himself enchanted. He suppressed the sensation. He had seen that sort of conspiratorial amusement on his mother's face. It had been a lie then and was likely one now, too. Ladies' smiles were not to be trusted, even if they were pretty and enticing.

'Petra, you really should not say such things,' Lady Marguerite said. 'It is all water under the bridge. While Compton Manor, then known as Bedwell Hall, did belong to our family, our ancestors supported the idea of a republic. After the Restoration, we lost the title and the land. Charles the Second bequeathed Bedwell to the Comptons, all except this cottage, which was occupied by an elderly lady who had maintained her loyalty to the King.'

'A very stubborn old lady apparently.' Once more Lady Petra's eyes twinkled. 'My family says I take after her.'

Lady Marguerite shook her head fondly at her sister. 'You are not stubborn, my dear, unless you do not get your own way.'

Both ladies laughed. Once again Ethan was struck by the younger sister's angelic beauty. Her laughter was a sweet light sound and her eyes gleamed with mischief. She was the sort of woman who stood out in a crowd and drew every man's eye when she smiled. The sort of woman who would lead a less sensible man a merry dance.

His suspicions about her having an ulterior motive returned in full force. He really should have declined this invitation. He certainly did not want to create any false impressions or hopes.

Lady Marguerite continued the story. 'It wasn't until the Stewarts were gone that our family wormed their way back into the good graces of the royals and were granted the property in Gloucestershire. Danesbury is where Westram has his seat now.'

'Yet you choose to live here in Kent?'

'Yes,' Lady Marguerite said, lifting her chin as if she expected him to take issue with her words. 'We like our independence.'

Lady Petra nodded her agreement.

Perhaps he was misjudging her motives after all.

The maid peeped in. 'Lady Marguerite, I am to tell you dinner is served.'

'Thank you, Becky,' she said, standing.

'May I?' Ethan offered both ladies an arm. He escorted them into a small dining room overlooking the garden at the back of the house. The French doors were wide open, admitting a light breeze along with the scent of roses.

He seated the ladies and then took a chair. 'Your garden is beautiful,' he said.

'That is Petra's doing,' Lady Marguerite said. 'She has a talent for making things grow.'

Lady Petra smiled. 'I have always had an interest in plants. How about you, Lord Longhurst?'

He grimaced. 'I enjoy eating what the land produces, my lady, but my knowledge beyond that is severely limited. But not for long, I hope.'

The little maid carried in an assortment of dishes, including a magnificent roast of beef, assorted vegetables and puddings.

Having carved the roast and made sure each lady's plate was full, Ethan got down to eating his own meal with a will. Food like this had not been coming his way recently.

The conversation, led by Lady Marguerite, revolved around the weather, the need for a church roof and some information about other families in the neighbourhood.

Finally, Ethan, put down his knife and fork. 'That was the best meal I have had in months, if not years.'

Lady Marguerite looked pleased. 'Surely you exaggerate, my lord.'

'Not at all. Everything was cooked to perfection. Your chef is to be complimented.'

'Actually, she is not *our* cook,' Lady Petra said. 'We hired her for the day.'

He frowned. 'Do cooks hire themselves out by the day?'

'Not as a general rule, but she is looking for a permanent post near to Westram. We do not need a full-time cook, unfortunately.'

Everyone needed a full-time cook if they could afford one. Again, his irritation at Westram's niggardliness with his sisters raised its head. But it was none of his business. Indeed, he had no idea why he would care.

'Perhaps you would like to hire her,' Lady Petra suggested idly. Too idly. He narrowed his eyes on her face. Why was she so interested in his household arrangements? The sort of arrangements that would normally be within a wife's purview. Was she seeing herself in that role? No doubt she thought an earl would be a very good catch.

Even so, the thought of having meals like this on a regular basis was so tempting as to make Ethan's mouth water.

'Are you sure I would not be depriving you of her services, if I hired her?'

'Oh, no,' Lady Petra said airily. 'Becky manages our everyday needs and, since we rarely entertain, we do not have need of a cook. Mrs Stone comes highly recommended. Indeed, she used to work at Longhurst Park years ago, so she should fit right in. And it would mean she could live at home with her family.'

The lady did protest too much. He frowned. 'Did you invite me to dinner so I might be convinced to hire this woman?'

Lady Marguerite looked embarrassed.

'Is it so terrible?' Lady Petra asked. 'Is it not our duty to help our neighbours and friends? Besides, what better way to know if she will suit than to sample her skills?'

She looked a little disgruntled. What? Had she not expected him to see through her ploy? Was she like so many others, including his father, who thought him lacking in intelligence because of his size?

Indeed, he also felt a little disgruntled. He had thought—well, perhaps vaguely hoped—she had invited him because she valued his company, but it seemed that it had been an attempt to manipulate him into hiring a cook. A very fine cook, to be sure, but he did not intend to be manipulated by any woman ever again, especially after his lucky escape from Sarah.

The maid entered with a tray containing desserts. A fruit compote, an apple pie and a lemon mousse. Everyone served themselves. Ethan partook of the pie and a little of the mousse.

Any idea of resistance immediately disappeared. Mentally he shook his head at what he knew would next be coming out of his mouth. Complete and utter surrender. 'Ask the cook to report for duty as soon as she is able.'

Both ladies seemed happy with his pronouncement, Lady Petra exceedingly so, blast the woman. O'Cleary would be delighted in the extreme. Ethan, however, could not quite shake his earlier sense of being ambushed once again.

From now on it would be best if he avoided Lady Petra completely.

Chapter Four

As was their usual wont on a Thursday, Petra and Marguerite walked to the village of Westram. Their first stop was the post office.

'Quite a few letters for you today, Lady Marguerite,' Mr Barker, the postmaster, said. 'And one for you, Lady Petra. Franked, they are.' He beamed, his red wrinkled cheeks looking like apples left too long in the sun.

All the letters had been franked by Westram or by Lord Avery's father—a duke, no less. Their connections to the nobility seemed to thrill Mr Barker, as if somehow the more noble the frank, the higher it lifted those who lived in the village.

'Thank you, Barker,' Marguerite said, stuffing the letters into her reticule after a glance at the sender's name and address.

'One is from Lord Westram,' Mr Barker said. 'Will he be visiting you any time soon?'

'Not to my knowledge,' Marguerite said, handing over her outgoing letters and opening her purse.

Perhaps Lord Longhurst will be good enough to

frank them for you?' he said, gesturing to the window with his chin.

Across the road, Lord Longhurst was talking to the Vicar's wife, Mrs Beckridge. 'That will not be necessary,' Marguerite said.

Marguerite hated asking anyone for anything. She was determined they would be completely independent. While she had not said anything at the time, she had been quite disturbed when their sister-in-law, Carrie, married so soon after they moved to Westram. Disappointed, Petra had thought, though Marguerite had hidden it well. It had certainly made their task of living independently a little more difficult, despite the fact that Carrie's new husband did all in his power to assist.

Their mail dealt with, they went back out into the street. Mrs Beckridge waved them over. Petra would have preferred to ignore her, since she tended to pry. Also, the thought of meeting the Earl made her feel hot and cold by turns. There was something about the man that fascinated her, she had discovered at dinner the other evening, and the strength of those feelings made her uncomfortable. However, since Marguerite was already crossing the street, she could hardly put her head down and walk the other way.

'Lady Marguerite, Lady Petra,' Mrs Beckridge gushed. 'How lovely to see you.'

Longhurst bowed. 'A pleasure, Lady Marguerite, Lady Petra.'

Petra curtsied. 'Lord Longhurst.'

'I was right at this moment telling His Lordship about the gypsies who have taken up residence in

Crabb's Wood at the edge of his land. I am sure you
ladies will agree with me when I say something really should be done about them.' She made the pronouncement in a voice of doom as if predicting the
end of the world.

'What sort of something?' Petra asked.

'Why, chase them off, of course. We don't need the
likes of them around here, stealing babies and wash-
ing off the line.'

Marguerite frowned. 'Whose baby did they steal?'

'No one's as yet,' the Vicar's wife admitted. 'But
as I mentioned to my dear husband this very morning,
it would be preferable not to give them the chance.'

'Utter rubbish,' Marguerite said with a shake of her
head.

'The Vicar thinks *I* should chase them off, does he?'
Longhurst asked.

'Well, it is *your* land they are sitting on. Disgraceful
people. Next, they will be knocking on doors selling
charms for warts or lucky heather. Most un-Christian
behaviour.'

'A gypsy band used to camp near Danesbury when
we were children,' Marguerite said.

'Our papa always hired them to help with the harvest,' Petra added. 'It was why they came back year
after year. We certainly never had any trouble with
them. Why not offer them the job of cutting your hay,
Lord Longhurst? I wouldn't be surprised if a previous earl used their services and that's why they set up
camp on your land.'

Mrs Beckridge made a sound of disapproval. 'Not with
my husband's approval, I assure you, Lord Longhurst.'

'What an excellent solution, Lady Petra,' Lord Longhurst said. 'When I enquired at the Green Man, I was told there was not a man hereabouts in need of gainful employment. I will ride over there tomorrow and see if I can hire them on.'

Petra looked up at the sky. Mare's tails were riding high above them. 'I would go today if I were you. The weather is about to change. You may have only a day or so before it rains.'

He looked startled. 'You can tell that?'

'Really, my lord,' Mrs Beckridge said. 'Do not encourage them to remain in the district. Please, send them to the right about, as my husband would say. We do not need their sort around here.'

'Your husband does not have several fields of hay in need of mowing and no men to help,' the Earl said with a pleasant smile.

Petra could not help herself. She beamed at him.

He recoiled slightly, as if he did not welcome her approval of what was a very sensible response to the Vicar's wife.

Mrs Beckridge shook her head. 'Far be it from me to dictate your actions, my lord, but were my husband here he would say the same thing.'

'I am sure he would,' Longhurst said. He bowed. 'If you will excuse me, ladies.'

All three ladies watched him stroll away. Petra had never seen anyone stand up so well to Mrs Beckridge's forceful personality. Perhaps he did not yet understand the lady's position and reputation in the village. No doubt he would when the Vicar heaped coals of fire on his head at the church service on Sunday. It would be interesting to see how he reacted to that.

'Why are you so set against these gypsies?' Marguerite asked Mrs Beckridge. 'I certainly have not heard of any abductions or theft associated with them.'

'Not yet, you haven't,' Mrs Beckridge said sullenly. She pressed her lips together. 'Likely, I should not make mention of this, but I fear I must warn you.'

'Of?'

Mrs Beckridge glanced about her and then drew closer, lowering her voice to a whisper. 'One of them tells fortunes.'

Marguerite shook her head at the lady. 'It is only a bit of entertainment, Mrs Beckridge. No one truly believes in it.'

Mrs Beckridge sniffed. 'People around here believe all sorts of blasphemous nonsense. All I can say is do not let yourselves be taken in.' She nodded her head and stalked off.

Marguerite sighed. 'More fire and brimstone to look forward to on Sunday. I should have kept my opinions to myself.'

'Perhaps she ought to have been a little less forceful in hers,' Petra said.

Marguerite chuckled. 'Every time I see the woman she rubs me the wrong way. If she said "Up", I would likely say "Down". I think your suggestion was the best. Give them some gainful work and leave them in peace. It is all anybody wants. Come along, I need to buy some bread.'

It would be interesting to see if the Earl actually went against the Vicar's wife and offered the gypsies work. They were people who really understood the land and who worked hard. And if they occasionally poached a rabbit, well, why not? The rabbits didn't belong to anyone any more than the blackberries did, even if the law said otherwise.

When Petra came in from the garden after a satisfactory hour of pulling weeds without any interference from Jeb, she found Marguerite in the hallway tying on her bonnet. 'Where are you off to?'

'Oxted. We are almost out of candles and the stall at the market there is cheaper than our shop in the village.'

'Not to mention that it would not do for our neighbours to know we are burning tallow in the private rooms.' Beeswax ones were kept for visitors and used only sparingly.

Marguerite pursed her lips for a second, then chuckled. 'Precisely.'

Marguerite always looked far too serious for her twenty-seven years. She was not the same person Petra remembered growing up in the Westram household in Gloucester. She had seemed to change after her marriage. She rarely laughed any more. It lifted Petra's heart to see her sister smile for once. 'I'll come with you. I have nothing else to do today.' It would be like old times, going shopping with her sister, even if it was a small village market and not London's Bond Street. Indeed, it would likely be more enjoyable.

Jeb had already brought around the pony and trap when they got outside and seemed ready to argue when he realised there would not be room for both him and Petra and he would therefore be left behind.

At a raised eyebrow from Marguerite he touched his cap and returned to the barn.

They set off at a spanking trot and as they passed the scene of the great blackberry robbery, Marguerite waved her whip. 'It seems Lord Longhurst took your advice.'

The field was more than halfway to being mowed by five men with their shirts off and expertly swinging scythes. Stooks of hay dotted the pasture. Petra could not help searching for one particular man, but she was disappointed. Lord Longhurst was not among the workers. 'It would seem so,' she said non-committally.

'It is good to see Lord Longhurst is taking his estate seriously at long last,' Marguerite said.

'It is indeed. Though I do not know how long he intends to stay. He prefers life in the army to life as a country gentleman, I believe.' As Harry had. Though Harry preferred life in town, he'd seen the army as a means of escape from an unwanted wife. She swallowed down her feeling of mortification. She had married the wrong man and she wasn't going to make that sort of mistake again.

The conversation turned to other topics, but Petra could not help wondering about the whereabouts of Lord Longhurst.

'I wonder if there will be any servants looking for employment at the fair,' she said.

'We cannot afford to hire more help,' Marguerite said sternly. 'I am not going to ask Red for more money when he is so hard-pressed.'

Their brother, the Earl of Westram, had inherited the Earldom only to discover its financial affairs in a state of disarray. When Marguerite and Petra had insisted on their independence after their husbands died, they had promised not to be an additional burden on their brother. Marguerite was determined to stick to their agreement.

'I wasn't thinking of us,' Petra said. 'I was thinking of Lord Longhurst. He needs a housekeeper and a butler.'

Marguerite frowned. 'I am sure it is not our place to be telling Lord Longhurst how to run his affairs.'

'I was not going to do any such thing. I simply thought if I saw any likely candidates I could mention Longhurst Park. Mr O'Cleary is not only looking after the horses and opening the front door, but he is serving tea—in his riding boots.'

Marguerite looked suitably scandalised. 'Very well. If you feel you must. But please do not let your kindness result in any sort of gossip or scandal. I do not want Red using it as an excuse to force us back beneath the family roof.'

It was not that they did not like Red; they did—indeed, they loved him dearly—but Red's idea of being a good head of the household was to find them each another husband. Neither of them wanted that. 'I promise you, I will be careful. Besides, there may not be any suitable people to be had so late in the Season. The Earl also needs a bailiff,' she mused, but one would not expect to find one of those at a fair.'

'Why don't you offer to take on the job?'

Petra's jaw dropped. Her heart gave an odd little thump. 'Me? Westram would never approve.'

Marguerite gave her an odd look. 'I was joking, Petra.'

Yes. She had to be. But the idea was just so appealing Petra could almost see it in her mind's eye. She'd followed Red about when their father was teaching him about the land before he went off to university. She loved the rhythm of the seasons, watching things grow and bear fruit. Unfortunately, Harry's father had been a mill owner and his only interest in land was how many sheep it had and how much wool it produced. And Harry had turned a pale shade of green when she'd suggested they live in the country.

She had been too blinded by his easy-going manner and handsome face to see the true man beneath. What a little fool she had been.

Their arrival at the Red Lion brought her uncomfortable thoughts to an end. Marguerite handed over the pony and trap to an ostler, and arm in arm they walked to the market held at the foot of Oxted's market cross.

Petra left Marguerite haggling over candles and wandered off to see what else was on offer. An enquiry led her to where servants were hiring out their skills, but there she found only a couple of dairymaids seeking employment. Lord Longhurst didn't have any cows as yet.

Oh, well, she hadn't really expected a housekeeper or a butler to fall into her arms. Which also meant she had no excuse to visit Lord Longhurst. Just as well, since she seemed drawn to the handsome man whose obvious ignorance about running an estate made him seem vulnerable. Seeing him at a loss made her want to offer her aid, when she should be keeping her distance if she didn't want the villagers to start gossiping.

Vulnerable? Longhurst? Surely not. Now she was making up stories in her head.

She wandered aimlessly among the stalls until she discovered a small crowd gathered around a shabby wagon sporting a pole from which fluttered an array of brightly coloured ribbons.

'What is going on?' she asked a portly farmer in a linen smock.

'Gypsies.' The disgust in the word was palpable.

'If you dislike them so much, why do you remain?'

His mottled red cheeks darkened to crimson. 'I heard as how they had a couple of horses for sale. The bidding will start shortly.'

'I see.' About to move away, she stopped at the sight of a young woman obviously far along in her pregnancy emerging from the wagon, grinning cheerfully. 'Madame Rose says it will be a boy,' she announced.

The farmer cursed beneath his breath. 'Fortune telling. Against nature that is.'

How odd. Mrs Beckridge had mentioned the gypsy camping in Crabb's Wood who told fortunes. Could this be the same one? Petra edged closer.

A man appeared at her elbow. 'Want your fortune told, miss?' He cleared his throat. 'I mean madam.'

How did he know? Was her widowed state written on her face or could he see the outline of her wedding band beneath her glove. She curled her fingers into her palm. 'I...er... Why not?' It would be the only way she would know if this was the woman the Vicar's wife had spoken of.

The man helped her up the steps. 'Cross her palm with a bit of silver and Madame Rose will tell you all you need to know.'

It would be interesting to see what sort of nonsense the woman came up with. Petra knew exactly what her future held. A quiet life in the country with her sister. She climbed the three steps and pushed aside the canvas blocking the way.

The interior of the wagon was a great deal larger than she had expected and lit by lanterns hanging from hooks. Bright red fabrics edged with glittering gold adorned a narrow cot and the table behind which sat a young woman, rather than the old crone Petra had expected. Clothed in brightly coloured scarves decorated with intricate gold stitching, with large gold rings hanging from her ears and a multitude of gold bangles jingling at her wrist, she looked exotic. The woman thrust out a hand, palm up.

Petra dropped the thruppence into her palm and the coin seemed to disappear. 'How did you do that?' she asked.

'Curiosity kills the cat,' Madame Rose said, her voice heavily accented. She grinned cheerfully. She was actually quite beautiful, with dark hair and eyes and skin the colour of polished oak.

'What do you want to know?'

Petra swallowed. 'Your man out there said you would tell me my fortune.'

The dark eyes stared at her unblinking. 'Is it the name of your second husband you are seeking?'

Petra froze. 'How did you know I am a widow?'

The girl shrugged. 'How do I know anything?' She shuffled a deck of cards with rather horrifying-looking pictures on their fronts.

A cold shiver trickled through Petra's veins. 'I have changed my mind.' She turned to leave.

Something grabbed her. She glanced down at the long fingers gripping her wrist. Strong, elegant fingers.

She raised her gaze to meet that of Madame Rose. The woman smiled. 'It is not the future that interests you. Most of all you wonder about the past.'

Petra squared her shoulders and turned back to meet the woman's scrutiny head on, for she had realised that, despite her youthful appearance, Madame Rose was a woman with a very old soul. 'I cannot deny there are things about the past that I question. But don't we all?'

The girl nodded. 'The person who could answer your questions has passed over.'

She shivered. 'Yes.'

'Sometimes the spirits are cruel with their answers.' She laughed and it was not unpleasant or mocking, rather it held sympathy. 'Your future is more easily discovered.'

It was too late to change the past, and besides, the woman was talking in riddles. 'Then I will settle for that.'

She removed her glove and held out her hand.

Madame Rose traced the lines across her palm. 'You are fortunate indeed. I see a long life, with two paths. One leads to discontent, the other to happiness. Yours is the choice.' She sat back. 'Good day, my lady.'

What? Petra stared at her, mouth open. 'That is it?'

'It is what I see.'

Behind her, the curtain at the door drew back, flooding the interior with harsh daylight, making the furnishings look tawdry and cheap and the young woman behind the table look weary and older than her years.

'This way, madam,' the man outside said.

Petra stumbled out and down the steps.

'What did she tell you, sweetheart?' one of the men

gathered outside called out. 'I'll marry you, if it's a husband you want.'

Petra smiled brightly. The man meant no harm. 'She said to avoid men like you at all costs.'

A chorus of laughter greeted this sally.

A hand grasped her elbow. She spun around, ready to defend her person. 'Lord Longhurst,' she gasped.

'Lady Petra. Allow me to escort you.' A fierce frown on his normally smiling face made her feel breathless. Her heart beat a little faster than normal. No, no, it was the stares of the crowd that had her feeling on edge.

'I would not put you to any trouble, Lord Longhurst,' she said, trying to maintain the easy brightness of her smile.

'It is no trouble at all,' he said in his lovely, deep, calm voice. 'Since I am going your way.' He held out his arm.

She cast him a look askance. 'How do you know where I am going?'

The twinkle returned to his eyes and his brow cleared. 'Naturally, I go in whichever direction you are headed.'

Was he flirting with her? 'Very droll, sir.'

He chuckled. A rich warm sound that started up a flutter in her stomach.

She felt oddly light-hearted. She repressed the urge to giggle like a schoolgirl. That was the Petra of old. She was a sensible woman now and a widow.

'You are not here alone, I presume,' he said rather more seriously. 'Your maid is nearby?'

'I am here with my sister. She is shopping in the market.'

'Your sister approves of your visit to the likes of

Madame Rose? Surely you do not believe in such nonsense?'

She felt herself bridle. Men always thought they knew best. Even lackadaisical Harry after they'd wed.

'You don't believe she can tell fortunes?'

'Certainly not.' He looked down at her from his great height and there was a troubled look in his gaze. 'Nor do I believe a sensible woman like yourself would believe it either.'

He thought she was sensible? Most men looked at her face and diminutive figure and decided she was nothing but dizzy headed. A warm feeling in her chest spread outwards.

'While I do not consider myself foolish, sir, it seems to me that there are mysteries in this world that cannot be accounted for by logic or the church would be doing a very poor trade indeed.'

His beautiful blue eyes widened. 'Such heresy! Mrs Beckridge would be aghast.'

She laughed. 'I trust you not to betray me, sir.'

'Upon my honour, I will not,' he said. 'I am a gentleman. Besides, I have to admit there is something of the truth in your words. It is my belief mankind does not know all the answers as yet.'

'I see.' She smiled. 'I presume you were not about to seek Madame Rose's wisdom yourself?'

He grinned. 'Lord, no. I came to bid on some horses.'

'Then I must not keep you from your transaction.'

'All done. Two plough horses and a carriage horse, much to Jack's relief.'

'Jack?'

'My mount. I brought him home with me from

Spain. He was not best pleased at the idea of doing all the work on the estate since all the horses were sold off by my cousin before he died.'

They strolled along the line of stalls. Merchants called out, encouraging them to inspect their wares.

'Better to sell them off than keep them eating their heads off to no good purpose. The land has not been worked for several years, I think.'

He sighed. 'If I had realised how badly my cousin had left matters I would have come sooner and found someone to oversee matters. With the war going badly and Wellington needing every experienced officer... Well, it is of no matter now. Hopefully I can come to grips with it and find the right man for the job.'

Her heart sank at the implication in his words. 'You maintain your intention to return to the army?'

'My place is with my regiment. While I do not wish to appear a braggart, I believe I am needed.'

Could he not see he was also needed here? What difference did one man risking his life on the Peninsula make to the war effort when so many people depended on him here at home? 'Your cousin had been ill for some considerable time, I gather. The locals say he rarely came to Longhurst. Had he come here more often, things might have gone better. I am surprised he did not discuss these matters with you as the heir apparent.' She winced. 'I beg your pardon. It is not my business to speak of your cousin in such a way.'

'He was a very distant cousin. I had never even heard of the man until the lawyers contacted me.'

Startled, she gazed up at him. His expression was grim. 'You did not know you were the heir?'

'No. I was unaware of the connection until I received a letter from a lawyer two years ago. They traced back three generations to find me apparently. The task was made more difficult by one of my great-great-grandfather's younger sons taking his wife's name and breaking all connection with his family.'

'But you did not return the moment you knew you had inherited.'

He shrugged. 'I saw no need to leave my duties until another person of whom I was not aware, a third cousin or some such, wrote to the General demanding my immediate release.' The disappointment in his voice was palpable.

'It is hard to imagine that someone would prefer the battlefield to the peace and quiet of the English countryside.' The very idea made her shudder inwardly.

'Is it?'

'Many families have lost sons and husbands in this dreadful war. Why do men have to fight and seemingly take pleasure in it?' The bitter edge to her tone came as a shock to her. 'I have to beg your pardon once again, my lord. I do not have the right to criticise. I am sure there is good reason for it, but—'

'You lost a husband to the war. Who better to criticise? I must also admit to having the occasional doubt. A man who does not is not using his brain. But I believe the freedom of our country is quite possibly at stake.'

Unfortunately, it was true. Still, she had the feeling that some men went off to war for the sake of glory and honour, without a thought for those left behind, rather than because they felt it was the right thing to do for King and country.

They walked in silence while he carefully guided her around knots of people chatting between the stalls.'

'I believe I see Lady Marguerite,' he announced.

Petra envied him his height. She could see nothing past the shoulders of people around her. Yet despite his height, he had managed to adapt his long stride to her exceedingly short one, when most men had her trotting to keep up. Indeed, it had been a most pleasant stroll and he hadn't once treated her like an ornament to be seen and not heard. Instead he had listened to her opinions as well as giving his own.

Harry had been charming and fun when he was in the mood, but often acted upon a whim and only asked her opinion when it was too late. Unfortunately, as a schoolgirl, his charming smile, teasing ways and seemingly undivided attention had completely blinded her to his true character. She had learned the hard way that one could not judge a book by its cover.

'Is something wrong,' Lord Longhurst asked, leaning closer. 'You look distressed.'

Oh, dear. Her thoughts were showing yet again. 'Not at all.' She forced her thoughts to take a more pleasant direction. 'I see you have made a good start with the haying.'

'I took your advice and visited the gypsy encampment. They were pleased to be offered work and got started right away. I also visited Lord Compton and he said I should come here today to look for horses. Thank you for the suggestions.'

Surprised by his open admission that she had been helpful, she gazed at him open-mouthed. The men in her family had always dismissed her ideas out of hand. They always thought of her as little more than a baby. Sometimes they had even used her ideas as if they were their own. 'You are most welcome,' she said, beaming at him.

He frowned slightly.

'There you are,' Marguerite said at their approach. She looked relieved. 'I could not think where you had got to.'

Petra waited for Lord Longhurst to inform on her, but he said nothing, although he was regarding her with a rather cynical light in his eye, as if he expected her to lie.

'I went to see if there were any possible housekeepers at the hiring fair. Lord Longhurst needs one, but there was no one suitable.' She took a deep breath. 'And then I stopped at Madame Rose's caravan.'

'Madame Rose?' Marguerite echoed, looking puzzled.

'A housekeeper?' Lord Longhurst said, sounding surprised.

'You had your fortune told?' Marguerite asked.

'Yes, Marguerite. Yes, Lord Longhurst, a housekeeper. I will continue to ask around.'

'Thank you. I do not believe I deserve such kindness.' He looked a little bemused. Oh, dear, did he think she was interfering? Before she could ask him, he bowed. 'Ladies, may I leave you to your errands? I have some horses to collect.'

She and Marguerite dipped curtsies. 'Good day, Your Lordship,' they chorused.

'Madame Rose!' Marguerite said again, turning back to Petra. 'What, pray, were you thinking?'

Blast it. Now Marguerite would not let the matter rest. Yet what else could she have done with His Lordship standing there looking at her as if he expected her to prevaricate.

Yet she felt better about it than she would have if she had kept the truth from her sister. 'I'll tell you all about it on the way home. Not that there is much to tell.' She certainly wasn't going to mention what Madame Rose had said about her finding a second husband. Because nothing like that was ever going to happen.

Chapter Five

'Where are you going, dearest?' Marguerite asked in an absent voice as Petra glided along the hall to the front door.

Blast. Petra should have known the slightest sound would alert Marguerite to her presence, although Petra had hoped to slip away unnoticed. 'Gathering chestnuts.' She held up her basket. 'There should be plenty on the ground by now.' Chestnuts were a treat eaten hot from the fire and would keep until Christmas in the pantry.

Marguerite closed her sketchbook and turned to face her. She frowned. 'Not from the tree on the village green, I hope. Mrs Beckridge would dine out on that for weeks.'

'Certainly not.'

'Then where?'

'There is a huge tree in Crabb's Wood.'

'Isn't that part of Lord Longhurst's property? If so, that would be stealing.'

'It is not stealing if one has permission.' She crossed her fingers behind her back. She did have permission of a sorts. He might not have included chestnuts specifically but he had said she was welcome to purloin his black-berries. She hardly thought he would have a different reaction in the matter of chestnuts.

Marguerite nodded. 'Don't be late for tea.'

Petra let go a sigh of relief. She'd half expected her sister to ask her not to go.

'Ask Jeb to go with you,' Marguerite added. 'He can pull down the lower branches for you.'

Dash it. Exactly what she needed. A nursemaid. 'Very well.'

She made good her escape and went in search of Jeb. He was mucking out. 'Want to go for a walk?' she asked.

He frowned. 'I have to finish this, Lady Petra. After that, I have windows to clean. Perhaps afterwards…'

She had done what Marguerite required, in fact at least, if not in spirit. 'Never mind. I will ask you an-other time.'

Duty done, she set off for Crabb's Wood with her basket over her arm. It had been a few days since she had been able to provide anything for their dinner table. Chestnuts weren't exactly a staple food, but they could help stretch a meal or make an evening fun.

A glance at the sky had her wincing. The weather had been fair for the past few days, but today's clouds had dark hearts and a less-than-friendly look about them. Hopefully she could gather enough nuts to make the outing worthwhile before it rained.

Instead of taking the winding lane, she took a short-cut across the corner of Lord Longhurst's land to where the river took a sweeping curve into Crabb's Wood, a copse mostly made up of ash and hazel and the odd oak. The ancient sweet chestnut trees were foreigners and had arrived in England with the Romans.

She followed the track along the river's edge for a while and then moved deeper into the woods. The woods had been ill tended for several years and she had to pick her way over fallen tree trunks and push through undergrowth. As she walked, she kept an eye out for distinctive spear-shaped leaves among the detritus.

She had a rough idea of the location of the tree she had spotted on one of her many walks, but it took a while to find it. After stopping to get her bearings a couple of times, she finally found herself standing in a golden carpet of leaves. She scuffed around with her feet to expose the spiny-skinned fruit. A few of them had turned yellowish brown and had burst open, making it easy to pick out the shiny brown nuts cupped inside. Most of the shells were still green and she carefully rolled them beneath her foot to break open the prickly casing. The thorns were so wickedly sharp they would easily pierce her gloves and did so when she extracted the exposed nuts if she wasn't careful.

After a half hour of shelling and picking up the glossy brown nuts, she had gathered what had fallen and looked up into the tree. There were still plenty of chestnuts on the branches. One of the branches was barely out of reach and her basket was nowhere near full yet. If only she could reach...

A thick branch the wind had brought down caught her eye. It might give her the two or three inches she needed. She dragged it over and stepped up. The branch rolled, she teetered and fell backwards, managing to land on her feet. 'Bother.'

This time she took more care, got her balance just right and reached upwards. She could touch one of

the leaves with her fingertips but could not quite...
get hold of it.

'Lady Petra! What are you doing?'

She fell backwards and was caught in strong arms
and held against a hard, warm chest. The owner of
the chest helped her get her balance and immediately
stepped back.

She spun around. 'Lord Longhurst!'

'What are you doing?' His voice held curiosity, not
anger.

'Gathering chestnuts. I was trying to reach that
branch.' She pointed upwards.

He glanced up at the tree. 'Ah, I see.'

'I have gathered all I can from the ground, but not
as many as I hoped.'

'Let me help you.' He easily reached up and brought
the branch down to eye level. She could not help watching the ease with which he forced the branches to bend
to his will. How she envied him his height and his
strength, but when he grabbed for a cluster of nuts, he
hissed in a breath and shook his hand. 'Why does anything tasty have to have thorns?'

She laughed, knowing he was also thinking of the
blackberries. 'I suppose it is the tree's way of protect-
ing its babies.'

He grinned. 'I suppose it is.'

'Pick them at the stem and drop them. I will peel
them.'

He threw down several bunches before letting the
branch go with a swish. He pulled down another branch
and another, until he could reach no more, while Petra
expertly stepped on the green prickly shells and rolled
the nuts free.

'So that is how it is done, is it?' he said, standing back and watching her. 'There were sweet chestnuts in Spain and Portugal, but I only ever saw the nuts themselves. The camp women gathered them. They gathered beechnuts as well, when they could, and turned them into flour and a concoction that tasted a bit like coffee.'

'I haven't seen any beech trees in these woods, have you?'

'There is one on the far side, closer to the house.'

Was he offering her the fruits of that tree, too? If so, he was a kind and generous man.

His big riding boots made short work of the rest of the chestnuts and now her basket looked invitingly full and was becoming heavy.

'I think that will do for now,' she said. 'It is time to head for home.'

'Let me escort you. Which way do you go?' He took the basket from her hand, not giving her an option to say no.

Mentally she shrugged. If he wanted to assist her, why not? 'Back to the riverbank, where the walking is easier, then to where the lane crosses the bridge.'

'Ah, so that is where the river goes.' He held back a branch so she could pass.

'What were *you* doing in this part of the woods?'

'I was following the river along to see where it went after it left my lake. I heard noises in the undergrowth and was wondering what sort of wild animal I would find.'

'Instead you found me.'

'And glad to do so. I was wondering if you might be a bear or a wolf.'

She laughed. 'In England?'

He grinned. 'Not really. I thought of a deer, actually.'

'Yes, there is the occasional deer. Are there wolves and bears in Europe?'

'There are.'

'And you slept in tents there?'

'Sometimes. But they don't come near the campfires and we would keep them going all night.'

'Oh, I see.'

At last they were back to the river and they could walk side by side in relative comfort. 'People must walk along here frequently,' Longhurst observed.

'I expect some of the villagers fish here.'

'Oh, so the villagers also poach on my land, do they?'

'I would not be surprised, since you do not have a gamekeeper. Despite their claims otherwise, they are no different from the gypsies when there is a chance of some free fresh food.'

'Not unlike you.'

She laughed and he joined in. 'Touché, my lord.'

They rounded the curve. A figure lay face down on the track ahead of them, face almost touching the water, one arm dangling in the river up to the elbow.

Longhurst dashed forward with a cry of alarm before Petra could stop him.

The lad leaped to his feet. One of the gypsy children. He looked terrified. He snatched up his jacket, dived past Longhurst, flew past Petra with his bare feet stirring up leaves and disappeared into the trees.

Longhurst stood, arms folded, watching him go. He shook his head ruefully. 'I thought he was injured.'

'Just another poacher, I am afraid,' she said with a smile.

'Poaching what? Frogs? If so, he's welcome to them.'

She winced. 'No, not frogs. If I am not mistaken he was guddling for fish.'

'Why would he cuddle a fish?'

She chuckled. 'Not *cuddle*. *Guddle*. Catching fish with his hands.'

'Not possible,' he declared.

'It most certainly is. I have done it myself. Did you learn nothing as a boy?'

'I didn't learn that. And how did a lady like yourself learn the way of it anyway?'

She rolled her eyes. 'I had two older brothers and a gamekeeper who didn't mind showing things to a mere girl, as it happens.'

'I had neither siblings, nor gamekeepers. I grew up in Bristol. All the fish I ever ate appeared on our table by way of the fishmonger.'

Clearly, his education had been sadly lacking. She glanced in the direction the boy had fled. 'Well, if you wanted evidence of the gypsies poaching, you have it now.'

'Never mind that. I want to learn how to guddle a fish. Can you teach me?'

A drop of rain hit her cheek.

She glanced up. 'Another day, perhaps. Apparently, it is about to rain.'

He glanced up, too. 'Dash it, you will get wet.'

'Rain is good for the complexion, so they say.' She picked up her basket. 'Good day, my lord.'

To Ethan, rain pattering on leaves had its own special sound. He'd grown up in a bustling city where the noise of wheels grinding on cobbles and the strident shouts of costermongers were constant. When he'd joined his regiment on its first march in Portugal, he'd been amazed by the different sounds and smells he'd encountered while sleeping rough.

The loamy smell of the earth beneath his feet intensified. Soon the trees would not protect them from the falling raindrops. He also knew all about the unpleasant sensation of being soaked to the skin. He really ought to find them some shelter. If she would accept it.

Never had Ethan met a woman quite like this one. She irritated and amazed him at one and the same time. Every word out of her mouth was designed to establish her independence. Since leaving home, he'd become quite accustomed to meeting strong-minded women, having met a good few of them during his time in the army. Even so, most of them were more likely to seek his help than rebuff an offer of aid.

Not to mention their attempts to attract his attention in other ways. Those sorts of entanglements he'd avoided like the plague. Other men's wives, no thank you. For some reason that seemed to make them chase him all the more. It seemed now this youthful and exceedingly attractive widow was turning the tables on him. She wanted nothing to do with him, which seemed to pique his interest all the more. It really was annoying to say the least.

Unfortunately, he could not allow her to walk home in a downpour unescorted and call himself a gentleman. He lengthened his stride, caught up to her and held out his arm. 'Allow me, Lady Petra.'

'Don't be ridiculous,' she said. 'I told you before I am quite used to walking by myself. Indeed, I enjoy it.'

Could she be any more brutally honest about her

lack of interest in his company? Likely so, given the opportunity. He simply continued to hold out his arm as he walked beside her. One did not argue with a lady.

Her foot must have caught in a tree root because she stumbled and grabbed for his forearm. Hmm, he hadn't noticed anything projecting from the dirt. Indeed, the path looked remarkably smooth and well worn. Perhaps she had manufactured a stumble, to take advantage of his arm without seeming to give in? Interesting.

'I must say I am impressed with your knowledge of agricultural matters,' he said. 'I have a great deal to learn.'

She brushed back a stray lock of hair from her cheek. 'I was a complete pest as a child and spent all my time following my father and my older brother around the estate. They called me their little limpet.' She chuckled. 'I don't think it was an endearment as much as an expression of exasperation. Nevertheless, whatever my brother learned from my father, I learned, too, along with my father's love of the land.'

'Does Westram feel the same way about his estate?'

'I think he sees it as his duty to pass the estate along in the shape my father passed it to him, if not better. There were several bad harvests that set us back somewhat. However, I am not sure that he loves it exactly.'

'I can sympathise.'

'Because you prefer the army.'

'I do.' He sighed. 'There is a great deal more to this farming business than I thought. The signs of neglect are readily apparent even to a layman such as me. I see it taking a great deal more time that I expected.'

'And a great deal of effort,' she added.

And a great deal of money that he did not have.

A flash of lightning turned her face a ghostly shade. 'Oh, dear,' she said, quickening her pace. 'It seems we are in for a thunderstorm. We should hurry.'

He could not agree more. Sheltering beneath trees was the worst place to be with lightning about. The wind tossed the branches above them hither and yon, the heavens seemed to open and what had been a gentle rain a moment before turned into a waterfall rattling on the leaves and their heads and shoulders. He whipped off his coat and put it over her head. 'This way,' he shouted, pointing down a fork in the path.

'The lane to the village is that way,' she protested.

'But we can find shelter this way.'

She nodded and he took her hand and hurried her along. The silly little sandals on her feet and the tight fit of her skirts were not conducive to speed. If she were not such an independent little thing, he would pick her up and run. Just the thought of her in his arms heated his blood despite the chilly water soaking through his shirt.

Another flash of lightning.

To hell with it. They were both getting soaked to the skin. He scooped her up and ran. No doubt he would pay for this indignity to her person, but better that than she catch a chill from spending too long out in what was now a downpour.

After a second or two, she relaxed and clung on around his neck, making his job easier. They reached the edge of the trees and the lake spread out before them. He ran for the odd little structure he had found the previous day while out walking. A series of man-made caves formed into a grotto like the ancients might have visited. In no time at all they were safely beneath the vaulted ceiling. He set Lady Petra down on her feet.

As a shelter against a storm it wasn't that wonderful. Water rushed down the walls and across the floor into the stream running down the centre. He took her hand. 'Come on.' He led her deeper into the cavern, until they reached the whole purpose of the ridiculous structure. A pool—and, glistening in the half-light provided by an opening in the roof, the statue of Venus in its centre—fed by the stream, its glassy surface of yesterday now broken by ripples as the raindrops splattered down.

Around the pool, stone benches at strategic angles provided visitors with a view of the statue.

Lady Petra shivered.

'I know. It's chilly,' he said, 'but at least it is dry.'

'And not as dark as I was expecting.'

'Stay here. I'll be back in a moment.'

'I'm not sure where else I would go.' The bravery in her voice gave him an odd sensation in his chest. He dispelled it with a chuckle that echoed around the chamber.

She also chuckled, her voice mingling with his in the dark reaches of the cave.

Yes, laughter was often the best way to be rid of discomfort.

Ethan ran back to the entrance, took a deep breath, bracing himself for the next dash of cold rain, and ran back into the trees. He managed to find some reasonably dry twigs and a thick branch and was soon back in the cave with his hoard.

He really wished he had thought to bring several large branches into the tunnel upon his last visit, but then he had not been expecting to be forced to shelter here. He carried his armful back to the reflecting pool and Lady Petra.

She had removed her sodden bonnet and set it on one of the benches while she perched on one of the others, clutching his coat around her as protection against the chill. The sight of her snuggled into his coat gave him a strange feeling of warmth inside.

'What do you have there?' she asked.

'The makings of a fire. We can try to dry out a bit while we wait for the storm to pass.'

'Oh. I see.'

He laid out the wood in front of her bench and reached into his pocket. In the army, he never went anywhere without his tinderbox and old habits died hard. He unwrapped it from its oilskin.

'Goodness me,' she said. 'You are well prepared.'

He wanted to grin like a schoolboy at her tone of admiration. Nonsense. The happiness inside him was simply gladness he would soon be warm and dry. He got the fire going without difficulty, and while it was only a small blaze, it offered a measure of comfort and a warm glow to the cold rocks.

'I had no idea this was here,' she said, glancing around.

'I found mention of it on one of the maps in the library and came to take a look at it a day or so ago.'

'Why on earth would anyone want to build such a thing?'

'In the last century they thought it romantic.'

'Oh.' She shivered.

'I must say, it is better when the sun is shining. Quite pretty, in fact.'

'I'll take your word for it,' she said, her tone dry. She shivered again and hunched inwards.

Of course, she was cold. She wasn't used to such hardships.

'Allow me,' he said and briskly rubbed her shoulders and arms. Damnation, her skirts were soaking wet and clinging to her very shapely legs. 'Get closer to the fire.'

She inched to the edge of the bench nearer the flames. 'The last thing I expected today was a thunderstorm.' She groaned. 'Marguerite is going to be so worried when I am late for supper.'

They stared into the flames in silence. How many nights had he sat thus on campaign, sitting around a campfire, wet and tired to the bone? Too many to count. There had been companionship with his fellow officers, but it was nothing like the feeling of contentment he had now, sitting next to this tiny woman in the depths of the English countryside.

The feeling of peace threatened his equanimity. As a boy, the brief periods of peace in his household usually presaged an enormous storm of passion between his parents far worse than the thunder and lightning of the storm outside their cave.

She shivered and leaned towards the flames. Shadows flickered on the walls and glimmers of firelight danced across Venus's pool. Silence descended.

'Do you think the storm will last long?' She glanced up at the fissure above the water, where the raindrops trickled down its edges and dripped into the pool.

They seemed to be falling a little less heavily than they had been. 'Let us hope not.'

She nodded and rubbed her upper arms beneath his coat.

Usually she sounded so sure of herself. Right now, she sounded uncomfortable. Some people were afraid of storms. 'Move up closer to me,' he said. 'We will be warmer if we share our body heat.'

At first, he thought she would refuse his offer of comfort. He wasn't sure why he felt this need to offer her protection against the elements, but when she shifted closer, he put an arm around her shoulders, holding her loosely so she would realise she could break his hold any time she wished. After a second or two he felt her relax and her trust made him feel warmer than any fire. He hoped some of that warmth would transfer through his skin to her.

To Petra there was something especially pleasing about the feel of such a sturdy forearm around one's back. She leaned closer, resting her head against his shoulder, and became aware of the strong, steady heartbeat against her cheek and the scent of his cologne. Something manly and spicy.

His calm solid presence kept the dark in the corners of the cave at bay. She'd hated the dark, ever since Jonathan had locked her in a wardrobe when she was a child and then went off with his friends. Jonathan had always been a bit of a beast.

She'd never told her brothers how much the dark terrified her, but Harry had winkled it out of her one night. And then he had teased her unmercifully as was his wont. Worse was when he came home drunk and blew out the candle on her nightstand, leaving the room horribly dark until she pleaded with him to light it.

Once it was lit, she would pretend she didn't care, but he'd laugh and tell her he would make love to her so she would forget all about her foolish fears. It never quite worked, but she never admitted that he sometimes left her less than satisfied, especially after he'd been carousing.

Sitting with Longhurst's arm lightly curled around her shoulders, she had the sense that he was not the sort to play cruel jokes on her or anyone else. How could that be? She barely knew anything about him. She wanted to know more. But she did not want him to think she was prying so she remained silent.

Warmth from his large body trickled through her skin and, what with him at her side and the fire at her front, she began to feel quite toasty.

Her eyes drifted shut and her breathing slowed. It was a lovely sensation: half-awake, half-asleep and knowing she was safe. A slight movement of his chest. A light touch to her hair. Tingles danced down her spine. Had he kissed the top of her head? Her breath caught. Dare she turn her face up to his and seek another, better kiss?

No. No. There had been no hint of interest of that sort from him. She must have imagined it. She held still, trying to recapture the peace and calm of moments before, but her heart was racing far too fast to do more than pretend to be at ease.

The sound of rain hitting the pool diminished to a steady drip.

'Lady Petra, I think the storm is over,' he said quietly, as if trying to awaken her gently from slumber. He removed his arm from about her shoulders and shifted away from her, leaving her feeling chilled.

She sat up slowly as if she had indeed drifted off. 'Oh, my goodness.' She patted her hair, smoothed it back from her face. The fire had died to a mere glow.

He rose and kicked the ashes about until the fire was no more, giving her time to recover her wits and retrieve her bonnet. When she went to remove his coat, he placed his hands on her shoulders. 'Keep it for now. Until we see how it is outside.'

She did as he requested, unwilling to lose the warmth of it. Or the scent of him that clung to it. He took her hand and led her outside into daylight.

She blinked in the brightness. What she had not noticed on their mad dash was a lake in front of the cave, set in a shallow depression and surrounded by trees. Long grass and rushes grew along its banks. At the other end, where the lake began to narrow, a grass-covered three-arched bridge crossed from one side to the other. Its reflection in the still water was one of the loveliest things she had ever seen. 'What a pretty view.'

'I thought so when I found it yesterday. It is too bad it is so overgrown. Another project to be undertaken once the land provides an income.'

She heard weariness in his voice. 'Hopefully it won't take too long,' she said encouragingly. Although, once he had his income, he would likely leave and return to his beloved army. Disgruntlement filled her. Why did people who did not care about the land get to inherit, while those who did care looked on in sadness? It was the way of the world, according to Marguerite.

He took her arm and they walked back through the trees to the lane. Petra found the silence oppressive, as if the real world had closed in on them and come between them.

Unable to bear it, she tried to think of something to say that would lighten the moment. 'Since you grew up in Bristol, I am surprised you did not choose the navy over the army.'

He made a scoffing sound. 'I'm a dreadful sailor. My father took me sailing once. I turned pea green and spent the whole time leaning over the side, hanging on for grim death. Father was not best pleased.' He grimaced. 'It was the same when I travelled to Portugal and back. The navy was definitely not an option for me. It is the only bad thing about going back to my regiment.'

In other words, he would not miss Longhurst Park. Sadness filled her. 'I see.'

'I was lucky that Mother's brother offered to buy me a commission as soon as I was old enough.'

'How generous of him.' What sort of uncle sent a boy off to get killed in the war?

'Yes, he was a generous man. He didn't have children of his own and I used to visit him from time to time as a lad. We became good friends over the years. I missed him greatly when he died.'

'And your parents, do they still live?' She winced. What a foolish question. He would not be the Earl if his father was alive.

'My father died of an apoplexy about ten years after I left home. My mother went into a decline and died shortly afterwards.'

'I am sorry.'

'Thank you, but there is no need. We were not close.'

How very cold that sounded. Her family had been so very loving, even Jonathan when they were younger. Longhurst's tone suggested he would not

welcome further questioning. And really, it was none
of her business.

A large puddle lay across the path at the edge of
the woods.

Without a word of warning, Lord Longhurst whisked
her up in his arms.

She cried out in surprise. 'My lord, I—'

A second later he was putting her down on the other
side. He glared at her. 'Don't tell me you would rather
have splashed through it in your sandals and soaked
the hem of your skirts,' he said gruffly.

Not at all. Being swept up in such a way for the
second time in one day, was rather…lovely. It made
her feel particularly feminine. She took a deep breath.

He held up his hand. 'Come, let us not argue about
such a trivial matter.'

His words gave her brain time to work. She could
certainly not encourage him in such outrageous behaviour by telling him she had thoroughly enjoyed it.
'Very well. But, my lord, you must leave me here to
continue my journey alone. The villagers are used to
seeing me walking by myself. To see you escorting me
through the village would give rise to all sorts of unwanted speculation.'

'My dear Lady Petra—'

Was she his dear? Her heart gave a heavy, painful thump. No, that she could never be. He was a soldier and a man who would leave here at the drop of
a hat and without a backward glance. 'Please do not
argue, my lord, unless it is your intention to ruin my
reputation.'

'Certainly not.' He sounded offended. No matter.
It was better to offend him than have the whole coun-

tryside gossiping about them and Westram getting to hear of it.

His expression became grim. 'While I cannot like the idea of your walking alone, I do take your point, my lady. I must therefore acquiesce to your request.' He frowned. 'However, before we part there is something I would like to ask you.'

For a second her heart seized. Ask her? Could he be thinking of a…proposal? No, no, what was she thinking? They were scarcely even friends. 'Ask away.'

'About the field you recommended we mow first. I've been reading about crop rotation and such and I was wondering if you would advise ploughing and planting this year, or leaving it fallow.'

Stunned by his willingness to ask her advice regarding such a complex matter, she stared at him.

His frown deepened. 'Is this not a sensible question?'

'Yes. Yes, indeed. Perfectly sensible.' But gentlemen did not ask ladies for such advice as a general rule. She swallowed.

'Perhaps you do not know?' He sighed. 'So far you are the only person to offer me anything helpful regarding the estate. All Mrs Beckridge suggests is that I chase off a band of gypsies, who as far as I can judge are doing no one any harm at all and are the only ones available to work in my fields.'

'Except they are poaching your fish and quite possibly your rabbits, you know.'

'As you so rightly pointed out the other day, things that exists in the wild belong to no one person. They are welcome to them. There are far too many of them anyway.'

He sounded so fierce, she wanted to laugh. She kept her face straight. 'To really give you a good answer to your question about the field it would help to know how it has been used in the past. I have not lived here long enough to know that myself, I'm afraid.'

He shrugged. 'I have been through the estate journals. But to be honest, they might as well have been written in hieroglyphs for all that I understand.'

She winced. 'It is quite possible. I understand that each bailiff has his own form of shorthand as a way of preserving their positions. I might be able to make sense of it, if I were to see the notes.'

'Would you be willing to look at them?'

She hesitated. What would people say? What would Red say?

His expression froze. 'I beg your pardon. I should not have asked.'

Why not? 'I would be happy to help.' Delighted, in fact. It was so long since she had anything truly useful to do.

'I'll bring them over tomorrow. We can go through them together. I am determined to understand this stuff.'

His eagerness was enchanting. As was his willingness to seek her advice. She stilled. Shook her head.

'No?' he asked.

'Perhaps it would be better if I come to Longhurst. No one will see me if I cut across country, or, if they do, they will think I am out on one of my rambles, but everyone will see you arrive at my door. And everyone will make assumptions. Before you know it, my brother will be knocking on your door asking about your intentions. Red is very dear, but completely misguided in matters regarding his sisters.'

His expression became serious. 'I would not like to go behind your brother's back.'

'Nonsense. We are simply making sure we do not incite gossip about something perfectly innocent.'

'Visiting a gentleman alone in his home is just as likely ruin your reputation.'

'Only if it becomes known. My lord, I am a widow. I am free to come and go as I please, provided I remain discreet.'

He frowned. 'Then it shall be as you wish.'

She shrugged out of his coat and handed it to him. 'I will come to Longhurst at around eleven on Friday.'

'I shall look forward to it.'

As she walked away, she was aware of his gaze following her down the lane until she turned the corner.

A few moments later the Vicar and his wife came driving along the other way. See, she was right. If he had escorted her home, there would have been all kinds of questions and innuendo.

The Vicar pulled up when he came alongside her. 'Good day, Lady Petra.' His gaze scanned her person. 'It seems you got caught in the storm.'

'I did. Fortunately, I found some shelter under a tree. I am only slightly damp.'

He eyed her up and down. 'You were fortunate indeed. It was quite a shower.'

Mrs Beckridge leaned forward with a sugary smile. 'My dear Lady Petra, you must hurry home before you catch a chill. I am surprised your sister permits you to wander around the countryside alone.'

Petra gritted her teeth but managed a smile. 'Thank you for your concern, but as you say, I really must be getting home. I bid you good day.'

She set off at a brisk pace, praying they would not turn around and offer to drive her to her door. There really was something about the Vicar's wife she did not like. The sound of the vehicle continuing on its way was a great relief. All she had to do now was think of an excuse Marguerite would believe to be out of the house for an extended period on Friday.

Or perhaps she should just tell her sister the truth.

And if Marguerite thought it a bad idea to visit Lord Longhurst in his home? Alone? Petra really did not want to fight with her sister.

She would think of something.

Chapter Six

Ethan paced his study. Lady Petra should have been here by now. He should not have listened to her worries and should have sent his carriage. After all, she could easily have brought her maid, or even her sister. It was not as if they were doing anything untoward. No matter how much he might like to.

He quelled that thought the instant it formed, but it did not quell the heat in his blood quite so easily, damn it.

A few moments with his arms around the woman, one brush of his lips against her hair, and he could not stop thinking about her. Which was simply not on. And if by seeking her aid, he was putting her reputation in danger, then he should cease and desist immediately. Particularly since his man of business had written to inform him the he believed he'd discovered the perfect heiress. The daughter of a foundry owner somewhere in the North.

If he wanted to take a look at her, he could meet her in town during the course of the Season, when Parliament resumed. He did suggest that Ethan should not delay in making his interest known, if she proved suitable, since more than one destitute lord was in the market for a wealthy bride.

Damn it all.

He strode for the window, looking out and squaring his shoulders. There was no help for it. Unless Lady Petra could see a miracle within the pages of the journals, he would simply have to buckle down and do his duty as his title demanded.

No matter how irksome. Still, once done, with the aid of a good bailiff and a wife to oversee things, he could head back to his regiment.

He swung around at a sound behind him. Lady Petra in the doorway with a smile on her face. Thank God. How long had she been there? He frowned, hoping she would not recognise the pure joy he felt at the sight of her. Joy? Nonsense, it was relief, that was all.

Like a beleaguered battalion upon the arrival of reinforcements.

'I am sorry I am late,' Lady Petra said, pulling off her gloves, revealing her dainty hands. 'My sister needed some last-minute help with the household chores.'

Why was a lady of her distinction required to do menial tasks? Why did her brother not take better care of his widowed sisters?

'Are you late? I had not noticed.' He certainly wasn't going to let her see how anxious he had been for her arrival. He knew only too well that women used such displays of weakness against a man. His own mother had been a master at the art.

Her face fell. 'I asked Mrs Stone to send up a tea tray. I hope you don't mind.'

The hesitant speech made him feel like a brute. 'Not

at all.' He gestured to the desk. 'I have set the relevant journals on the desk, if you would care to take a look at them.'

After his boorishness, he wouldn't be surprised if she refused.

She removed her bonnet, tucked her gloves inside it and looked around. 'I see you have managed to get rid of the furniture in the hall.'

'O'Cleary and I carted it into the barn. We thought we would put it in the attic, but it is already completely full of yet more furniture.'

'What will you do with it all? Sell it?'

'If anyone wants it. Or burn it, perhaps. I cannot keep it in the stables for ever.'

She winced. 'It seems like a terrible waste, I must say.' She made her way to the desk and looked at the stack of journals he'd set there. 'I suppose I should get on.'

In no time at all she was seated at his desk, poring through the entries, cross-checking between the various years and flipping back and forth.

With her head bent over her work and the sunlight from the window catching her hair and making it glint like gold, she looked lovely. Such a pretty woman. The recollection of her cuddled up against him in the grotto made him wish for an excuse to hold her again. He pushed the thought aside and paced the room, waiting for her judgement.

O'Cleary brought the tea tray and collected it again, and still she studied the ledgers.

Finally, he could bear it no longer. 'What do you make of it?'

She glanced up as if startled by the sound of his

voice, as if she had forgotten he was present. A humbling thought.

Then she smiled and he forgot all about books and estates and titles and could think only of how much he would like to kiss those pretty lips. He froze.

She tipped her head as if she saw something in his reaction, then stared back at the pages before her. 'Bring a chair and I will share what I have understood so far. But I need your help.'

He sat beside her, aware of her arm so close to his, drinking in the sight of her delicate nape as she pointed to an entry in the ledger before her. He forced himself to focus on the page.

'I can understand what it says with regard to what was planted and when, but I cannot for the life of me understand where.' She pointed to a series of letters and numbers.

He stared at them. 'Those look like map references to me.'

'Really.'

He searched through the pile of papers and pulled out a dog-eared map which had neatly printed letters and numbers and arrows pointing in all directions scattered all over it. 'Yes, I saw this earlier and couldn't make head nor tail of it, except that it's obviously a map of the estate.' He pointed to the number she had indicated in the journal and then to a corresponding section on the map. 'Those coordinates refer to this location, I believe. It is not done exactly correctly, but it is plain this location is what is meant.'

'Oh, my goodness. Very well, what about this one?'

Slowly but surely, they worked through it together and a pattern emerged, linking the ledgers to the maps.

'Well done, Lady Petra. Finally, there is clarity.'

She beamed. 'Well, without your knowledge of maps, I would never have figured it out. This is very dissimilar to the way my father's bailiff recorded his journals. Now we have figured out the key, next we have to understand exactly which field was used for which purpose.'

'Can I help?'

'Of course.' She handed him a sheet of paper and the ink stand. 'I think we need to focus on the hundred-acre field that you mowed and see if we can trace exactly how it has been used these past four years. Seven would be better, if you have the information.'

He shook his head. 'There are no records older than four years as far as I can determine.'

'Then we must work with what we have.'

The determination in her voice was heartening. And he was equally determined. Though it had surprised him, he was glad his map-reading skills were as useful here as they had been in the army. He had a knack for it. It had been part of the reason he had risen to the rank of Major. That and his attention to duty.

They worked through the details in the journal, matching them to the map, until they had recorded each of the previous years.

'Judging from this, I would say you should plough now and plant root crops,' she said, leaning back in her chair with a smile that held not a little satisfaction.

The urge to kiss her mouth was almost overwhelming.

He straightened, putting distance between them. 'I agree. That accords with what I have been reading in the agricultural journals.' He grimaced. 'Now I need to buy a plough and hire a ploughman. Not to mention find a bailiff.' This business of caring for the land was indeed an expensive proposition. All the outlay came ahead of any income.

He turned the pages of the most recent journal until he reached the last few pages. These were written in a different hand. A more flowing script, albeit one that looked a bit shaky in places. There were names, dates and amounts beside each one, along with letters and numbers that must be some sort of code. 'Do you have any idea to what this might refer?'

Lady Petra shook her head. 'I have no idea what it is. It is like nothing else in the ledger.'

As he had thought. He grimaced. 'Unfortunately, these I believe I understand all too well. It is a record of enormous expenses. The only thing I can think of to account for these large amounts are gambling debts. This must be why there is no money left in the coffers.'

She looked as shocked as he had felt the first time he saw them. 'Oh, dear.'

'Exactly.' He closed the journals. 'Is it not time for you to be heading home?'

She glanced at the clock. Her eyes widened. 'Four o'clock? Already? I told Marguerite I would not be gone above two hours.' She chuckled. 'I'll be in trouble again. Poor Marguerite. I really am a sad trial.'

'Next time I see her, I will thank her for allowing me to take up so much of your time. I wish I had some way to thank you, as well.'

She gazed at him with a soft glow in her eyes. 'Nonsense, my lord. It has been my very great pleasure.' She grimaced. 'However, I think it would be better if you did not say anything to Marguerite. I simply told her I was going for a walk.'

He glanced at the pile of ledgers. 'And there are still a great many more puzzles to solve. We have only tackled one field.'

'I know. Would you like me to help you with the rest of them?'

He could not believe what he was hearing? 'You would do that?'

'As and when I can. If you think it would be helpful.'

He could do it by himself, but it would take a great deal longer than it had taken them together. Relief filled him. 'Helpful does not describe the value of your contribution.'

A smile lit her lovely face. 'Then I shall come as often as I can.'

'In the meantime, I'll see if I can borrow a plough from Lord Compton, because it seems my cousin cared nothing for farm implements and sold them off with the horses. Ploughing cannot be that hard.'

Her eyes widened. 'You mean to plough it yourself?'

'Why not? Drive up and down in straight rows. How difficult can it be?'

'I do not know. I have never tried, but I do recall my father saying a good ploughman was worth his weight in gold.' She glanced down at the journals. 'Like a good bailiff. Yet it is possible to learn.'

'Then I shall learn.'

She laughed, stood up and stretched, revealing the delights of her petite figure in a very intimate way. No doubt she had no idea what the sight of her breasts pressing against the fine fabric of her gown did to a man. For although she was a widow, she seemed almost too young and innocent to have ever been a wife.

He frowned at the wayward thought.

'I will come again when Marguerite goes to market next Friday, unless something untoward occurs,' she declared as she tied her bonnet and pulled on her gloves. 'There are a great many more acres for us to worry about. One by one we shall solve the mysteries of the estate.'

Her confidence was heartening. Perhaps his sojourn in England would be shorter than he had at first thought. For some reason, that thought did not make him feel as glad as he would have expected.

'No mail today,' Petra sang out as she entered the drawing room.

Marguerite threw down her pen. 'Dash it. Are you sure?' She looked worried.

'Of course. Why what were you expecting?'

'Final approval of the drawings I sent off to a publisher last week.'

'Your drawings are being published?'

She blushed. 'I was asked to colour some drawings of parts of plants for a book, and they requested some samples of drawings of specific flowers. I am hoping they might use them.'

'That is wonderful. Amazing.' She rushed to her sister and gave her a hug.

Marguerite sighed. 'It would be wonderful if they accept the drawings. Colouring pays very little.' She had the household ledger open in front of her.

Petra's heart sank. 'Is there a problem?'

'We don't have enough money to last us through the winter, if they reject the work.'

'They must pay for work they requested, surely?'

'They made no commitment. They rejected the last one I sent.'

Petra recalled how upset Marguerite had been. 'But your work is wonderful and now you know what they are looking for, I am sure it will be fine. The letter will likely come tomorrow.'

'I hope so.' Marguerite did not sound convinced.

'I could set some traps for rabbits to tide us over.'

'You won't find any rabbits in our garden. Jeb has made sure of that.'

'No, I'll set traps the in the field Longhurst had mowed a few days ago. I've seen rabbits there.'

'Did His Lordship give you permission?'

He had said he didn't mind if the gypsies poached his rabbits or his fish. He had also given her permission to purloin what she wanted in the way of blackberries. 'He did.'

'He gave you permission to hunt rabbits?'

'Not rabbits exactly.'

'Oh, no, Petra. I am not having my sister arrested for poaching. I want to see permission in writing.'

'Very well, I will send him a note.'

Marguerite nodded and went back to her ledger. 'Perhaps we can do with less coal if we don't heat the bedrooms.'

Petra sat down and scribbled off a note, then went in search of Jeb to deliver it. He was nowhere around. Then she remembered that he had said he was going to take Patch to the farrier, since she had a loose shoe. She would just have to take the blasted note herself, even though she knew Marguerite would not approve. On the other hand, perhaps it was better this way, because if Ethan was home and gave permission right away, she could set her traps on the way back.

She put on her hat and coat and marched across the fields to Longhurst, picking hazelnuts from the hedgerows as she went. If Longhurst wasn't home, then her trip would not have been completely wasted.

As it happened, she met Lord Longhurst riding up his drive as she crossed his lawn from the other direction. He really was a fine figure of a man on a horse. Her unruly feminine side gave a little sigh of appreciation. It had apparently lost all sense of decorum.

He dismounted as soon as he came up to her. 'Lady Petra, to what do I owe this pleasure? I wasn't expecting you today, was I?'

'No. I came to ask permission to trap a few rabbits on your land.'

He looked surprised, but then smiled. 'You are an endless source of surprise. Help yourself. You know you may.'

He looked so handsome when he smiled she almost forgot her manners. 'Thank you. Would you like one?'

He grinned. 'I didn't like to ask but, yes, O'Cleary and I would appreciate some fresh meat.'

'Very well. Either tomorrow or the day after. In the meantime—' she held out her note '—would you write your assent to my trapping on your land? That way Marguerite will not live in fear of my imminent arrest for poaching.'

He chuckled heartily. 'I will do better than that.' He tore a leaf out of a small notebook with a pencil attached and scribbled his permission. 'There you go. You did promise to teach me to guddle, don't forget.'

'So I did. Would you like to go tomorrow afternoon? I can check my traps at the same time.'

'I would be delighted. Fresh fish for dinner will be a welcome change.'

'Good. I'll meet you at the stream where we saw the boy.'

'You *are* still coming on Friday, as promised?'

Her heart picked up speed. At this rate she would be seeing him every day this week. She really ought not to do that. 'I will.'

'Excellent. May I offer you some tea before you leave?'

She was sorely tempted, but if she did not leave now, then she would not have time to set her traps before dark and it would be two more days before they would have fresh meat on the table.

'I will take tea when I come on Friday, if that is all right. I really must be getting along.'

He bowed. 'Until tomorrow, then.'

'Yes. Tomorrow.' She headed back across the lawn, before she changed her mind and went for tea instead.

Ethan arrived ahead of the appointed time. A good officer always checked the lie of the land before he engaged in a sortie. He'd also organised things the way he wanted them and had ascertained there were no gypsy boys lurking about. Now he would meet Lady Petra before she entered the woods. He strolled along the path to the spot where the river emerged into sunlight. From here he could see the bridge, the lane and anyone walking along from the village.

The next person to come along was a farmer on a

wagon. He pulled up at the bridge and Petra jumped down, giving him a wave as he started his horse moving again. She waited until he was out of sight, then hopped over the stile.

Ethan waited until she was close enough to hear him. 'Lady Petra.'

She smiled.

And it was if the sun had come out from behind a cloud. He glanced upwards. There wasn't a cloud in the sky. But the day definitely felt brighter and warmer. He shook his head at such nonsensical flights of fancy. They walked into the cool of the woods and when they were out of sight of the road, he tucked her hand in the crook of his arm and matched his steps to hers. He was pleased that she made no demur about his escort.

When they reached the chosen spot, she released him with a sound of surprise. 'You brought a blanket?'

He had spread it out where the boy had been lying. 'I didn't think you would want to get your gown dirty.'

She chuckled. 'Well, I did wear something old for the task, but it was thoughtful of you. Thank you.' She raised her eyebrows. 'I see you also brought fishing rods. Is that in case my method of catching fish does not work?'

'Insurance,' he said. Perhaps he should have had a bit more confidence in this guddling of hers, but, when O'Cleary had explained fully what the term meant and since the gypsy boy clearly had not caught anything by this method, Ethan had decided that reinforcements might be required.

'Well, let us see, shall we?'

She removed her gloves, her spencer and her bonnet. She was wearing a dark blue gown with the tiniest little sleeves. She stretched out on her stomach on the rug, so that most of her shoulders hung out over the water. 'Come on, then,' she said to him, 'you cannot learn the way of it standing there.'

He stretched out beside her.

'Lie very still,' she whispered, 'and look down into the water until you see the trout.'

At first, he could see nothing but ripples and waving weed and pebbles. Slowly, his eyes became accustomed to the watery scene and the shapes became more defined. A brown fish was right beneath him, all but his head hidden by the bank's overhang. One really had to look hard since the fish seem to blend in with its surroundings. 'I see it.'

'First you gently ease your hand into the water, about a foot away from him.' She suited her actions to the words. 'You stay like this until he stops noticing you.' The fish shifted position as if to take a look at her hand. Fascinated, Ethan watched her dangling hand. It did not move for a very long time. Eventually, the fish returned to its original position.

She slowly moved her hand a little closer. She repeated this until the fish no longer took any notice of her at all as she gently and rhythmically stroked along its side.

The fish seemed to go into a trance.

'Now,' she whispered, 'I will catch him beneath the belly and toss him up on the bank.'

With a twist of her wrist, she flipped the fish up on to the bank. It stared up at him in puzzlement. 'Poor thing,' he said. 'I can't believe that a fish would let you tickle it, then simply pull it out of the water.'

'There is something they like about having their skins stroked. It seems to send them to sleep.'

'It feels like a mean trick.'

'But a good way to get dinner on the table if you do not have a rod.'

The fish began to jump around. Petra dispatched it and pulled out a knife to gut it.

'I'll do that,' he said firmly, taking the knife from her hand.

'Do you know how?'

'I have seen it done many times.'

'Seeing and doing are not the same necessarily.' She sat back on her heels and watched. She nodded when he was finished. 'In your case, it seems it is.' She turned back to the river. 'Now it is your turn to try.'

They lay side by side, staring into the water.

'I see one,' she said. 'There.' She pointed.

He saw it, too. He took off his jacket, rolled up his sleeve and lowered his arm into the chilly water. He did exactly what she had done and the fish flicked its tail and disappeared.

'Slower,' she said.

They found another one and he lowered his hand at a snail's pace.

It worked. Soon he was also stroking down the fish's side with a fingertip. The scales were slippery. The fish's gills slowed. It let him close his hand around its belly.

He tossed it up on the bank. Petra fell upon it.

'What a beauty,' she said.

They continued fishing and soon had a good haul.

'What are we going to do with all this fish?' he asked. 'I certainly can't eat that amount in one sitting.'

'Take what you want for dinner and I will take the rest. I will smoke what we cannot eat right away. It will help us get through the winter.'

He sat up and dried his arm on his shirt tails. He was looking forward to fresh fish for dinner. Smoked fish he could do without. He had eaten far too much of it during his army days. Smoked fish. Dried meat. Hard biscuits. He certainly did not miss the food.

They had caught ten good-sized trout and they worked together to get them cleaned, tossing the offal back into the water, where it would feed other fish.

She grinned at him. 'You brought your rods for no purpose.'

'I am assuming that guddling is not always an option?'

'No. The conditions have to be right. We would have been glad of the rods had it been cooler or cloudy.'

'Well, I must thank you for my lesson.'

'You are a good pupil. My brothers were hopeless at it. They could not sit still long enough. Sometimes you have to get into the water with the fish. We are lucky here, the overhanging bank makes it a perfect spot.'

He touched the bare arm that had been in the water. 'You are freezing. You need to put on your coat.'

'I am not in the least bit cold,' she objected.

He gave her a look. 'You will not be pleased if you catch a cold.'

'Believe me, I don't catch cold so easily. I must go now. I need to prepare this fish so it does not spoil, and I want to check my traps.'

He shrugged. 'As you wish.'

She frowned as if surprised he did not insist more.

Why would he? She would only take him to task for fussing.

He could not, however, stop himself from saying one thing. 'I will see you on Friday as you promised.'

'If I can get away. If I am not there on Friday, I will come at the first opportunity.'

And with that, he had to be satisfied. He rolled down his sleeve and put on his coat. Once they had split their haul, they went their separate ways.

Or at least, she headed back the way she had come. Ethan followed her from a distance, moving quietly through the undergrowth until he was sure she was safely back in the lane. Why had he not simply insisted on escorting her?

Because she would refuse and he really did not want to have to insist. If he did that, she was sure to turn cold on him.

Chapter Seven

Petra hurried along the path in the woods. She had not been able to get away to help Lord Longhurst with his books for five days now. She had been so busy with smoking the fish they had caught and dealing with the rabbits, then a storm had blown in, leaving Marguerite with a bad headache. Today was the first day she was able to slip away.

The ring of metal against wood rang out through the forest. A woodcutter clearing up the deadfall, no doubt. It seemed Lord Longhurst had taken her advice on that matter also. She smiled. Not only was he a handsome, charming man, he was also the most sensible male she had ever met.

Deciding to avoid being seen, she circled the clearing, but could not resist a peek. She started as she realised it wasn't a woodcutter at all. It was His Lordship stripped to the waist once again and swinging an axe. The muscles in his arms rippled with each powerful strike. Sweat gleamed on his sculpted torso. The man was so beautifully proportioned with his wide strong shoulders and tapered waist he might have been used to model Atlas himself.

Unable to resist, she crept closer to get a better look. And stepped on a twig. At the snap, he turned. Their gazes met across the clearing. Heat shimmered in the air. She could scarcely breathe for the pounding of her heart as she remained fixed in his bright blue gaze for what felt like a very long time, but must only have been seconds.

He lowered the axe head to the ground. 'Lady Petra.'

'Lord Longhurst.' My goodness, how breathless she sounded. She forced herself to take a deep breath and draw closer, as if he was not half-naked and radiating heat from his exertions. Indeed, he was the most tempting sight she had ever seen. 'I was on my way to see you.'

'I thought you had given up on me, to be honest, so I have been plodding along on my own and making a bit of headway.'

Was he saying he no longer needed her assistance? Disappointment filled her. Sadly, she stared at him, drinking in the sight of him as if she was about to lose something precious and dear to her heart. Shocked by her reaction, she cast him a bright smile that felt brittle and false. 'I am sorry I was unable to send you a note on Friday to let you know I would not be coming as promised.'

'Never mind. You are here now and I have some questions.'

Relief flooded through her. Impulsively, she touched his arm. His heat permeated through her cotton gloves and his muscles shifted slightly as if surprised by her touch. The strength beneath her fingers inspired awe. 'I am so very happy you still need my help.'

She gasped even as the ill-thought-out words left her lips. Yet they were honest, were they not? The truth.

His eyes widened a fraction, as if he, too, sensed more to the words than their actual meaning.

She swallowed. 'I mean—'

'I missed you,' he said gruffly. 'Your help. Your smile. I—'

And then, without knowing who had made the first move, she was in his arms and kissing him as if her life depended on it.

His mouth moved over hers, his lips soft yet hungry, his tongue tracing the seal of her lips, requesting rather than demanding entry. She parted her lips and welcomed the blissful strokes of his tongue and tasted the nectar of his kiss.

She pressed against that beautiful broad expanse of chest, loving the hard feel of him against her soft flesh. Her insides tightened unbearably and she arched her back, aligning her body as close to his as possible. The blood rushing through her veins made her dizzy with excitement.

A large warm hand lay flat on her back, holding her steady so he could explore her mouth fully. His other hand stroked over her derrière and gently pulled her close as he rocked in counterpoint to the movement of her hips.

Pleasure became an exquisite ache in her core. Wild with desire, she ran her hands over his back and up to his lovely shaped head, where she speared her fingers through the damp curls at his nape.

Finally, when she thought she would never draw breath again, he broke their kiss and rested his forehead against hers, breathing hard.

'Ethan,' she whispered.

'What is it, my...dear?'

His little hesitation gave her pause. What had he been about to say before he changed it. *My love?* Surely not. Perhaps he had been going to say *my lady* and had realised it did not really fit the circumstances. That was far more likely.

'Should I apologise?' Ethan asked, his voice gentle. 'Because you know, I am not at all sorry.'

She laughed, the awkward moment forgotten, and stroked his beard-roughened cheek with the tips of her fingers. 'It is I who should apologise. I believe I caught you unawares. But I am not at all sorry either.'

He chuckled softly. 'You have no idea how glad that makes me.' He let out a sigh. 'I cannot deny that I find you attractive in the extreme and knowing that you reciprocate makes me happy.'

Her heart lifted, then plunged as he stepped back.

Sorrow filled his expression. 'What has happened here, between us, makes it clear that we must not meet alone again.'

'I don't understand.' Heat rushed to her face. Why was she arguing? Why was she not simply shrugging and accepting his rejection as any sensible woman would? But after the joy of that kiss she needed to know what held him back. 'What harm do we do?'

He grimaced. 'None. We clearly enjoy each other's company. And your knowledge has been invaluable. Indeed, if I had a choice, Lady Petra, I would request your hand in marriage, we are so well suited.'

Her jaw dropped. He wanted to marry her?

'But needs must. I have to marry for money. There is no help for it if I want to rescue this estate.'

She laughed awkwardly. 'I certainly cannot help you there, my lord. I do not have a penny to my name.' She fixed her gaze on his face, willing him to listen. 'Nor am I on the marriage mart. I do not seek to marry again. And since, at least for the moment, we are both free to seek our...' How did one put this? Heat rose in her face, but she soldiered on, for was this not one of the only advantages to being a widow? 'To seek our entertainments where we please. Does it not seem opportune that we have found each other at this moment in time? As if the fates have brought us together? There can be no doubt that there is more than mere friendship between us.'

His eyes widened.

She tried not to flinch. 'Oh, dear, now I have shocked you with my boldness. I apologise.'

He caught her hand in his, brought it to his lips, and kissed it gently. 'Not so much shocked, my dear, as pleasantly surprised. You are a desirable, beautiful woman. The attraction between us strikes me anew, each time we meet. But for your sake, I would not dishonour you by proposing anything untoward. Or anything that you do not want.'

Her heart soared at his reluctant admission that he also desired her. She wanted this. She wanted him. And she was free to indulge herself, provided she did not make a scandal. Why should she not enjoy the attentions of a man she had come to like very much?

She moved closer, ran her free hand down the bare expanse of his chest and was delighted by the way his nipples hardened in response. She looked up into his face, unable to hide her feelings of hope. 'Then it seems we are perfectly in accord in our desire for a brief affair.' She glanced around at their surroundings. 'And who knows how many opportunities the future will offer us to be alone? Should we not make the most of it right now?'

His voice deepened and became husky. 'I am honoured that you trust me enough to make such an offer.'

'But?'

He groaned. 'But nothing. I have no willpower where you are concerned.' He pulled her close and kissed her deeply. After a few heady moments he drew back and gave her a small peck on the cheek. He left her side and she felt a sudden chill until she saw what he was about. He collected a bundle on the ground she had not noticed before. His coats and shirt and, of all things, a blanket.

'I planned to eat luncheon out here, so I could get as much work done as possible today,' he explained at her quizzical look. He spread the blanket on a patch of soft green moss beneath the limbs of a large oak. 'A soldier learns to take along what comforts he can,' he said, grinning up at her from his knees on the grey wool blanket. He held out his arms to her with the expression of a naughty boy who has just found something wonderful, like a grasshopper or a frog, and had plans for it.

'How exceedingly fortuitous for me,' she said, shaking her head at him and going to him with laughter bubbling in her chest.

She hadn't felt quite this giddy since she was a girl. She sank down on her knees beside him and he undid the strings of her bonnet. He carefully removed it and set it aside. 'Now I can see your pretty face properly,' he said with satisfaction. 'And kiss you properly, without fear of crushing your hat.'

He did just that and as she gave herself up to kisses that were almost magical, he gently eased her back on to the blanket so that he was leaning over her, kissing her lips, nuzzling at her throat and exploring her ear, until she felt like she would explode with the heat and pressure building inside her. Her core ached for his touch, for the pressure of his body against hers. Out of pure self-preservation of her sanity, she took his hand and placed it where she needed it. He lifted his head and smiled down at her.

'Anxious, are we?'

She was panting and scarcely breathing for the excitement bubbling in her veins. Why had she never felt such overwhelming sensations before? It was almost unnerving. She'd enjoyed making love with Harry, mostly. It was really the only time that it seemed as though she'd had his full attention, once they were married. But the storm going on in her body right now was making her dizzy. She did not understand it all. 'It would seem so,' she gasped.

Realisation dawned on his face, along with a hint of regret. His dropped a small kiss on her nose. 'Yes. Of course. You have missed your husband.'

That wasn't it all. But how could she explain the wildness inside her that had been building since the moment she met him?

He smiled as if he understood her silence, though he could not possibly understand anything at all. 'Let us do this properly, shall we?' he said.

'Is there any other way?' she said more boldly than she actually felt at that moment. A doubt niggled at the edges of what remained of her brain. Would she meet his expectations? Harry had accused her of being boring and after a few short weeks had gone elsewhere for his pleasure.

Ethan gave her a sweet smile. 'Let us hope not.'

Lying on her back, her face eager, bright and flushed, Petra looked strangely innocent for all that she was so bold. He liked her daring. Certainly, he would not have let things go so far had she not made it perfectly plain what she wanted.

He'd been wanting this for days when he usually didn't allow himself to want anything at all. One day at a time had been his philosophy for years. It avoided disappointment. That was until he met Sarah. He'd allowed himself to dream of a different future then. And hadn't that been a stark reminder of why his usual philosophy worked so well?

The here and now was what counted and he was going to make sure she enjoyed their encounter as much as he did. More. Because not only was that what a gentleman did, it was what he wanted for her. It was what she deserved.

Luckily, he had been blessed with the tutoring of one of the most accomplished courtesans in London while he kicked his heels waiting for his orders to come through. She'd had other moneyed clients whom she charged a fortune, but for some reason she had picked him to be her lover on the side for those few short months. Perhaps she'd felt sorry for him. Or enjoyed showing off her prowess to a younger man. He'd never asked. One did not look a gift horse in the mouth. And it was certainly a gift that was being offered to him now. A liaison with a widow, with no strings attached.

But Petra was a different proposition to a courtesan.

Or even Sarah. Beneath her prickly outer shell, he sensed she had a delicate centre that would be easy to crush. A soft heart that had likely been crushed in the past.

The thought gave him pause.

'You truly are sure you want this?' he asked, gazing into her deep blue eyes already hazy with desire from their kissing.

'Positive,' she said, smiling at him. A shadow passed over her expression. An expectation of hurt? 'Unless… you've changed your mind?'

He didn't want to hurt her for the world. 'Not a chance,' he said, kissing first her chin and then her collarbone where it peeked at him above the neckline of her muslin gown. He swirled his tongue around the little hollow of her throat and she shuddered. 'I simply want you to be sure.'

And he did not want her to feel as if she did not have a choice.

'I am sure.' Her eagerness sent the blood from his brain straight to his shaft.

'I am happy to hear it.' He smiled down at her and she smiled back. It was if they shared a secret, though he had no idea what it was. But whatever it was, it deserved a kiss.

As they kissed, he undid the bow at the neck of her gown and eased it down over her shoulders. Such delicate pale skin compared to his, which was bronzed by the sun of many summers abroad. Reverently he traced the rise of her breasts where they swelled above her stays and chemise. Small breasts, but beautifully formed. He kissed them one at a time and she gave a soft moan and arched towards him.

It would be easy to hike her skirts and lie between

her thighs, but he wanted to reveal all her loveliness, to pleasure her as she deserved. 'Let me help you out of your gown,' he murmured close to her ear.

He helped her to stand and turned her around, kissing her lovely nape as he undid the tapes of her gown and her stays. They fell to her feet and, stepping out of them, she turned to face him with a shy and mischievous smile.

He really liked those smiles. He never wanted to see her sad or unhappy. He drank in her beautiful shape, tiny yet with curves in all the right places, and marvelled at his good fortune.

She raised her eyebrows and pointedly glanced down at his breeches, where his erection must be evident through the tight fabric. 'Do you need help?'

Good lord, he must have been standing here staring at her like some besotted fool. Quickly, he disposed of his boots and stockings and, turning his back, peeled off his breeches.

When he turned to face her, she was once more sitting on the blanket, watching him with an avid expression. He felt like preening.

Inwardly, he laughed at his schoolboy inclinations around her. He'd always told himself that one lover was like any other. That women in general were to be treated with kid gloves and not to be trusted, but with this one he seemed to be constantly battling to retain his guard.

When she opened her arms to him, her high, pert breasts pressing against the filmy fabric of her chemise, he forgot all about such thoughts and fell to his knees beside her, losing himself in her kisses, savouring the hot dark warmth of her mouth with his tongue.

While his lips paid homage to her mouth, his hand found one small breast, its tip furling tight as he circled it with his thumb. With a last lingering kiss to her mouth, he lowered his head and kissed the hard little nub. He suckled, the muslin a sensual counterpoint to the silkiness of her flesh against his tongue.

She sighed her pleasure and her hips arched towards him. He pushed the chemise up to her waist and gazed down her length. The pale gold curls at the apex to her thighs were damp with her desire. He petted the pretty curls and she parted her thighs, giving his fingers access to her hot wet core. He stroked his fingers along her slit until he found the source of her pleasure. She made soft keening noises that drove him nearly insane with desire.

And when her fingers curled around his shaft, squeezing and stroking with a knowing hand, his mind went dark. The urge to plunge into her rode him hard. But he was so bloody big and she was just so tiny.

He rolled over on his back, bringing her with him. She squeaked in surprise, but when she found herself straddling him with his erection pressing against her belly, she smiled and rose up and took him in.

How he survived the first shock of sliding into those tight warm depths without losing control he didn't quite know, but he gritted his teeth and hung on. At first, she seemed uncomfortable with the position, but with his hands clasped around her waist he helped her find a rhythm and depth that suited her and soon she rode him with the skill of a woman who knew what she liked.

The pleasure on her face was nearly his undoing. He shifted within her until he found the spot that sent shudders rippling through her and made her cry out. A few swift strokes and she came apart.

As she collapsed on his chest, he withdrew from her body, and his own petite mort racked him from head to toe.

He lay panting and boneless for what seemed like for ever. At long last, his breathing returned to normal and a great lassitude came over him. He forced himself to lift her off his chest and cleaned them both up with his shirt tails.

With a sigh of satisfaction, she curled up against him. He enfolded her in the crook of his arm and covered her with his shirt. Hopefully, she would not regret the gift she had bestowed on him when she awoke. He fell into warm darkness.

A heavy weight pressing on her hip brought Petra to her senses. What…? Oh, yes. Ethan. Warm and alive and one exceedingly heavy thigh across hers. Recollection flooded in. The way he had given her control. The unbelievable pleasure. The complete loss of herself in those last few moments, like falling apart and reforming as someone new.

Had he felt the same thing? Was it something that happened only occasionally during lovemaking? Nothing in her marriage had prepared her for such a shattering experience.

Yes, there had been pleasurable sensations when Harry made love to her…but that explosive ecstasy she'd just felt? No. Compared to the way Ethan made love, Harry seemed clumsy and rushed. As if he'd always been in a hurry to be done with her. The withdrawal thing she did understand. Harry also had not wanted children. He'd wanted to wait. He'd been having far too good a time as a newly minted member of the *ton*.

The warm heavy weight shifted as Ethan rolled away. She quelled a shiver at the loss of his heat. 'Oh, my goodness,' she said, opening her eyes, surprised to see the sun still shining and glinting through the leaves above their heads. She felt as if she'd slept away a whole night when in truth it must have been only a few moments.

He rose on one elbow to look down at her. 'Are you all right?'

She stretched. All right? She felt wonderful. Full of energy and lax all at the same time. She smiled into his concerned expression. 'I am more than all right. Thank you. That was lovely.'

A warm smile lit his face and his eyes danced. 'My pleasure, I assure you.'

They both laughed.

'I think perhaps we should dress in case anyone comes along,' she said, running her hand over his heavily muscled flank and down over the hard, round buttocks. They were positively delicious. So masculine and firm. Sensual. It was going to be a shame to cover them up.

'Yes, I suppose we should,' he murmured, leaning forward to lick at her breast.

Her nipples hardened instantly. Tension began building deep in her core.

She glanced down at his now-flaccid member resting against his magnificent thigh. Even at rest it was impressive. And already hardening.

As quick as that, she wanted him again. Wanted to

live through that amazing exquisite delight. If it was
possible to feel such things a second time?

He rolled away and rose to his feet. 'You are right,
my dear. We do not want to be discovered. Think of
your reputation.' He pulled on his shirt and helped
her to rise.

Disappointed, she sighed, but nodded agreement.
They had already risked a great deal out here in the
woods where anyone might trip over them. Discovery
would without a doubt put paid to her and Marguerite's
independence. She really could not do that to Marguerite. She must be more careful next time.

Oh, heavens, was she already planning a next time?
Was she really so wanton?

He helped her into her stays and gown, fastening
them with all the expertise of a ladies' maid. Clearly,
he had done this before. A pang of jealousy took her
by surprise.

To hide her chagrin, she sat down to put on her
sandals. 'If I am to help you today, we should hurry.'

He hunkered down beside her and took over tying
the strings. His hands were large, but he accomplished
the task with meticulous dexterity. He shook his head.
'I think you should not come to Longhurst today.'

She froze. He didn't want her at his house? Did he
think less of her because of what they had done? Had
he found her lacking in some way as Harry had done?
Cold trickled into her chest.

'I told Mrs Stone I would be gone all day,' he said. 'It
might look strange if we were to arrive there together.'

Cold was replaced by a flood of warmth. He was
thinking of her, not himself. Oh, how she loved—
appreciated—his generous nature. Harry had only

ever thought of himself. 'You are right. I shall come tomorrow.'

'If it is convenient.'

'I will make it convenient.'

'I will give Mrs Stone an errand in Sevenoaks.'

She giggled. 'Perfect.'

'Do you want to know what is even more perfect?' he said, smiling and picking a leaf out of her hair.

'What?'

'There are beds at Longhurst, with nice, soft mattresses.' He grinned in triumph as if he had produced a rabbit out of a hat.

She could not help laughing. 'It sounds heavenly.'

Chapter Eight

Over the next week or so, Petra had found every excuse to be out of the house. Hazelnuts ready for gathering, elderberries ripening in the hedgerows and even a visit to a sick neighbour on the other side of the Parish when Marguerite was otherwise engaged.

While they were not ladies of the manor, since Longhurst had no wife, someone had to take on the role, particularly since Mrs Beckridge found the idea of visiting ill people distasteful.

Petra never went home to Westram Cottage without completing her stated task, but always managed an hour or two in Ethan's company, either in his arms or poring over the journals. Or both. Little by little, together they uncovered all the secrets in the journals. And little by little, she grew closer to Ethan until on the days she could not go to Longhurst for one reason or another, she felt lost.

Today was one of those days. She put aside her needlework and went to the window to see if the rain had abated. She had not seen Ethan for two days and she missed him terribly. She felt as if she could not breathe. No, it wasn't only him she missed, it was the enjoyment of working with him, of imparting all her knowledge to someone who sincerely appreciated the help.

And, if she was honest, she adored their interludes in bed where she'd experienced that indescribable pleasure each and every time.

Sadly, there was no sign of a break in the weather.

'What on earth is the matter, Petra?' Marguerite asked, putting down her pen. 'That is the third time you have looked out of the window.'

Petra winced. There really was no excuse she could think of for going out on such a miserable day. She flopped down into a chair. 'I am bored.'

A pained look crossed Marguerite's face. 'Are you, dearest?'

Petra hated giving Marguerite pain. 'It is this weather, getting me down, that is all.'

'Perhaps life in the country does not suit you after all?' Marguerite sounded as if she had an idea on her mind.

Petra straightened. 'What are you saying?'

Marguerite glanced down at the letter she had been writing. 'I was thinking a visit to London might do us both good.'

A chill entered Petra's chest. 'Are we running out of money? Do we have to return home to live with Red?'

'No. At least, not yet. But things are getting a little difficult, as you know.' She glanced at the empty hearth. They had agreed to hold off lighting the fire, despite the growing chill of autumn, and were both wrapped in warm shawls.

'So how will going to London help?' Petra tilted her head. 'You can't be thinking about marriage.'

'Certainly not,' Marguerite said swiftly, sharply. 'I need to meet with the publisher, personally. I am owed some money.'

'But Red—'

'It will never come to Red's ears. Unless you tell him.'

Petra gasped, 'I would never say a word. But someone is sure to tell him we are in town.'

Marguerite smiled grimly. 'I will tell him we are in town. He will understand perfectly, when I say we need to shop.'

Oh, indeed. Petra grinned. Red assumed that all women wanted to do was spend money in the shops. His series of mistresses had trained him well, poor dear. But to leave Westram and go to London meant leaving Ethan. She wasn't sure she wanted to do that.

'You go. I will stay here and look after things.'

Marguerite folded the letter and added it to a bundle of folded papers, which she proceeded to wrap in brown paper. 'Nonsense. I could not possibly leave you here alone. And anyway, I'm not yet sure whether I will be going at all. It will depend on the answer to this letter.'

Petra went to her side as Marguerite daubed sealing wax on the strings around the parcel. 'What is that?'

'Some drawings that I am hoping to sell. I saw an advertisement in the newspaper for a sketch artist.'

'Is there anything I can do to help?'

Marguerite pressed her lips together. 'I don't know if my sketches will be accepted, but if they are you will need to take on more of the housekeeping. I hate to burden you with it.'

Petra gasped, 'Do you think I am so spoiled I would not willingly do whatever is needed?'

Her sister closed her eyes briefly. 'It is not that. Of course it is not. You have always done your share and more. It is my fear that it may all be for nothing.' She sounded…mortified. 'I am not sure they are any good.'

Marguerite was sensitive about her art. She rarely let anyone look at it.

'They are sketches of what?'

'Samples of my work. Diagrams. Watercolours. So they can see what I can do.' She shrugged. 'It is for a book.'

'There is more to it than that.' Petra just knew it.

'I am trying to make sure of our independence,' Marguerite said. 'And that is all that needs to be said.'

Petra eyed the package. There was no address on the outside. 'Do you want me to take it to the post office?' It might give her an excuse to run across the fields and visit Ethan, if only for a few minutes.

Marguerite snatched it up. 'I prefer to take it myself. I won't be long. When I come back, we will see if we can turn some of the elderberries you collected into cordial before they go bad. I am sure we have enough sugar on hand. Perhaps you wouldn't mind taking them off the stems in the meantime.'

She whisked out of the front door and was off down the lane with her umbrella over her head before Petra could argue.

Dash it all. Why was Marguerite being so secretive? But then they all had secrets, didn't they? Petra wandered into the kitchen and eyed the basket of elderberries she had picked two days before. She sighed. If she was going to bring fruit home, then she really ought to be prepared to deal with it. She pulled the scissors out of the drawer and began snipping off the stems.

What would Ethan be doing on such a wet day? Would he be staring out of his window, hoping she might come? Likely he would not expect her in such weather. Perhaps he was out riding his estate, verifying the information in the journal, as he so often did on the days she could not go to him. Or paying a visit to Lord Compton. The two men were becoming fast friends. Or at least that was how it appeared.

More to the point, would he be disappointed if she and Marguerite went off to London before she had finished helping him with the journals?

She sighed more deeply. Really. Be honest. Ethan now knew exactly what needed to be done before the start of winter. He simply did not have the money to do it. All they had done recently was try to prioritise which things must be done and in what order, until he came up with a way to finance it.

Two days later, Ethan glanced at the library clock. If Petra was coming today, she would have set out by now. The rain of the previous few days had cleared out and it was a bright crisp autumn day. Ethan shrugged into his coat. He really did not like her wandering the countryside alone. If he left now, he would likely meet her before she had got too far across the fields.

She always scolded him for going to meet her, but he could tell she was also pleased. And seeing her pleased made him happy. Made him forget the dire future looming over him, though the future was rapidly becoming the here and now.

It would soon be time to present himself in London. He had received several letters from other peers of the realm asking for his support on one issue or another in the next session of Parliament. Those letters had reminded him that if it turned out he could not continue to be a soldier, there were things he could do in government to help with the war effort. Things that might improve the lot of the men fighting for their country.

And then there was the matter of the potential bride his man of business had discovered. The man had more or less indicated that if Ethan didn't stir his stumps in regard to the marriage mart, she'd be snapped up by some other poverty-stricken nobleman.

He opened the library door and discovered Petra walking down the hallway with a couple of rabbits dangling from a string. He grinned. 'Poaching again, I see.'

She laughed. 'Marguerite makes a wonderful stew. Send them over with O'Cleary and come for dinner tonight, so you can find out for yourself. It is Mrs Stone's day off today, I believe?' Her eyes twinkled saucily.

'What a clever girl you are,' he said and kissed the tip of her nose, pulling her into the library and closing the door so he could kiss her more thoroughly. How he was going to miss this closeness once he brought home a bride.

Although... No, he would not disrespect any woman who became his wife, despite the fact that many married men kept a mistress. And he certainly would not disrespect Petra by persuading her to continue their relationship after his marriage, no matter how much the idea appealed.

'Wonderful. I shall have Jeb deliver a note of invitation when I get home.'

He took the rabbits and, finding O'Cleary in the stables, gave him the necessary instructions. By the time he returned to the library, Petra had removed her bonnet and her spencer and was seated in his chair at the desk.

'I have had another thought,' she said, peering at the map they had carefully drawn together. 'If we—'

He went around behind her and kissed the delicate nape of her neck.

She shivered, then laughed. 'Don't you want to hear my idea?'

He removed the pins from her hair, watching in delight as the fine golden tresses tumbled around her shoulders. 'I always want to hear your ideas,' he murmured into her ear, delighted to see the fine hairs on her arms stand to attention.

She turned her face up to his, offering her lips for a kiss. He took full advantage and words were forgotten as he brought her to her feet without breaking the kiss, taking her place in the chair and seating her so she straddled his lap.

She moved slowly and sensually against his groin.

He groaned and undid his falls and she sank down on to his erect cock. 'I missed you,' he groaned. He missed her the way he would miss an arm or a hand. He felt incomplete when she wasn't there. He kept waiting for the feeling to die a natural death, but each time they were together it only grew stronger.

Not that he would ever admit such feelings out loud.

He would never give a woman that sort of power over him. Those wild sorts of passions led to a great deal of unhappiness and jealousy as he'd seen first-hand with his parents. No, he did not like feeling this way about Petra. Which was why he was willing to consider the northern heiress as a bride. A sensible convenient marriage was all he would ever need. One that would allow him to return to the war, if at all possible.

He sank lower in the chair and gave her free rein to take her pleasure as she pleased. He loved watching her face as she moved on him. Loved the sensation of hot wet tightness around his shaft. The slide of her inner muscles stroking him brought him close to the edge and it was almost beyond his control to wait for her to find her release. While she pleasured him, he undid the bow at her neck and unfastened the hooks and eyes of the front-closing stays she had taken to wearing just for him. It was always a delight to expose her beautiful breasts to his gaze and his hands and his tongue. He loved their firm softness and the way her nipples hardened to the touch of his tongue.

He suckled. A few moments later she fell apart. Desire beat a demand in his blood. He lifted her clear and she grasped his member and brought him to completion, expertly catching his seed in the tails of his shirt before collapsing against his shoulder.

He curled his arms around her. If only he could protect her from the future. He could not. He lifted her so she sat comfortably in his arms. Entwined in his chair, satiated and content, the minutes passed. If he was honest, he had never been this contented in his life. A very foolish admission. 'I missed you, too,' she said sleepily.

His heart ached in a painfully sweet way at her words. Foolish sentiment. He was a soldier. An earl. Sentiment had no place in his life. 'Tell me your idea.'

She sat up and he helped her straighten her clothing and she lifted up so he could button his falls.

'It is about using the fields for grazing animals.'

'I have no cattle to graze.'

'Exactly. Why don't we lease out the fields to those who do?'

'Are there people who need grass for their animals?'

'Yes. There is an article about it in this journal. The demand for wool from sheep is going unfulfilled at the moment, because France is blocking ships from reaching us. There is not nearly enough grazing land for the growing number of flocks and people are leasing out patches of land all over the place.'

She shuffled through the papers on his desk and found a journal he had not yet had a chance to read. She flipped through the pages until she found what she sought. 'Here. This is it.' She handed it to him.

He scanned the article. 'How do we locate such a person?'

She gave him a smile of triumph and took the journal back. She opened it to a page at the back and pointed to a paragraph set in bold type. 'We advertise.'

We. It was if this situation between them could go on for ever, even though she knew full well it could not. On numerous occasions she had indicated that it must end soon. Pain sliced through his chest. He swallowed.

She stared at him, concerned. 'You don't like the idea?'

He shook his head to clear it. 'I like it very well. Indeed, it is brilliant.'

'Would you like me to draft up something for you to send in to the journal? Merino sheep would do very well on your fields and they fetch a good price at market. Their grazing would bring a good income, I should think. We will have to look into what sort of prices others are asking. Lord Compton might know. I believe he pays for grazing for some of his cattle.'

She pulled a sheet of paper and a quill towards her.

A sound made him look up. The sound of a door opening. He frowned. Was O'Cleary back from Westram already? If so, he must have ridden—

The library door swung back. Mrs Beckridge stared at them, slack jawed.

'My lord,' she gasped. 'Lady Petra. Oh! Oh!'

Petra leaped from the chair, but it was far too late. With her hair in disarray around her shoulders, her gown obviously askew and sitting on his lap, there was nothing she could have said that would have done any good.

Instinctively, Ethan rose to his feet and put Lady Petra behind him. He gave the Vicar's wife his best parade-ground stare. 'Madam, what right have you to intrude on my privacy in this way?'

Attack was always best when faced with an enemy.

'Well, I never. Wait until the parish hears about this revolting spectacle.'

Anger rose in a red haze before his eyes. 'If I hear one word about your visit here today, your husband will be looking for a new living.'

She turned white, then a mottled shade of red before she turned and fled.

'That's torn it,' Petra said flatly, coming out from behind him.

'Marry me,' Ethan replied, knowing it was the only thing he could say.

She looked aghast. 'Certainly not. She won't say anything. Not with her husband's livelihood at risk.'

He didn't trust the woman an inch. 'It is the only way.' Though God knew how he would support her.

She stared at him for a long moment and he was sure he saw longing in her gaze. She brushed her hair back from her face and gave him a bright smile. 'I am a widow. I can do as I wish. In our circles it is quite normal. No one would say a word. That woman had no right barging in on you like that.'

If he'd been able to afford a butler, she wouldn't have been able to barge in on him. 'Think of your reputation here in Westram.'

'Oh, pooh. Even if she does say something, who is going to take any notice of that old bat? The villagers despise her.'

'People love scandal.'

'Well, I don't care a fig for it.'

'Petra—'

'No, Ethan. I won't be forced into a marriage neither of us wants and that is final.'

Her rejection stung, whereas he should have felt relieved. He ought to argue with her. Make her see things his way, but if she truly did not want him..., Well, he certainly wasn't going to force her, was he? The last thing he wanted was an unwilling wife.

She went to the mirror, pinned her hair up neatly and donned her outer clothing. On her way to the door,

she paused. 'I don't think dinner tonight will be a good idea, do you?'

He closed his eyes briefly. 'No. I do not.'

She smiled sadly and left.

At first everything seemed normal when Petra and Marguerite entered the church the following Sunday. She'd certainly heard not a word of gossip that would lead her to believe that Mrs Beckridge had spoken a word of what she had seen at Longhurst Park.

Petra could only be thankful that the busybody woman had not entered a half hour before.

She and Marguerite took their usual seats in the second row. Ahead of them in the closed pew, Ethan was already seated, his broad shoulders in his tight-fitting coat a most enjoyable sight for any woman. And especially enjoyable for her, because she knew intimately what lay beneath the snug blue fabric.

As usual the service began right on time, but Petra felt the back of her neck prickle as if someone was watching her closely. Using the excuse of adjusting her hassock, Petra glanced back and met Mrs Beckridge's piercing and challenging glare. *How dare you show your face in the house of the Lord*, the look said.

Petra pretended not to notice and, staring to the front, lifted her chin.

No other member of the congregation sat beside them, but that wasn't unusual. The villagers usually occupied the seats further back and while Mrs Beckridge occasionally sat with them, it was her wont to visit herself upon various families over the course of the weeks, as if it was an honour to be bestowed.

It wasn't until the sermon began that she realised

the reason for the challenge in that unfriendly look. The Vicar read from Corinthians chapter six regarding sexual immorality and preceded to call down hell and damnation upon anyone who ignored the warning contained in the scripture. Petra's face became hot. She prayed no one could see her blushes. Ethan's shoulders squared and he kept his gaze fixed firmly on the Vicar's face, but even from this distance she sensed his anger. Oh, heavens, what if Ethan said something to him? Might people conjecture and put two and two together? They had met other parishioners from time to time when out on their rambles around the estate.

Petra forced herself not to look around at the congregation to see if anyone was looking at her, but a glance at Marguerite's grim face made her heart sink. Had Mrs Beckridge said something to her sister?

At the end of the service, Marguerite nodded stiffly to Mr Beckridge and hurried to climb into the pony and trap before anyone else left the church yard. They set off at a spanking pace. Heat and cold flushed through Petra by turns. Had the Vicar spoken to Marguerite? Or had Marguerite guessed the reason for her many absences from home this past month?

'Insufferable man,' Marguerite snapped. 'He was looking right at me.'

Petra gaped at her. 'I thought he was looking at me.'

'What reason would he have to look at you? No, it was me he was looking at. Once or twice he has cautioned me about the temptations of two women living

alone. Horrid man. How could he think such things? I should have known better than to...'

'Than to?' Petra asked.

Marguerite gritted her teeth. 'I gave him a piece of my mind. Blast it, I told him it was none of his business what I did or who I did it with... I should simply have agreed and assured him nothing of that nature would cross our minds.'

Petra's jaw dropped. 'He thinks we are Sapphists?'

'He is an idiot. He didn't precisely say we are living in sin, he just hinted that we might be tempted to do so.'

'Where would he get such a peculiar idea?'

'From his wife, no doubt. Oh, heavens, if he says one word of that sort to Red I am going to strangle him. You know, I really think it would be better if we went to London tomorrow, instead of waiting until next week. Out of sight is out of mind. We will start packing as soon as we get home.'

'Marguerite, you were not the object of that sermon. He would not dare make such an unfounded accusation.' Inwardly she winced. 'However, there is something I must tell you.'

Marguerite slowed the horse to a walk and turned in her seat. 'What?'

'Yesterday, Mrs Beckridge caught me sitting on Lord Longhurst's lap in his library.' How angry he must have been at the Vicar's sermon.

Marguerite let the reins go slack and the pony stopped. 'She what?'

Petra swallowed. 'She barged in on us. He and I have been having an affair.'

Marguerite closed her eyes and tipped her head back. 'So that is all it was.'

'All?'

She pursed her lips. 'Well, of course, it is a serious matter, but nowhere near as odd as his other accusation. And besides, I assume Longhurst made you an offer? Or if he did not, he certainly will now.'

She took a deep breath. 'He did make me an offer and I refused.'

'What? Why?'

'Because I don't wish to marry again. I certainly don't wish to marry a man forced to the altar by Mrs Beckridge. Besides, we all agreed we could take lovers if we wished when we came here.'

'As long as we were discreet about it!'

'I was discreet. The woman walked in on us unannounced.'

'Typical.'

'Of me?'

'Of Mrs Beckridge! Blast it. This is sure to get to Red's ears and he'll be racing down here—'

'Ethan—' she winced at the slip '—Lord Longhurst said that if she uttered one word to anyone, Beckridge would lose his living. I don't think either of them would dare say anything outright.'

'I see.' She picked up the reins and set the pony in motion. 'Well, we are still going to London tomorrow. And, Petra, it would be better if you did not visit Lord Longhurst again, in case someone else stumbles in on you. Someone who can't be forced to remain silent.'

It was what she had already decided. Particularly since his offer of marriage. Somehow, him making the offer and her turning it down had felt like the world had shifted, leaving them on opposite sides of a crevasse too wide to cross. It was too wide to cross. Over and over, Ethan had talked about returning to the army. She would never marry a man who cared only for war. She'd lost one husband to it, she certainly didn't want to lose another. And losing Ethan would hurt far more than losing Harry had.

She stilled. Was that true? Was she really so smitten with Ethan? If she was, it was exceedingly stupid of her. She should know better.

'I'm sorry, Petra,' Marguerite said softly.

'Do not be.' Petra smiled brightly. 'I had already come to the same conclusion.' After shedding a few tears.

Marguerite patted her hand. 'You know, if my errand in London is successful, in time we can buy a cottage of our own and not be dependent upon Red.'

And everyone would be happy.

Then why did she still feel so terribly sad?

Chapter Nine

Ethan watched the Westram ladies depart from the church in haste. He had his temper in check. Barely. 'Interesting sermon, Vicar,' he said through gritted teeth.

'Thank you, my lord.' Beckridge rubbed his hands together. 'There are a few members of our little congregation who were squirming in their seats.'

He actually had the gall to look smug.

'And your reason for selecting that particular message today?' Ethan could not keep the dangerous note from his voice, no matter how hard he tried.

'Actually, it was my dear wife who suggested that it had been a while since we had last addressed the topic. The ladies employed at the Green Man are no better than they should be and have been getting bolder by the week. A little reminder never goes amiss.' The Vicar beamed.

A sly and clever woman, the Vicar's wife. Ethan could hardly object to a sermon directed at the village's round-heeled wenches. Not without raising suspicions in the Vicar's mind. But it was a fine line his wife was walking. A very fine line indeed and Ethan would not hesitate to make good on his threat if one shred of gossip impinged upon Petra's reputation.

Unfortunately, since she had not accepted his offer of marriage, he was honour-bound to end their idyll. And since that was the case, he no longer had an excuse to put off going to town to take his place in the House of Lords. It was also time to meet his prospective bride before making a commitment.

'There is another matter I wish to raise with you, my lord,' the Vicar said.

Ethan eyed him warily. 'And that is?'

Beckridge glanced at the departing congregation. 'If you would care to honour me by taking a cup of tea in my study, my lord, we could discuss the matter in private.'

The hairs on the back of Ethan's neck rose. He narrowed his eyes on the Vicar's face, but he saw no guile, nothing untoward. Damn it all. It looked as if this was a discussion he could not avoid.

It would be as well to discover what the man had on his mind and, since the Vicar's abode was beside the church, it should not take long to dispense with the matter.

Once they were seated in the small study each with a cup of tea and the maid had closed the door behind her, the Vicar leaned forward in his chair. 'It is about these gypsies.'

Gypsies. Ethan felt the stiffness leave his body. The result of a protective urge that seemed to overtake him in regard to Petra, when he knew that lady could take care of herself. 'What about them?'

'The last time my wife raised this matter, you indicated you knew of no wrongdoing on their part which would make you require them to move on.'

This was likely the reason for the woman coming to his house in the first place. And no doubt now she thought she had the means of getting what she wanted by making Petra's life uncomfortable. Yes, Mrs Beckridge was indeed a clever woman, but he was not one to be held to ransom. He'd learned a great deal about strategies for dealing with enemies in the army. He was known for it. 'And you have some knowledge of their wrongdoing you would like to impart?'

'No direct evidence, my lord.' He shook his head. 'But two reports of stolen laundry in the past week lead me to think they are up to their usual tricks.'

'Have these thefts been reported to the constable or the magistrate?'

'I am not aware that they have.'

'Then they ought to be.'

The Vicar waved a hand in dismissal. 'The villagers do not like to bother such people with trivial matters, my lord. Indeed, it is unlikely that either of those persons would lower themselves to investigate the theft of a couple of handkerchiefs and a chemise, not when the matter can be easily resolved by moving the gypsies along.'

'And if it is not the gypsies, laundry will continue to disappear and I shall have lost useful labour.'

The Vicar goggled. 'You continue to employ them, my lord?'

'I do. They are currently harvesting the deadfall in Crabb's Wood.' He'd arranged it when he realised he wouldn't have time to finish the work before he removed to London for the opening of Parliament.

'How do you know they will not steal the wood from you?'

'If I am not concerned, I do not see why you should be, sir.'

Looking very unhappy, the Vicar drew out a kerchief and blew his nose loudly. 'I see.' He was no doubt wondering how to break the news of his lack of success to his wife.

Ethan took pity on him. 'When that task is done, they intend to move on to their winter quarters in the south country.'

The Vicar beamed. 'Soon?'

Ethan nodded. 'Very soon.'

The Vicar reached down and opened his desk drawer and pulled out a small bottle. 'A drop of brandy to liven up your tea, my lord?'

The man was a tippler. No wonder with a wife like his. Ethan accepted a splash of brandy in his tea and sipped appreciatively. 'Are there any other matters we need to discuss, Beckridge?'

'Nothing at all, my lord.'

Ethan was very glad to hear it.

When Red had learned of his sisters' intention to visit London, he'd sent his carriage for them. To their surprise, he was waiting for them on the doorstep of the family town house in Grosvenor Square, looking as pleased to see them as they were to see him.

Red rarely left Gloucestershire. Their visit to town seemed hardly likely to draw him forth, but they accepted that it had with gladness.

He kissed them both on the cheek and escorted them indoors. By the time they had gone up and removed their outer raiments and directed the staff with regard to their belongings, the tea tray was awaiting them in the drawing room.

At first, Petra had been so pleased to see her brother, she had noticed nothing amiss. However, now she had a chance to observe him more closely sitting beside Marguerite on the opposite sofa, the lines around his mouth and eyes seemed deeper than they had been a year ago.

Yet, despite his drawn looks, he was beaming at them as if he was genuinely pleased to see them, so she refrained from commenting on his appearance.

'I knew you would tire of the country eventually,' he said to Marguerite.

'Nonsense,' Marguerite said. 'We simply need to refresh our wardrobes, that is all.'

Red nudged her with an elbow. 'Who needs a fashionable wardrobe stuck out in the middle of nowhere? Unless some country squire has sparked your interest.' He waggled his brows.

Petra's cheeks heated. Not that she'd ever felt any need to alter her dress for Ethan. He had never seemed to notice what she was wearing. Indeed, he seemed to prefer her wearing nothing at all. Her whole body went hot.

Marguerite also coloured.

Petra frowned. Had her sister met someone and not seen fit to mention it? More likely she was embarrassed because she did not intend to tell Red her real reason for coming to town. No doubt she was worried that he might see her being paid as an artist as something less than desirable.

'We still go to church every week, Westram,' Marguerite said reprovingly. 'You would not have us attend with worn hems and flounces turned more than once, I assume?'

His face fell. 'Certainly not.' He drew in a breath. 'I should tell you, however, that the moment I heard you were coming, I accepted several invitations on your behalf. Thought you might like to get about a bit.'

Marguerite glared at him. 'Now, why would you do that without asking us?'

'Because people would think the worst of me if you visited London and were not seen in polite company. That is why.'

'Think the worst of you? What nonsense. What on earth would give you such a notion?' Marguerite said. 'Besides, no one would be any the wiser about our presence here, unless you told them. Really, Red, could you not have consulted me first?'

He stiffened. 'Actually, it was Miss Featherstone who said it would look most odd if it appeared you had gone into hiding from the public eye.'

'Miss Featherstone,' Petra echoed. 'What business is it of—'

His face darkened.

'Red!' Marguerite's voice rose in volume. 'You have finally offered for her.'

He gave a shamefaced grin. 'I did.'

A flicker of emotion crossed Marguerite's face. Worry? Then she smiled. 'Congratulations, my dear. I wish you both very happy.'

'Oh, Red, if it is indeed what you want, I am so pleased for you, too,' Petra said.

Petra and Marguerite had never understood his devotion to the lady in question. She was so high in the
instep as to be insufferably rude to everyone she met.
But the match had been arranged between their parents years ago, before they were born, and he had never
looked at another woman. Not a respectable woman
anyway.

'Have your finances finally come about?' Marguerite asked.

He grimaced. 'With my prospective father-in-law's
help. In addition to advancing funds for improve-
ments to the estate, he has made a great many...er...
helpful suggestions with regards to its management
over the past year. Within a month or so I will be sol-
vent and there is no longer any reason to put off the
wedding.'

No reason, except that Petra could not imagine a
worse sister-in-law than Miss Featherstone. While the
world generally described her as handsome, Petra always thought of her as horse faced. Not that there was
anything wrong with horses. Nor would she dislike
anyone simply because of their looks. She was not so
petty.

Unfortunately, Miss Featherstone had never liked
Red's sisters and had called them spoiled and frivolous.
Naturally, the scathing words had got back to Petra
by way of her friends. She had never told Marguerite.

'What else does Miss Featherstone think?' she asked
Red sweetly. 'Perhaps she thinks it is time we married again?'

Red looked distinctly relieved. 'As do I, my dear
Petronella.' Red only called her by her full name when
he thought he could lord it over her. When she was a

child, she'd always stuck her tongue out at him when he had done so. Right now, she felt like hitting him over the head.

'Well, it doesn't matter what she thinks,' she said briskly. 'Or what you think for that matter. I am not marrying anyone.' She couldn't bear to think of it after the way she felt about Ethan. She froze. She didn't mean it quite that way. Ethan was a friend. A close friend whose company she enjoyed to the fullest. As a widow it was permitted. It was a delightful affair that was now over. 'And you cannot force me to do so.'

'Or me,' Marguerite said quietly and with a great deal less heat.

Red rubbed the back of his neck, something he did when faced with a conundrum. 'Unfortunately, it is... I mean my whole future happiness depends on... You have to understand—'

'Spit it out, for heaven's sake,' Marguerite said. 'I am assuming you have made us part of your agreement with her father.'

'I agreed that I would ensure that I was not carrying any more expenses than the estate can afford. As he pointed out, the income Westram Cottage would bring would be a boon if I could rent it out.'

'We will pay the rent,' Marguerite said immediately.

Petra gasped, 'Marguerite, how can we?'

Marguerite squared her shoulders. 'You will let me worry about that.'

Red looked unconvinced. 'I am sorry, my dears. I wish I could simply let you have your way in this, but you must either find husbands or come and live with me and Miss Featherstone once we are wed.'

A shudder rippled through Petra. Living as a poor

relation under that woman's roof would be utterly in-
tolerable.

'Perhaps Carrie—' she started to say.

'What are you suggesting?' Red snapped. 'Would
you have it said I refused to care for my widowed sisters? Lady Avery is not even a relative.'

'She is our sister.'

'She *was* your sister-in-law and has now married
into another family altogether.'

'Anything would be preferable to—'

'Petra,' Marguerite said calmly. 'Let us not get into
a brangle with our brother. Red, if I can prove to you I
can support Petra and myself, will you accept that you
are no longer responsible for either of us?'

Red eyed her warily as if anticipating some sort of
trap. 'If you could prove it to my complete satisfaction,
I suppose so. Provided you are not planning to go into
trade again. Miss Featherstone was appalled when I
told her of your foray into the world of commerce.'

She would be appalled if they as much as breathed
fast. Heaven knew what she would do if she learned
about Petra and Ethan. Probably die of apoplexy. In
which case, she maybe ought to tell her. She squashed
the uncharitable thought.

If the woman made Red happy, who was she to criticise? But if he was happy, why did he look so care-
worn? He looked years older than his twenty-five years.

'At the end of one week and I will pay you three
months' rent in advance and show you that I have
enough keep Petra and me in style. If I cannot do this,
we will agree to abide by your wishes.'

Investments? Agree? 'You might be willing to
agree—' Petra said hotly.

'Trust me,' Marguerite said, the look of appeal in her gaze so intense Petra felt compelled to acquiesce.

'Very well, sister,' she said, forcing a smile. 'I will trust you.' But she hoped like anything she wasn't making a huge mistake.

Red nodded his satisfaction. 'In the meantime, I shall be happy to foot the bill for one ballgown each. You will need them for my wedding, therefore I will make you a gift of them. And, my dears, it really would please me greatly to see you out and about in society while you are here.' He gave them a pleading smile.

Who could resist when he asked so nicely? And Petra had to admit it would be pleasant to catch up with old friends and all the latest on dits. She glanced at Marguerite, who nodded grimly.

Petra put down her cup. 'Very well. We shall attend these events.'

Red rubbed his hands together. 'Excellent.'

Marguerite rose. 'I think I need a rest after our journey.'

'I'll join you,' Petra said. 'I hope you know what you are doing,' Petra added when they were on their way up the stairs.

'So do I,' Marguerite said quietly. But she did not sound at all certain.

Petra felt as if she had jumped from the frying pan into the fire.

For one mad moment, she felt like running back to Ethan and telling him she had changed her mind about his offer of marriage. She forced herself to remember he had offered for her only because he had been honour-bound to do so. She reminded herself that Harry had been similarly forced to offer for her and had clearly resented it. Not to mention that, as delightful as a man could seem before a wedding, once married, they held all the power and had no qualms about doing exactly what they wanted.

So far Ethan had shown nothing but good qualities. But then she had thought the same about Harry. One never knew for certain what lay beneath a person's surface until they had no reason to hide.

She'd been disappointed once. She would not take the risk a second time.

Ethan was in London but had yet to contact the lawyer who was supposed to introduce him to his prospective bride. Instead, he'd been investigating other alternatives to return his estate to its former glory. While he knew he had to marry, eventually, he wanted to do it when *he* was ready, not because of financial exigencies. Unfortunately, none of his enquiries to his fellow peers had borne fruit. While marrying an heiress was his very last choice, no other solution had come to the fore. The day when he would have to knuckle down and admit there was no other way was drawing ever closer.

The image of pretty little Lady Petra floated across his mind. Too bad she was not a wealthy widow. He pushed the wish aside. It was pointless thinking about how much he enjoyed her company. Or how well they suited. His emotions when it came to Petra were far too strong. He did not want that sort of marriage. He wanted peace in his house.

Her suggestion of leasing out his fields had been a good one, but upon deeper investigation he had concluded it would not bring enough income. His barns needed repair as did the cottages for the people he needed to employ on the estate. To put it bluntly, he needed a huge infusion of funds. If only there was some way other than marriage…

A diminutive lady with bright yellow hair swirling around on the dance floor caught his eyes.

Petra? His heart leaped with joy.

For a moment he thought his eyes were deceiving him. She always looked lovely, but tonight in a ball-gown of a celestial blue that matched her eyes and her hair elaborately dressed, with jewels at her throat and wrists, she looked ethereal. Otherworldly. Not in the least like herself. Yet stunning. Was this the real Petra rather than the woman who tramped across his estate in all weathers to lie in his arms?

Clearly, she was enjoying herself thoroughly. He glared at her partner, a handsome man with rich auburn hair. Apparently, it hadn't taken her long to attract an admirer, for there was no denying the warmth in her gaze as she gazed at this man.

Lord Pelham wandered over to stand beside him. 'I hear you are going to make your debut in the House of Lords next week, Longhurst?' He'd briefly met Pelham at an event earlier in the week.

He bowed. 'I am.'

'Where do you stand on the Corn Laws?'

Ethan frowned at the older man. He'd been reading about the matter, about the artificially high price for bread. 'It is hard to justify keeping the cost of such a basic food item so high.'

'And yet without the necessary protection of our in-come, men like you and I will be ruined and the men who buy bread will have no work and no money at all. Trust me, it is for the good of the country that we landowners must stand together.' The older man gave him a hard look.

'Thank you for your advice.' Ethan wasn't convinced. He needed to read more from both sides of the question before he made any decision.

Clearly assuming he had a convert, the other man beamed. 'You are most welcome. If there is anything else I can do to help you, let me know.' He bowed and moved to join a group of men on the far side of the room.

Petra had concluded her dance with the tall red-haired nobleman and was now standing beside her sister, whose severe manner of dress and air made her appear more unapproachable than usual. One could not imagine Lady Marguerite dancing. She also looked very much like... Of course. The man Petra had been dancing with must be her brother, the Earl of Westram.

A feeling of relief rushed through Ethan. He made his way to Petra's side and bowed. 'Lady Marguerite. Lady Petra. What a pleasure to find you here.'

Petra beamed. 'Lord Longhurst, I had no notion you were coming to town.'

She had. He'd mentioned it. Was that why she was here? Hardly likely, she'd already turned his proposal down. Unless she had changed her mind? If so, would he be glad or sorry? Good Lord, he had never felt so conflicted in his life. Or at least not recently. 'Would you care to dance?'

The request left his lips before he had time to think about the possible implications.

Petra's eyes widened a fraction and then she smiled.

She glanced at her sister, who made a shooing motion with her fan. 'Just don't leave the ballroom.'

Good lord, had Petra told her sister of their affair? The back of his neck became hot, much as it had in the church when that idiot Beckridge had lectured the congregation about sexual morals.

He led Petra on to the dance floor.

Their opportunities for conversation were limited and their words easily overheard, so he restricted himself to pleasantries until the end of the dance.

'May I bring you some refreshment?' he asked politely.

'That would be lovely,' she replied in kind.

He led her to a chair beside a small table at the edge of the ballroom and then sent a footman off to fetch a cooling glass of punch.

She laughed when he sat down beside her. 'Handled with the efficiency of a major.'

He raised an eyebrow. 'I didn't spend twenty years in the army and not learn something.'

'How lovely to see you here.'

'And you. You look as at home here in town as you do in the countryside.'

She sighed. 'I had forgotten how much I enjoyed dancing. Perhaps we can convince the landlord of the Green Man to hold the occasional assembly. We would need subscriptions from enough people to make it worth his while.'

She was going to be returning to Westram.

For a moment, he felt incandescently happy. Until he remembered his purpose for coming to London. When he returned to Longhurst, he would likely be returning as a prospective bridegroom, if not married already. His mood darkened immediately.

'You don't like the idea?'

He forced himself to smile. 'I think it an excellent plan.'

'Mrs Beckridge will not like it,' she mused.

'Then together we will rout her.'

She smiled. 'As you did the other day.' She blushed. 'Oh, I should not have mentioned that.'

'It is hard to forget. The woman was gobbling like a turkey when she left.'

She laughed out loud. 'It is a sight I shall never forget as long as I live.'

The sight he would never forget was Petra as she came undone.

They gazed at each other and he knew he was going to miss her for the rest of his life.

'Would you really make Beckridge leave if she starts to gossip?' Petra asked curiously.

He sighed. 'I would not turn him out, but I must say I find his sermons highly unpleasant and his wife even more so. I am thinking I might try to offer him some sort of lure to make him leave of his own accord.'

Petra nodded her approval of his idea.

Her sister walked purposefully over to where they sat, clearly intent on breaking up their tête-à-tête.

Regretfully, Ethan gave up his seat. 'May I fetch you some refreshment, Lady Marguerite?'

'Please,' she said with a stiff nod.

He did as he was bade and sent a footman over with the glass of ratafia since he had already used up the requisite amount of time with the ladies and had no wish to give the gossips fuel for their conjectures. On moving away from the table, a guest touched his arm. When he turned he saw it was Pelham. 'May I introduce my niece? Ermintrude, this is Lord Longhurst. Longhurst, my sister's daughter, Miss Lambton.'

Nonplussed, he stared at the girl. Why... He kept his face expressionless, but inwardly he cringed. This was the way the marriage mart worked. Pelham would not be so anxious to make the introductions if he knew the state of Ethan's finances. So far, he and his man of business had managed to keep that to themselves. He bowed. 'I am pleased to meet you, Miss Lambton.'

Finally, the girl raised her gaze to his face. She did not look at all happy to meet him. 'My lord,' she said, her voice dull.

Her uncle whispered something in her ear and she forced a smile.

Pelham rolled his eyes and leaned close. 'She's nervous,' he whispered.

Ethan set out to make the lady feel more comfortable. While he could not say that she warmed to him, she did deign to walk the circumference of the room on his arm. She responded to his remarks in monosyllables for the most part, but when a new set formed she agreed to dance with him. She danced with precision, but not with Petra's grace and verve.

When he allowed himself to glance over to the table where he had left Petra, she was gone. He had wanted to tell her what the future held. Clearly a ball was not the place to reveal his intentions.

Perhaps she would consent to drive out with him. He'd discovered a natty curricle among the myriad articles in the back of the stables at his town house. It would be easy to rent a pair of horses to pull it. Unfortunately, the town house was included in the entail or he would have sold it in a heartbeat. The place was also in need of care and attention and a good clearing out. It, too, was stuffed to the gills with furniture and assorted knick-knacks. In fact, it was even worse than Longhurst Park had been.

Chapter Ten

Petra should have been surprised to receive Ethan's note three days after the ball, asking if she would drive out with him at the fashionable hour. She was not. She was, however, surprised at how thrilled she felt at the notion.

Marguerite absently agreed that it would be perfectly all right for her to accept the invitation. Her older sister clearly had other matters on her mind. She had been disappearing on errands of her own. On one occasion, two days after their arrival, she'd seemed particularly dispirited. When Petra had asked her point-blank what was wrong, Marguerite had smiled vaguely and said she would reveal all when the time was right. Then she'd locked herself away in her chamber for two days.

Did Marguerite have a secret lover? Had she been rejected? Or was she still pining for Saxby and this visit to London had brought all her memories of her late husband back? Petra's heart ached for her sister, but what could she do if Marguerite would not talk about her troubles?

Ethan arrived a few minutes early, but Petra was

ready and waiting in the drawing room when his curricle pulled up outside.

With Marguerite nowhere to be seen, or to remind her of the proprieties, she dashed down the stairs before the doorbell rang. When the butler opened the door, she beamed at Ethan, who looked splendid in a coat of blue superfine with silver buttons. He whipped off his hat and bowed. 'Lady Petra, how good to see that you are ready.'

One of her brother's footmen had taken charge of the horses and he held them steady while Ethan helped her up and once more took control of the reins. In just a few moments, they were moving out into the traffic and heading for Hyde Park.

Ethan pulled around a parked brewer's dray and neatly avoided a hackney carriage coming in the other direction.

'The traffic is busy today,' Petra remarked.

The offside horse started at a piece of paper blowing across the road, but Ethan held him in check. 'It is always busy in London, I think.'

'And noisy,' she added when three hawkers competed for attention for their wares at the corner of the street.

He grinned at her and nodded. It was only a little less noisy when they turned into Hyde Park given the many carriages making their way sedately up the row, in order that their occupants would have plenty of time to see and been seen. And, of course, there were the pauses while acquaintances greeted each other and looked each other over.

Fortunately, the weather, while cool, did not threaten rain.

'That is a very fetching bonnet, Lady Petra,' Ethan

said, looping the reins expertly around one hand and half turning to face her.

'Thank you. I made it myself.'

He looked surprised. 'You are very accomplished, I must say.'

She smiled at the compliment and addressed the thought uppermost on her mind. 'Did you have a purpose for inviting me to drive today, or was it merely for the pleasure of my company?'

His lips twitched. 'You are also very forthright. Which I like very much,' he hastened to add.

'Do you, indeed? Then I shall never hesitate to speak my mind when I am with you.'

A short pause ensued. 'I did advertise my fields for grazing and, as luck would have it, Compton needed somewhere to put his dairy herd, since one of his fields flooded and it will be weeks before it is fully drained. He also loaned me an old plough share. It needs repairs, but O'Cleary thinks he can mend it.'

'That is good news.'

He shook his head. 'It is a step forward, but it is nowhere near enough.'

'Perhaps you can lease out more fields.'

'I will lease as many as I can, but even if I had animals on every field, it will not be enough to cover the expenses, unfortunately.'

Dash it. She had hoped— 'Perhaps you need to marry an heiress,' she said, thinking of her brother and Miss Featherstone. She had decided that was the only reason Red could possibly want to marry the woman, hence the reason for his haggard appearance.

'You are not the first person to make that suggestion.' His voice was dry.

A pang seized her heart at the thought of him marrying someone else. Or perhaps it was because he, too, seemed content with something so cold-blooded as a marriage of convenience. She tried not to show her disappointment. After all, she had known he would have to marry sooner or later, but for some reason she had hoped it might be later. The back of her throat ached with…unshed tears? Surely not. She must have a cold coming on.

'Do you have someone in mind?' she asked calmly, hoping he would notice nothing amiss with her voice. 'Or would you like me to make discreet enquiries among the ladies of my acquaintance? They often know about these things.' She winced, fearing she sounded a little bitter.

'You would do that for me?' He frowned.

'If you wish it?' Was she mad? She hated the idea.

'I see.' He urged his horses a few steps forward and lifted his hat to a group of ladies walking along the path. 'There is actually someone waiting in the wings, but I have not yet met the young lady in question.'

He didn't sound happy; he sounded stoic.

'You would rather not.' She felt a little more cheerful.

'It is not my first choice to be sure.'

Naturally he would not say more because he was a gentleman.

'When you meet her, you might be pleasantly surprised.'

'Why, Lady Petra, you sound as if you are trying to marry me off.' His laugh had a hollow ring, though his blue eyes were twinkling. He was trying to make them both feel better about what was to come. And for that she was grateful.

'What about selling your town house?' she asked.

'Entailed. It seems that the Longhursts have been

a feckless lot and decided to make sure the property remained in the family.'

'There is nothing else of value?'

'Only my horse, but I would only have to buy another, so selling Jack would be a false economy. Even if I lease out the town house *and* the estate, it won't bring in enough income to put the estate into anything like order.'

Together they had worked out just how much would be needed. It had been an enormous sum.

Back to the heiress, then… 'Yes. It seems your hands are tied. I can think of nothing else you could do that would result in vast sums of money.'

'Nor me.'

People did marry for money and often they were happy. Sometimes they were not and if she were going to wish something for Ethan, it would be his happiness. 'Would a bank give you a loan?'

'It would, if I had any collateral.'

They reached the end of the row and turned out of the park. Their hour was up.

He sounded like a man preparing to lead a forlorn hope. 'Perhaps you should think about it for a day or so. Something might turn up.'

'I have done nothing but think about it.' He heaved a sigh. 'I can certainly wait a day or two more, since the duns are not yet at the door.'

'I am very glad to hear it. Do you go to the Frobishers' ball next week?'

'I have not replied to the invitation, but I can do so. Do you go?'

'Yes. Perhaps by then one or other of us will have come up with a solution.' Other than marrying an heiress. She really hoped so.

* * *

Ethan sighed and threw the agricultural journal aside. He'd spent all afternoon going through every last article to no avail. There really were no shortcuts for a landowner. It took five years at least for every damned thing to get to a point of profitability.

He'd received word from O'Cleary that the plough had been repaired and asking which field was to be turned over first, and could he please see about hiring a man to do the work. But if Ethan didn't have money for seed, what was the point in laying out money on hiring a ploughman? He'd have to go home and see to it himself.

Someone thumped on the front door with a fist. Ethan started. He'd not hired on any servants for the London town house, because he had decided that even though he slept here each night, he would neither pay calls nor receive any here. The house was a mess and it had to be cleared out before he could think of entertaining anyone. Another expense he'd have to face soon.

In the meantime, if someone wanted to meet with him, then he met them at his club, where he took all of his meals, thus keeping his expenses to the minimum.

Not having O'Cleary's help here in town had been an inconvenience, but he was perfectly capable of dressing himself and shaving.

The knock came again. He got up and looked down into the street and saw a very familiar face looking back up at him from beneath her umbrella. Lady Petra. Standing in the pouring rain.

He wasn't exactly dressed for afternoon callers, but nor was he going to leave her standing on his doorstep for any old passer-by to see. He tightened the belt on his dressing gown, wended his way round the multitude of furniture that took up every inch of floor space and opened the door. He quickly pulled her inside.

She took in his state of undress and beamed. 'I am sorry if this is an inconvenient time to call, but Marguerite went out and I had an idea.'

'An idea?' Hope lifted his heart. 'Let me help you out of that wet coat.' She undid the buttons and he eased her out of the nonsensical thing. The thin fabric offered almost no protection against the elements and barely skimmed the high waist of her gown. Her skirts were soaked at the hem.

'Yes.' She looked about her. 'Sell everything. All the furniture. The lamps. The rugs. They can't possibly be included in the entail. Surely that would help?'

He gave her coat a shake and draped it over a chair. She took off her bonnet, stripped off her gloves and handed them to him. He draped them over another chair. He shook his head. 'They won't fetch anything approaching what is needed. Like the stuff at Long-hurst, most of it is only fit for the rag-and-bone man or the fire.'

'You already thought of it.' She sounded disappointed.

'I had a man come round yesterday. He offered to take it all away as a job lot.'

'You must pay him to take it?'

'Yes. Only then can I lease out the house.'

Her face fell. 'And here I thought I had the answer.'

'Thank you for the attempt, but you know you really shouldn't be visiting me here. Wasn't I supposed to see you at Frobisher's ball tomorrow night?'

'We are not going after all. Marguerite came home

after lunch and announced that we are going home first thing in the morning.'

'Why the haste? What has happened?'

'I have no idea. Red is furious with her, but apparently she was able to pay him three months' rent in advance for Westram Cottage so we can go home.'

'And you came here because you thought you ought to let me know I would not see you at the ball.'

She nodded. She gazed up at the picture in the hall. Like all the paintings in the house it had acquired a thick coating of dust and grime. 'This picture looks familiar.' She touched the surface and her fingertip came away with a black smear. She frowned and looked at the picture again. 'It looks like a painting Marguerite tried to copy from a book when she was going through her Italian phase,' she said slowly. 'She enthused about it for an hour at least. His name is Canal something. I remember that because that was mostly what he painted. Venice canals.'

Ethan knew nothing about art and artists. he simply knew when he liked something. The dealer who had come to value the furniture had only looked at one painting and had declared it a copy of a Reynolds, and a poor one at that.

'There was a diary at Longhurst recording the grand tour of one Joshua Trethewy,' he said. 'The previous Earl's father. I didn't take much notice of it when I realised it didn't have anything to do with the estate, but one of the pages I opened recorded several purchases in Venice of what he called "scribbles" that his mother had asked him to buy.' Along with recording a great deal of other nonsense, like masquerades and the licentious behaviour engaged in by young men out on the town. If the tone of the journal was anything to go by, Joshua would indeed have bought second-rate copies of artwork and spent the bulk of his money on the ladies of Venice, about whose beauty and sensuality he waxed on and on.

Petra turned away from the picture and stared at the clutter of furniture littering the hallway. Footmen's chairs, carved chests, sculptures of assorted sizes and materials all higgledy-piggledy. 'My goodness, it is the same as it was at Longhurst. Your cousin had some sort of problem, I think.'

'All the rooms are the same. Let me show you around. If you can see anything worth salvaging, I would be glad to know it.'

They moved from room to room. Each chamber was full to overflowing with items. 'It is awful,' she exclaimed. 'Who needs five beds in a bedroom?' she asked, peering into one of the guest chambers where the beds were in pieces and the mattresses piled in a corner. 'All these things must have originally cost a fortune.'

'I should think so. And I doubt any of it is worth more than a farthing or two it is so out of style and ugly.'

'What a terrible waste,' she said with a sigh.

'If he would have only spent half of it on the upkeep of the estate…' He let his words trail off. He did not want to mention his need to marry money yet again. If he was honest with himself, instead of trying to pretend otherwise, he really wouldn't mind marrying Petra, if she would have him. He felt comfortable with her. She had become a good friend. Not to mention he thoroughly enjoyed their lovemaking. The fact that she also made his heart beat a fraction too fast was something he could control. Unfortunately, since she had no fortune, it was not to be.

Finally, they reached the only room in the house that was anything like normal, the state bedroom where he slept. Even it had three armoires.

She walked into the room and stroked the beautifully embroidered counterpane. 'I suppose, since you will soon be offering for your heiress, this is the last time I shall see you alone.' She gave him a shy little smile that held a world of meaning.

His heart sank at the thought of them parting, even as his body tightened at the blatant invitation in her words and glance. 'I suppose it will.'

'It would be a shame to waste the opportunity,' she said, holding her arms out to him.

He pulled her close and kissed her.

Ethan's kisses were simply lovely. When he held her in his arms she felt precious and feminine. It was easy to believe that they could be together for ever, when they really could not. As the daughter of an earl, she understood that the nobility married to advance their influence or fill their coffers. Her father had been indulgent in allowing her to choose her husband for love.

It hadn't worked out terribly well.

Ethan would be a lot happier marrying his heiress, knowing that his family line was safe and his estate could be brought back from the brink of disaster, than marrying a poverty-stricken widow but, oh, how she wished she had money. But then he would be marrying her for her money, just as Harry had been convinced by his family to marry her for her connections.

No, she really would not want that. She sighed.

He pulled back and gazed into her face. 'Sweetheart, what is wrong? If you do not want this, please say so. I would not have you regret this for the world.'

She managed a smile. 'Of course I want this.' She gave his shoulder a push. 'It was my idea.'

'Then why the sigh?'

'I was thinking how I would miss this, being with you.'

'Me, too. Let us not think about the future, but enjoy the now. It will be a good memory for us both.' The concern in his face touched her heart.

'Yes, I would like that. It has been a lovely friendship, but in future we will meet as mere acquaintances, in the village and at church, but we will each have our memories.' It would be hard to meet him under those circumstances, knowing there would be no more memories to make.

'First I need to get you out of that wet gown. I don't want you catching a chill.'

'That is your excuse anyway,' she said, laughing and undoing the ribbon holding the bodice closed. He lifted the gown over her head and stepped back as if to admire the view. A moment later he was tugging at the laces on her front-closing stays. 'These will just be in the way, don't you think?'

'Most definitely.'

He pulled her close and his kiss was hard and seemingly as full of longing as her own and she gave herself up to the wooing of his lips and the soft strokes of his tongue and the shivery sensations caused by his caressing hands. She wanted this to be wonderful for him, too. A fond memory of the bliss they created together.

She certainly could not imagine herself ever doing this with any other man.

She pulled the pins from her hair and let it fall around her shoulders. He speared his fingers in her tresses. 'Mmm...' he murmured against her lips. 'I love the feel of your hair. It is so soft and silky.'

'It feels good to me, too,' she said, hot prickles running down her spine.

He picked her up and lay her on the bed. He gazed down at her. 'It looks like spun gold spread out on the pillows.'

She wrinkled her nose. 'Sadly, it is only hair or I would give it to you to sell.'

He shook his head and gave her the smile that always made her heart tumble over. 'I couldn't bear for you to part with it.'

She held her arms out to him. 'Come to bed, dear Ethan. Let us not waste time talking.'

He divested himself of his dressing gown beneath which he was wearing nothing at all. What a beautiful man he was in his bare skin and fully erect. Gorgeous. And clearly interested in her as a woman.

He toed off his slippers and climbed up to lie beside her. Leaning on one elbow, looking down at her, he took a lock of hair and raised it to his nose. 'I will never smell lavender without thinking of this moment, or taste blackberries without remembering how we met, or eat a trout without seeing you in my mind's eye stretched out on your stomach on a riverbank.'

A pain pierced her heart, so agonising she could scarcely breathe. 'Ethan,' she murmured, hoping her laugh did not sound forced to his ears, for she wanted him to believe she was happy, 'you say the loveliest things.'

He shrugged and gave her a sweetly shy smile. 'It is the truth.'

She thought for a moment. 'I will never pass a field of hay without recalling you swinging a scythe with your muscles glistening in the sunlight and shifting beneath your skin. I will never eat fish without remembering your expression when you guddled the first time. It was adorable.'

He gave a gentle tug on her hair. 'Now you are teasing me.'

'It is the truth. And I will never ever pick chestnuts without wishing you were there to lend your help.' She reached up, pulled his head down and plundered his mouth for if she did not kiss him right then and there she might very well cry.

As if sensing her anguish, he kissed her back and gently palmed first one breast, then the other, making them feel full and heavy, with her nipples tightened to hard little peaks. She rolled towards him, aligning their bodies, seeking blindly for the closeness she needed.

He groaned and kissed her with urgency and abandonment, until she could no longer think about anything but the demands of her body, her longing for him to be inside her and her need to feel his weight.

She parted her thighs and he came over her, settling his body into the cradle of her hips. The muscles in his chest became hard ridges, as he supported himself on his hands, as did those on his belly. He really was too beautiful.

'Ah, sweetheart,' he said. 'When you look at me just so, I believe I could move mountains.'

Slowly he entered her body and began to move in long delicious strokes.

She moved against him, lifting her hips in counterpoint to his thrusts. The pleasure built and she brought her legs up and around him. Bringing him even deeper inside her body.

He suckled on one nipple, then the other, while she hugged him close, holding on for dear life as she reached for the delicious undoing of body and soul.

The sweet pain of it tore her asunder. She had never experienced such undoing before Ethan and likely never would again. He withdrew from her body and reached his own climax. Sated and lax, she lay panting beneath him. He pulled the counterpane over them both and she fell asleep in his arms, knowing it really must be for the very last time and trying with a monumental effort not to cry.

Chapter Eleven

With winter approaching, Petra found herself more and more housebound. But then she had no real reason to go anywhere, did she? Longhurst Park remained unoccupied while His Lordship stayed in London, no doubt wooing his heiress and preparing to take his seat at the opening of Parliament the following week.

She would have liked to have been there for that. She would have felt so proud of him.

A letter arrived from Red while she and Marguerite were at breakfast one morning. Miss Featherstone had agreed that their wedding would take place in the spring.

'Finally,' Petra said. 'Though I don't understand why they would wait yet another six months.'

'She is a fortunate woman,' Marguerite remarked. 'I hope she appreciates him the way she ought.'

Petra laughed. 'No doubt she expects him to appreciate her.'

Marguerite sighed. 'Poor Red.' She rose to her feet. 'Time to get back to work.'

'How is it coming along?'

She winced. 'It's hard to come up with new ideas.'

'You haven't shown me any of your drawings for weeks.'

Marguerite looked out of the window. 'That's because there hasn't been much to show. I am working mostly on the drawings from nature the publishing house contracted.'

'They certainly take up a great deal of your time.'

She gave an uncomfortable laugh. 'They do indeed. It is dull stuff, I assure you. It is mostly the insides of flowers, their reproductive organs. Very technical and tedious. I'll show you the one I am working on before I send it off.'

'I'd like that.'

'I was wondering if you wouldn't mind going to market with Jeb today, so I can finish it. I need to get it in the post tomorrow.'

Mind? She'd be thrilled to get out of the house. Anything to take her mind off missing Ethan.

She dressed warmly and went out to tell Jeb the good news that he would only have her company for the drive to Oxted.

He grinned good-naturedly and helped her up into the trap. 'When be His Lordship returning from London?' Jeb asked.

Petra stiffened. 'I have no idea, Jeb. Why do you wish to know?'

'Me ma says it ain't the same cooking for no one but Mr O'Cleary and him taking all his meals in the kitchen, like.'

'I am sure he will be back as soon as his business in London allows.' And then Mrs Stone would have two more mouths to feed.

Her throat filled with unwanted tears. She swallowed them down. 'Are there things you need for the stables?' she asked.

'Yes, my lady. I need corn for Patch here and some nails. We got a board or two coming loose on the potting shed.'

Petra added the items to her list.

Shopping at the market in Oxted was uneventful, though she found the haggling to get the best price tiring and rather distasteful. It ought to have been enough to keep her mind busy, but she still had to stop herself from thinking of Ethan every time she noticed a tall fair-haired man. He wasn't living at Longhurst and therefore he would not be at the Oxted market.

While Jeb went to buy feed, she purchased the items on her list. No more tallow candles either. The advance from Marguerite's contract had allowed for a few little luxuries.

She counted the money left in her purse once she'd bought all the required items. She had enough remaining to buy some good-quality tea. She wandered along the stalls. A hand clutched at her shoulder.

She swung around, half expecting to find a cutpurse at her elbow. To her surprise it was Madame Rose. She was not wearing her gaudy outfit today, apart from her large hoop earrings and her bangles that tinkled softly as she moved.

'My goodness,' Petra exclaimed. 'You gave me a start.'

'I beg your pardon, my lady,' the woman said in her heavy accent.

Petra smiled politely. 'Was there something you wanted?'

The woman narrowed her eyes on her. 'You are sad.'

Petra frowned. 'Nonsense.'

'You miss the one who makes you unhappy. You will see him soon.'

'If you are talking about my husband, you are barking up the wrong tree,' she said with an airy laugh. 'I won't be seeing him any time soon.'

'I speak of the big man. The fair lord.'

Why did everyone suppose she knew Ethan's movements? She glared. 'If you mean Lord Longhurst, of course I will see him. We are neighbours and he will be returning to Longhurst with his wife before very long.'

Madame Rose shook her head, her earrings swinging back and forth, until Petra could not help but wonder if they might hurt her. 'You can see the future, my lady?'

'Of course I cannot see the future. I simply know of his plans.'

The woman smiled knowingly. 'There is many a slip between cup and lip, and many a child born of love.'

Petra's mouth dropped open. Unthinking, she pressed her hand against her belly, before she recalled it wasn't possible. Things had all gone as they should this month with her courses.

Madame Rose raised her eyebrows and her eyes danced wickedly. 'Give a message to the lord when you see him. The woods are finally all cleared and we are wondering if he has other work for us to do since it is too late now for us to seek other quarters for the winter.'

'You plan to stay at Longhurst all winter?'

'If His Lordship will allow it.'

'You should speak to Mr O'Cleary. He is sure to be in touch with His Lordship.'

'You will see His Lordship first.'

She didn't want to see Ethan. It would only remind her of how lonely she had been since she left him in London and how lonely she would continue to be. Sometimes she wished she had never set eyes on him at all. At other times she knew that she would not have missed their few weeks together for the world.

Madame Rose patted her arm. 'It is all right, little one. You will find the man of your heart.'

Dash it all, these platitudes of hers were annoying. 'Please speak to Mr O'Cleary.' She turned and hurried back to find Jeb.

Since Jeb wasn't much of a conversationalist, on the way home Petra found herself reliving her conversation with Madame Rose. Mrs Beckridge was right. The woman was a charlatan, playing on the emotions of unhappy women. Petra was sorry the gypsy band had chosen to linger in this corner of Kent.

As they passed through the village, she told Jeb to pull up so she could collect the mail from the post office.

She jumped down from the trap and went inside.

Mrs Beckridge was at the counter. When she turned to leave and saw who was waiting behind her, she recoiled, a look of disgust on her face.

Petra flinched inwardly, but pretended not to notice the look or Mrs Beckridge. But the woman wasn't satisfied with being ignored. She leaned close and hissed, 'You think yourself so high and mighty, but you are no better than the wenches at the Green Man. Tell Lord Longhurst those gypsies have to move on. No one dare hang out their laundry while they are still about.' With a stiff nod, she hurried out.

The postmaster eyed Petra askance.

'How are you today, Mr Barker?'

'Fair to middling, Lady Petra.' He frowned. 'It really is a shame His Lordship lets those gypsies stay on his land, you know.' He gave her such an odd look; her stomach fell away. Had Mrs Beckridge reported what she had seen to others despite Ethan's threat?

'Then you take the matter up with His Lordship,' she said matter-of-factly. 'Do you have any mail for Westram Cottage?'

'Ah, I would, were I to see him. My wife lost her best petticoat this week. Right cross she is about it, too. Perhaps if you hadn't agreed with His Lordship that it was all right for them to stay...' He checked his pile of letters. 'Nothing for you ladies today.'

'Thank you.' She made her way outside.

So that was what the artful Mrs Beckridge was about. Letting people blame her for Longhurst's decision. How ironic that she was just as unhappy with their presence in the area as everyone else. Perhaps there was something she could do. Madame Rose had said they had finished clearing the woods, so perhaps Petra could convince her and her family to move on.

Or better yet she should write to Ethan and tell him that the problem with the laundry continued and his presence was required.

That was a much better idea.

She didn't feel comfortable talking to Madame Rose after what the woman had said to her.

Ethan could not wait to see Petra and to tell her his news. Her letter about the gypsies had come at a most opportune moment. He pulled up outside her cottage and jumped down. Petra was on her hands and knees working on her garden.

She got up at the sound of his footsteps and her gaze filled with pleasure. 'Ethan.' She started forward, then stopped, her cheeks turning red. 'How good to see you, Lord Longhurst.' She glanced towards the cottage. 'I didn't know you were back from London. May I offer you tea?'

He'd arrived late last night. Too late to visit Westram Cottage.

'Thank you, that would be delightful.'

Inside, she offered him a seat and rang for the tea tray. 'How was your journey down from town?'

'Excellent. I left the moment I got your note, though I cannot stay long. I have to take my seat in Parliament on the fourth.' It was a task he would be glad to have out of the way. He had planned to speak with Petra after that, but receiving her note had changed his mind and he'd come straight away.

She nodded. 'I wish I could be there to see you make your first speech.'

'It is not a speech as much as a question. Pelham advised me to keep it short, unless I have plans to become a great orator, which, I assure you, I do not.'

He frowned. She looked paler than usual. Unhappy. 'What is this issue you are having with the gypsies?'

'Apparently, they are stealing laundry left and right.' She gave a short unhappy laugh. 'As predicted by Mrs Beckridge.'

'You know for certain they are involved?'

She got up and went to the window, looking out as if she did not want to see his reaction. Or maybe to hide hers. There was more to this than met the eye.

'Who else could it be?' she said evasively. 'I know I did not agree with Mrs Beckridge at first, but it seems we both might have been wrong. Now they have finished clearing the deadfall, could you not ask them to leave?'

'I told them they could stay for the winter if they wished. I do not generally go back on my word.'

Damn it all. This was not what he wanted to talk to her about. And yet he was loath to discuss a more delicate matter while this topic put them on opposite sides of the fence.

She turned to face him. 'What if they were caught in the act? Would you ask them then?'

He closed his eyes briefly. 'It would certainly be in their interests to go if one of their number was caught in a criminal act.' He narrowed his eyes on her face. 'It is not the only reason you have for wanting them to leave, is it?'

She sighed. 'No. The villagers seem to be blaming Marguerite and me for their continued presence here. Because we took their part against the Vicar's advice. They don't say anything, but they are not as friendly towards us as they once were.'

'The Beckridge woman again, I suppose.' Damn her. If she couldn't make trouble one way, she found another to accomplish her ends.

'Most likely.' Petra smiled unhappily. 'Though I think she didn't need to say much on the subject to have them up in arms after the loss of valuable items. Next, they fear their homes may be pillaged, I am sure.'

As a landowner, it was his responsibility to protect his neighbours. Both the villagers and the likes of the two lady widows. And he wasn't having her made unhappy because of a point of honour. 'You say they have not yet been caught in the act?'

'Unfortunately, no. I was thinking of setting a trap.'

He started. 'You would need to be very careful. Any creature who is cornered can be dangerous, but it is a good idea.'

'That was why I wanted your help. I was thinking of spreading one of our tablecloths on the laurel bush in the front garden. It wouldn't be the first time we have used it to dry larger items.'

'You are going to use yourself as bait?' He did not like that idea at all.

'Who else can I ask? Besides, the villagers might be grateful to us if it was Marguerite and I who were the ones to finally capture the thieves.'

'You really care what these people think of you, don't you?'

'Naturally. We live here. To be ostracised by our neighbours would be horrible.'

Well, he had a different answer for that problem, but now was not the time. 'When do these thefts occur?'

'Usually in the evening. Honestly, I had no idea how often people forget to bring their laundry in at night, though I believe they are being a lot more careful now. We have not had any incidents for two days.'

'Then this is what we shall do. I will return here after dusk and set up a perimeter with O'Cleary around the laundry and we will nab our thieves.' He stood up. 'Wait to put out your linens until after I have gone.'

'Thank you, Ethan. I knew I could count on you.' His heart warmed at the words he'd never heard from a woman before.

She came forward, hands outstretched, and he took

them in his. So tiny. So easily broken. He raised one to his lips and brushed his lips against her knuckles. 'You know you can call on me for anything at any time.'

Her eyes went moist for a moment, as if tears were close to the surface, but her bright smile made him think he was likely wrong. 'I know it,' she said huskily. 'Though I will try not to take advantage of your kindness.'

He wanted her to take advantage of him as often as she wanted. The idea pleased him and he smiled back. Only just in time did he stop himself from taking her in his arms. That would come later, after he put paid to the petty thieves who were causing her concern.

Instead of folding her into his arms, he picked up his hat and gloves. 'Once you have put out your laundry, stay inside the house with the door locked.'

Petra could hardly sit still. Every little sound made her jump. Putting aside her book, she glanced out of the window and shook her head at herself. It wasn't fully dark yet. Soon, though. She could scarcely see to read. Was Ethan out there already? What if he came too late?

He wouldn't. He was a man one could rely on. It was one of the things she liked about him. She got up, lit the candles and pulled the curtains closed as they usually did at this time of the evening.

Marguerite raised her head from the stocking she was mending. 'Is something wrong, dearest?'

'No. Why do you ask?'

'You sighed.'

Oh, dear. She really did not hide her emotions very well. 'I am not finding this book as entertaining as I thought I might.'

'What is it?'

Petra looked at the cover, having chosen it from random off the shelf and not read a word. '*The Vicar of Wakefield* by Oliver Goldsmith.'

'You do not like it? I found it vastly entertaining. Indeed—'

Petra tossed the book aside. 'I am simply not in the mood.'

'Then I suppose you are not in the mood to read it to me,' Marguerite said, laughing. 'Take out your mending, my dear. I know you have some.'

Petra winced. How could she bear to sit reading or sewing when Ethan might be outside apprehending a criminal? What if the man was dangerous? 'I will read it to you when I return from the privy.'

'You are surely not going outside now?'

'It is not yet full dark. I won't be but a moment.'

Marguerite grimaced. 'Surely it would be better to—'

Petra whisked out of the room before her sister could finish. It was all very well using the chamber pot, but it then had to be emptied—besides, the privy was simply an excuse. She snatched up her cloak and quietly unlocked the back door, intending to sneak around to the front garden to see if her tablecloth remained where she had left it. Of course, she could have gone upstairs to look out, but it would be difficult to see exactly what was going on.

She hadn't gone but a few steps when someone grabbed her from behind and covered her mouth with a large warm hand. The scent of cologne gave her attacker away. Ethan. She relaxed. He turned her around and lifted her hood over her head. 'That bright hair of yours,' he whispered.

Oh, she had forgotten about that.

'I might have known you would not wait indoors,' Ethan muttered in her ear. He pulled her down the path and into the shelter of the hedge.

'No one came?' she whispered.

'Not yet.'

'Is Mr O'Cleary here also?'

'Yes. Hush.'

She subsided into silence, pleasantly tucked against his large warm body. Petra prayed Marguerite would not come looking for her as the minutes ticked by. A squeak of hinges. A burly shape freezing at the sound, then tiptoeing along the path and across the grass. In a second, the tablecloth was torn from the bush and bundled beneath the interloper's cloak.

Ethan and Mr O'Cleary stepped forward. 'Hold,' Ethan ordered sternly.

The thief squawked, made a dash for the gate and was caught around the waist by O'Cleary, who raised his fist, then stepped back, startled.

'I have a pistol,' Ethan warned.

The thief made a choking sound. Mr O'Cleary uncovered the light of a lantern he must have brought for the purpose.

A scared face scrunched up at the sudden glare.

'Good Lord!' Ethan exclaimed.

'Oh, goodness!' Petra gasped. 'Mrs Beckridge?'

The woman drew herself up straight. 'Someone had to do something to get His Lordship to listen to reason.' Despite her bravado, her voice shook.

'Nonsense,' Petra said curtly. 'How dare you try to

put the blame for the thefts on the gypsies? And what is more, you will return everyone's belongings first thing in the morning and apologise for giving them such a scare. Lord Longhurst I assume you will deliver this woman to her husband?'

'That I will. And I will be having a few words with that worthy gentleman.'

Mrs Beckridge moaned.

'Lady Petra,' Ethan said, 'I will call tomorrow to let you know the conclusion of tonight's events.' He bowed and grabbed Mrs Beckridge's arm. 'This way, madam.'

The front door opened. Marguerite stood framed in the doorway with the light behind her and a coal shovel raised above her head. 'Who is out there? Show yourselves,' she quavered.

'It's all right, dearest,' Petra called back. 'It is only I.'

'What on earth is going on?'

'A slight case of mistaken identity,' Petra said, going to her side. She hooked her arm through her sister's and drew her back indoors, trusting Ethan to handle the matter satisfactorily.

She trusted him more than ever she had trusted Harry. She liked him, too. A great deal more than she should for someone who had sworn never to marry again.

Chapter Twelve

Ethan was disappointed when it was Lady Marguerite who met him at the door, but her greeting was
warm. 'Quite the adventure last night,' she said, smiling at him.

'Indeed, it was.'

'I assume the Beckridges will not be remaining
in Westram?' She sounded pleased. Everyone had
sounded pleased.

'They are packing up and preparing to move as we
speak.'

She nodded. 'Petra is dying to hear all about it. And
she will tell *me* all about it later. You will find her in
the kitchen garden. She is expecting you.'

Finally. 'Thank you.'

'Go around the side of the house. I would offer to
take your hat and coat, but the wind is rather chilly
this morning.'

He did as she suggested and found Petra on her hands
and knees weeding an herb garden. She sat back on her
heels at his approach. 'Lord Longhurst.' She laughed.
'You always catch me at the worst possible moments.'
She gestured to her muddy hems and gardening apron.

As far as he was concerned, any moment he caught her was a good one.

He took her hand and helped her to her feet, inhaling the scent of lavender and thyme and rosemary. 'I am probably earlier than you expected. I apologise, but I thought you might be anxious to hear about the rest of last night's adventure.' That was his story and he was sticking to it. At least for now.

'I am all agog.' She gestured to a wooden seat overlooking the rest of the small garden and the view of the fields beyond. 'Come, let us sit and be comfortable and you may apprise me of all that occurred after you left here.'

He seated her and sat beside her. He crowded her a little more than he ought to, but that was how he felt at the moment. The need for closeness.

'I could not have been more shocked to discover our thief was the Vicar's wife,' she said.

'Nor could Beckridge. At first, I thought they may have schemed up the idea together, but his shock was real enough. He had assumed his wife was tucked up in bed with a headache. His jaw almost hit the floor when she appeared with us on his doorstep.'

'What on earth did he say?'

'Well, it seems Mrs Beckridge rules the roost in that household, so he tried to support her in her exaggerated claims about the gypsies, but when I threatened to call the magistrate and the constable, he collapsed and admitted she was in the wrong.' Though she had threatened to reveal all that she had seen in his study the day she had barged in on him and Petra. A few pithy words had convinced her husband to ensure her silence. He'd also made sure she understood that in his noble circles, widows did as they wished, as did gentlemen, and that neither he nor Petra gave a damn what people like Mrs Beckridge and her social ilk thought.

That the woman believed that about Petra simply proved her stupidity.

'She really is an awful woman,' Petra said.

'Beckridge is a fool to let a woman lead him around by the nose.'

She stiffened slightly.

He frowned. 'I mean in regard to his vocation, his dealings with his flock. He should have known better.' He wasn't sure he had made things any better. The ground beneath his feet felt a little slippery.

'Did you call the constable?'

'Not when Beckridge agreed to leave immediately.'

She nodded. 'That sounds fair.'

He breathed a sigh of relief. 'He said he had been thinking about going to America anyway. He had a letter from someone he knows out there indicating they were in need of a pastor. He asked for references.'

'Did you give them?'

He was back on dangerous ground. 'I said I would think about it.' He took a deep breath. 'I did tell him that I would only do so if he promised not to let his wife run amok again.'

'It would be better if you extracted that promise from Mrs Beckridge.'

He gazed at her, at the tightness around her mouth. Of course. This was where he was going wrong. And he definitely did not want to be going wrong at this moment. It would not do at all given his real purpose in coming here today.

'You are right,' he said. 'And so I shall insist.'

Her posture relaxed. Hallelujah.

'There is another matter I wish to discuss with you,' he said.

She perked up. 'About the estate?'

'In a manner of speaking. You will recall the painting you noticed in the hall in my town house. The view of Venice.'

'I do.'

'Well, upon your departure, I got to thinking about the agent who initially offered to take all the items in the house off my hands. He was also quite eager to look at what we had put out in the barn here at Longhurst, with a view to disposing of them. There was something familiar about his name.' He could not keep the note of excitement out of his voice.

'Ethan?'

'I recalled a bill of sale among the papers my cousin left. When I located it again, it was a receipt for a French table and the price was exorbitant, except that someone had scribbled on it the word *Versailles*. I asked around and eventually was given the direction of an agent who purchases French items for the Prince of Wales. He came and looked at the piece and confirmed it indeed could well have been purchased for the Palace of Versailles along with several other items that he looked at. For the paintings he recommended another expert. It turns out the picture you spotted is the genuine article by Canaletto.'

She was staring at him, wide-eyed. 'It must be worth a fortune.'

'My cousin's collection is almost priceless apparently.'

'Oh, my word. What are you going to do?'

'Sell it.' He shrugged. 'Or most of it. My predecessor should never have spent the money he did on all that stuff when the estate needed funds so badly. I am assured that there are several collectors, including the Prince himself, who will be more than happy to pay a fair price for the artwork and the furniture as soon as the provenance is fully documented. And he saw no problem at all with that.'

She beamed at him. 'That is amazing. Wonderful. I am so pleased for you.'

He grinned back at her. 'Now I can finally put the estate to rights. Which leads me to the last reason I came here today.'

He sought the item he had tucked in the watch pocket in his waistcoat and went down on one knee. He smiled at her. 'I think you know how fond I am of you, Petra. I believe you do not hold me in aversion either. I would like to beg for the honour of your hand in marriage.'

At first, she looked surprised—nay, shocked. And perhaps a little pleased. Slowly, though, her expression turned to one of dismay. 'Oh, please. Do not.' She averted her face.

Pain seized his chest. What the hell was the matter with him? He should have known better than to have expected her to behave in a rational manner. His mother never had. One day hot. One day cold. He got to his feet staring down at her. 'I beg your pardon. I must be under some misapprehension about your feelings towards me.'

'No. No. I like you very well, Ethan. Truly I do. I do not wish you to feel that you must marry me, because of what Mrs Beckridge might say to others. I will not do it.'

He shook his head. 'My offer has nothing to do with that woman, I assure you.'

'Are you saying you...love me?'

Love? Did she really expect such a thing? His mother and father had thrown the word around as if it meant everything and nothing. He had certainly not felt more than mild affection for them, as one must for one's parents.

'I am fond of you. I have affection for you. We deal well together. I can now offer you an estate with good prospects which we can build together. Is that not a more solid foundation for a marriage that some passion that is likely to be over within a few months of marriage?'

Her face drained of colour. What had he said to make her react so?

She inhaled a deep breath and rose to face him, or rather look up at him, she was such a tiny thing. He stepped back a little so as not to overwhelm her. She gave a faint smile at that.

'Ethan, I am truly honoured by your proposal. Deeply touched.'

She didn't sound touched, she sounded hurt. As hurt as he felt. He gritted his teeth.

'As you know, I am determined not to marry again.' She winced. 'I do hope we can remain friends, but I think it would be better if we did not see each other again for a while.'

Friends. As clinically as a surgeon with a knife, the word sliced something in his chest to ribbons. It was the oddest and most painful sensation he had ever known.

Even more painful than his mother's frequent rejections of him. As he had when he was a boy, he bore the pain in silence. He bowed. 'As you wish, Lady Petra.'

He walked away.

Was that a sniffle he heard?

Hardly likely. Perhaps she was laughing at him.

Heart aching so painfully she could scarcely breathe for the pain if it, Petra watched Ethan walk away. Had she really suggested they remain friends? It would not be possible. Meeting each other, even casually, would cause the utmost embarrassment for them both. She should have tried harder to express how honoured she was by his proposal, but truly, receiving such a cold offer was worse than knowing he had intended to marry an heiress for her money.

She sank on to the wooden bench.

What was wrong with her that the men she fell for could only manage a lukewarm affection for her rather than love? What was it Harry had said?

I'm very fond of you, old thing, but this marriage was all your idea. I wanted a commission in the army. Once Pa realised he could be related to an earl, there was no talking him round. It was marry you or be kicked out on my ear. No one ever said anything about love. Besides, in our set no husband hangs off his wife's sleeve. I'd be ridiculed.

She'd loved him so desperately from the age of about fourteen she hadn't realised it had been all one-sided. She'd been so angry at his words she'd told him he would make a terrible soldier. A few days later, he'd entered into that silly bet with her brother Jonathan and Neville Saxby and all three of them had gone off to prove their worth.

All they'd managed to do was get themselves killed.

Well, she knew better than to enter into that sort of marriage again. But, oh, she was going to miss Ethan. Somehow, turning down his offer of marriage this time seemed a whole lot worse than saying their lovely goodbye when they knew there was no choice for him but to marry an heiress. Likely because for a moment she had actually thought he was requesting her hand because he loved her.

But he didn't.

And since she loved him, she'd be right back where she was with Harry. Watching her husband sneak off to make love to whichever woman caught his fancy and knowing that her love was not returned. Not to mention that now he had all the money he needed to set the estate to rights, he'd soon be dashing back to the war and his beloved career. No, turning him down was the right thing to do. For them both.

She closed her eyes to ease their burning. When on earth had she fallen in love with Ethan anyway? It really should not have happened. It was meant to be a fling, nothing more. She really was the worst sort of fool.

She brushed the back of her hand across her eyes and it came away wet. Dash it all. What did it matter that he didn't love her? She had been perfectly all right before he came along, and she was perfectly all right now.

She went back to her weeding. Unfortunately, she had no idea what sort of plant she was yanking from the ground. She could not see them through her tears.

She didn't care.

* * *

Petra walked alone to the village a few days later to discover her neighbours still abuzz with the news of the Vicar's departure and the mysterious reappearance of their missing articles.

'His Lordship said it was all a mistake,' Mr Barker said, scratching behind his ear when he held out a small stack of mail. He tapped one of the notes. 'Franked by Lord Westram, that one there is.'

Petra smiled, though her cheeks felt stiff. 'Thank you.' She didn't feel much like smiling these days, but Barker didn't seem to notice the falseness. Nor did he release the letters.

'Odd that. The Vicar going and the laundry reappearing, don't you think, Lady Petra?'

Gossip. The villagers loved gossip and conjecture. She had delayed going to the village as long as possible in order to avoid this kind of discussion, but Marguerite had been worried about the mail piling up and had been too busy to come herself. 'I really have no idea.' She tugged at the letters and finally he released them.

'He said it weren't the gypsies after all.' He sounded doubtful.

'I am sure he knows what he is talking about.'

Barker shook his head. 'Odd, I call it. Very odd.'

Petra turned to leave.

'Don't forget your package, Lady Petra.'

Why could he not have mentioned a package right away? She frowned. 'I do not believe I am expecting a package?'

'It is quite large. Shall I have my lad deliver it?'

'How large?'

He went behind his counter and pulled out a huge square parcel and set it on the counter. 'Heavy it is, too.'

'Who is it from?' Marguerite often sent parcels out, but nothing so large and she had never had one in return.

'From London. Sherman's Antiquities and Fine Art.'

It must be one of Marguerite's pictures, then. 'Thank you.' She eyed the package. 'I think I can manage it.'

When she stepped out into the street, it was still raining hard and she tucked the package awkwardly under one arm while she opened her umbrella. Intent on getting out of the rain as fast as possible, she put her head down and started walking. She collided with someone coming the other way. The package slipped sideways. She grabbed for it and dropped her umbrella. Blast.

'Why can't you look where you are going?' she said as she snagged the handle.

'I beg your pardon, Lady Petra.' A deep, rich and terribly familiar voice.

Heat rushed to her face. The pain around her heart intensified. 'Longhurst,' she snapped and whipped the umbrella back over her head. 'Good day. I am in a bit of a hurry.'

'Allow me.'

He neatly extracted the parcel from under her arm.

'There is no need,' she protested, reaching for it.

'There is every need.' He tucked the parcel under his left arm and it fit there easily. He then held his other arm towards her.

Short of giving him the cut direct there was little she could do. She rested her hand lightly on his sleeve.

She raised her umbrella over her head and they walked in silence. Like an old married couple. And yet like strangers. She had burned her bridges with Ethan and this sort of reminder was just too much to bear.

Finally, she could stand it no longer. 'I can manage the rest of the way by myself.' She sounded stiff and unfriendly.

He did not break his stride. 'I will see you to your door, Lady Petra.'

Blast. If she had acceded to the offer of the postmaster to send his lad, she would not have had to suffer this.

'Do you think it will clear up later?' he asked in the most normal of tones.

She glanced up at the sky. 'I think it is set for the day. Marguerite said she was feeling a headache coming on.'

'Ah. I wondered why you were walking alone.'

She gritted her teeth in case she told him to mind his own business. She wasn't angry at him exactly, merely the circumstances. But there *was* something she needed to say to him. 'The villagers are putting two and two together with respect to the Beckridges's departure and the reappearance of the missing laundry.'

'I expected it, to be honest. I went to see Compton the morning after we caught her in the act. I decided that, as magistrate, he should be made aware of the whole. It is bound to come to his ears and better he heard about it from me. He suggested we let them work it out for themselves, so they do not continue to blame our gypsies.'

'Our gypsies?' she said, surprised.

'My gypsies, I suppose, since they are on my land. I have spoken to their leader and told him what happened. I explained that as long as nothing else untoward happened during the course of their stay in Crabb's Wood, then the villagers would understand that they were not to blame. He understood completely and then informed me that their plans had changed. They had received word of work from another band and had decided to move on after all.'

'How ironic. Mrs Beckridge would have been so pleased to know that her efforts were successful.'

'Though not in the manner she intended.' He sounded amused.

She glanced at his face and saw he was smiling. Unable to resist, she smiled back. 'All's well that…'

'Ends well,' they finished together and laughed.

It was strange that they could be so in accord on some things and so on the outs with regards to others. Her heart gave a little pang. Regret. It was going to be a long time until she did not feel regret.

He opened the front gate for her to pass through and followed her to the front door. Under the porch she closed her umbrella and stood it in the corner to dry. Fortunately, it was their maid's day to work and she opened the door before Petra needed to search for her key. Longhurst handed her the parcel. Petra turned to face her escort and forced a bright smile. 'Thank you for your help, Lord Longhurst.'

'You are very welcome, Lady Petra. It was nice to be able to assist you for a change.' His smile turned a little wry. He bowed and walked back out into the downpour. He didn't so much as flinch when the rain beat down on his shoulders.

Oh, mercy. What was she thinking? She should have offered him her umbrella. 'Lord Longhurst,' she called out.

When he turned she held it out. He waved it off and continued on his way.

She ought to have felt proud of how she had handled their chance meeting, instead she felt more miserable than when she had set out for the village.

'I put the package on the dining room table, my lady,' the maid said, helping her out of her coat and bonnet.

Petra glanced in the mirror to straighten her hair. 'Can you let Lady Marguerite know it has arrived?' Whatever it was.

'But it is addressed to you, my lady.'

'Oh.' She hadn't as much as glanced at the name of the addressee. 'What can it be? I haven't ordered anything.' Something from Red? Or perhaps from Carrie? She was a frequent correspondent, but Petra could not think what she could be sending that was so large.

'You will have to open it and see, my lady.' Becky bustled off.

Petra wandered into the drawing room and inspected the parcel. It was indeed addressed to her. She untied the string and peeled back the paper. A painting.

'Oh, my word!' She sank down on to the nearest chair.

The maid hurried in. 'Is something wrong?'

'I— No, nothing is wrong exactly.'

'That is a nice picture, my lady. What place is that?'

'Venice,' Petra said faintly. He had given her the picture of Venice. She gazed at the signature, now easily visible since the picture had been cleaned. Canaletto. Out of curiosity, she had asked Marguerite about him on her return from visiting Ethan that day. She had gone on and on about the fellow, but at the time Petra had assumed Ethan's picture to be a copy. This painting was worth a fortune.

The maid gathered the brown paper up. 'There is a note enclosed, my lady.' She handed it over. It was from Ethan.

I want you to have this.

Without your help this picture and many like it would have been given away to an unscrupulous dealer.

Keep it or sell it. It is yours to do with as you wish.

Longhurst

Oh, the wretched man. How could he? And he had carried it for her all the way home and not said a word. He must have known exactly what it was.

The tears that she thought had been all used up burned the back of her throat and forced their way from beneath her eyelids.

'You don't like it, my lady?' Becky asked worriedly.

Petra wiped her cheeks. 'It is not that. It was just the surprise.'

And the generosity.

And the foolhardiness.

Chapter Thirteen

'A package for you, my lord,' O'Cleary said. 'And your new bailiff, a Mr David Carter, is waiting in the hall.' O'Cleary set the large square parcel on a chair.

Ethan frowned at it. It couldn't possibly be what he thought it was. 'Show Carter in.'

He got up and tore a corner of the paper. Yes. Unfortunately, it was. Damn it.

'Good day, Lord Longhurst.'

The young man standing on the threshold had been recommended to him by Lord Compton when he had visited him to discuss the Beckridge affair.

Ethan shook hands with the young man and gestured for him to take a seat. He rang the bell for O'Cleary and gave him instructions as to what to do with the painting Lady Petra had returned.

She wasn't going to like his solution.

'There is a great deal to do here, Mr Carter,' he said, resuming his seat.

'Yes, my lord. I took a bit of a look around before I came here. I can see that things have been let go for a while, but with a bit of work it will soon recover.'

Petra would like this young man's attitude.

'Excellent. When can you start?'

Carter looked surprised. 'Don't you want to see my references, my lord?'

'Compton's recommendation was enough of a reference for me,' Ethan said. He himself was also a good judge of character. Most of the time.

He hadn't been too smart in regards to the art-dealer chap. But then he knew nothing about that sort of person. Fortunately for him, Lady Petra had an eagle eye.

She would no doubt like the look of this young fellow.

Damn it. Every time he thought about something, he tried to imagine what she would say, what she would think. Sometimes he even heard her voice in his head, laughing or teasing. He really would have to stop thinking about her. She had rejected his offer and that was that.

'You should still take a look, though, my lord.' Carter handed over a sheaf of folded references.

Ethan went through them. They were all glowing. And all from men who were known to be honest.

He put down the last one and raised his eyebrows. 'So when can you start?'

The other man blushed and smiled. 'In a month's time, my lord. My current employer has sold the property and the purchaser has his own bailiff.'

'How very fortunate for me,' Ethan remarked and entered into negotiations about terms and conditions and salary, based on yet more suggestions offered by Lord Compton.

* * *

'This has to stop,' Marguerite declared. 'This is the third time this painting has come back to us.'

'I can't accept it,' Petra replied exasperatedly. 'You know I cannot. What on earth would Red say to a gentleman offering a lady who is not related to him such a priceless object?'

'I shall go and speak with him,' Marguerite said.

'No. I will go and speak with him.' This time he would listen to reason.

'What did his note say this time?' Marguerite asked curiously.

'If you don't like it, sell it.'

'That was it?'

'A lot of nonsense about paying back a debt to me and his sincere gratitude. It isn't seemly.'

'It might have been more seemly if you had not bedded the man.'

Petra stiffened. 'That is not nice.'

'It is the truth.'

And it was the real reason the painting had to go back. They had been lovers. If Mrs Beckridge had not walked in on them, if there was no possibility of anyone ever learning of their affair, then she might have gladly accepted the gift in recognition of her help with his estate. But since the truth might one day come out, accepting the picture might well look like the spoils of a paid-off mistress. It was that she could not abide.

She had loved Ethan, still did love Ethan, and despite that he did not love her in return, she did not want their relationship tainted by what could be perceived as some sort of commercial transaction.

'It is too bad we cannot sell it, though,' Marguerite mused. 'It would solve all our financial problems.'

'I thought we were out of the woods.'

Marguerite pursed her lips. 'They accepted three of the four botany pictures. I have not yet received another commission.'

'What happened to the fourth one?'

'They decided not to use it.'

'Still, they will have paid you for the work, surely?'

'I have already told you before, that is not how it is done.'

Petra turned back to the package leaning against her chair. She hadn't even bothered unwrapping it. She could not keep it, no matter what. It would hurt too much every time she looked at it. And she certainly could not sell it. 'I will return it myself this time. Do you need the trap today?'

'No. I am going to be working indoors all day.'

She didn't sound happy. Marguerite used to love her painting and drawing. 'Don't do it if it bothers you,' Petra suggested. 'We can find some other way to get income.'

She'd had a million ideas when it came to Ethan's property, but then there were a great many more opportunities to be had on a large estate like Longhurst Park. Their cottage had none.

Marguerite smiled. 'I'm sorry. I am being defeatist. I can do this. I know I can. Take Jeb with you to Longhurst, dearest. Please.'

She didn't need to be reminded to play the part of a proper lady, but she let it pass. There would be no more sneaking into Ethan's home for her and if it made Marguerite feel better to play her part as the responsible elder sister, so be it.

Walking across the lawn, the sight of the little trap travelling up his drive both gladdened and saddened Ethan's heart. An oddly disturbing mix of emotions he did not like to recognise. He certainly knew the purpose for the visit, however. He put down the chair he was carrying and waited for the trap to pull up.

'Good day, my lady,' he said when Petra halted beside him. He nodded at Jeb. 'Your mother is baking biscuits today. You'll find O'Cleary hanging about in the kitchen getting in her way.'

O'Cleary had been helping move the furniture out of the barn, but at the sight of the trap he had developed a sudden need for biscuits and tea.

Jeb grinned. 'I'll take this inside, shall I, my lady?' He hauled the painting out from behind the seat.

'Please do,' she said, her expression cool.

Ethan waited until Jeb was out of earshot. 'All right. You win. I will not send it back again.' There really was no point. She not only did not want him…she clearly did not want anything *from* him.

'Thank you,' she said quietly.

Now she thanked him. Damn it all.

She flicked her whip in the direction of the chair. 'What are you doing?'

He gestured to the growing pile of furniture on the lawn. 'Making a bonfire.'

She gasped, 'You are going to burn it?'

'No choice. It is full of woodworm. That pile is from the attic, but the rest of it is just as bad. I am advised that if I do not want woodworm getting into the structural beams and bringing down the house, it must be burned. It certainly cannot be sold.'

'The pictures, too?'

'Not the pictures themselves. Only the frames.' He shook his head. 'My cousin must have bought something that was infected and they have been having a feast. I really hope I am in time to save the house. I had a chap come down from London to look at it and we have to cut out a couple of diseased sections from the joists, but he says that fortunately the furniture was keeping them too busy to do much damage elsewhere, though it was only a matter of time. I hope he's right.'

Shock and then sympathy filled her expression. Sympathy was better than nothing. He'd take what he could get.

She stared at the pile. 'What a terrible waste.'

He'd been shocked himself. 'Fortunately, none of the items in the town house are similarly affected and the stuff here was less valuable to begin with. The items in London were collected by my cousin's great-uncle.'

'And these?'

'My cousin collected what was here at Longhurst Park. He did not have as good an eye as his predecessor. Most of these are reproductions or badly made to begin with. They wouldn't have fetched much even without the woodworm.'

'I see.'

'Honestly, the previous Earl clearly had no clue what he was doing. He simply could not help himself. Whatever he saw he had to buy. That list we found in my study was not a record of his gambling expenses, but a record of everything he bought for outrageous sums.

I wish he'd had the same compulsion with regard to farm implements. Those we could have made use of.'

'Do you think he suffered from some sort of mental imbalance?'

He narrowed his gaze. Was she wondering the same about him? 'I have no idea.' He looked over at the pile. 'There are one or two items I wish I could have saved, though.'

'Is there no other alternative?'

'There are treatments, I'm told, but nothing is guaranteed. I won't take the risk of losing the house over sentimental rubbish.'

She looked puzzled.

'I had to get rid of the desk in the study. And the chair.'

She gave him an oddly wry smile. 'Sentimental rubbish indeed.'

Damn. He'd obviously said that wrong. 'The memories are all I need.'

Her eyes widened.

A hit. He forced himself not to smile.

'Well, I am truly sorry things turned out so badly for the items here.'

'Me, too. Right now, I'm sleeping on the floor and we still have a great many more rooms to clear.'

'We?'

'Me and O'Cleary. Until the paintings and furniture in London are all evaluated and sold, I still don't have any ready cash to hire the extra help I need and I refuse to go into debt over something I can easily do myself. The dealer thinks we should start seeing income from the auctions at the town house in about two to three weeks.'

'I can lend you Jeb to assist, if you could use his help. He has little enough to do at Westram Cottage at the moment.'

His first instinct was to refuse her offer the way she had refused his painting. But that would be cutting off his nose to spite his face. 'I will accept, provided you allow me to pay his wages for the time he spends here.'

She smiled so sweetly something in his chest clenched and the pain was suddenly so intense his knees buckled. He locked them tight.

'Yes,' she said. 'That would be fair. You can pay him when you have sufficient funds.'

He grinned at her. For a woman she really was quite sensible. 'Good. Send him over in the morning, if that suits you.'

'I'll do better than that. I'll have him set to work now.'

'Even better. By the way, I should tell you I hired a bailiff. He is to start in a month's time.'

'Excellent.' Her tone was just a little too hearty. Could it be that she did not like the idea of him replacing her help? He held that thought close to his heart. It eased the pain somewhat.

'I am sure he would be delighted if you could pass on any of the information you learned over the last few weeks,' he said, hoping for another hit with her. Which was just plain daft at this point. 'I will, of course, try to do so, if you feel it would not be appropriate to speak with him yourself, but you understand it all so much better than I.'

Ah. Yes, there it was. That brightening of her expression that he liked so much.

'I would be delighted to assist him, if needed. But

you should not be so modest. You learn quickly and I am sure you have a good grasp on what is required.'

And so, like the picture, she neatly returned the compliment.

Clearly his case was hopeless.

They waited in silence for Jeb to return so Petra could give him his instructions. It wasn't many minutes before he and O'Cleary arrived on the drive.

'Jeb, His Lordship needs your help for the next few days. Mr O'Cleary will find you a place to sleep.'

Jeb frowned. 'I should ask Lady Marguerite first.'

'No, you should not,' Petra said firmly. 'If she was here now, she would say the same thing. We can manage very well without you at Westram Cottage for a few days.'

O'Cleary grinned. 'A right welcome sight he will be, me lady. Big strapping lad like that is worth ten of me.'

Jeb grinned at the compliment and his ears turned pink. 'You does all right,' he assured O'Cleary kindly. 'I will do as you bid, my lady, but if I am needed back at the cottage, just send word by one of the lads from the Green Man.'

'I promise I will.'

Ethan looked down at her and wanted to kiss her for her kindness. He rolled his aching shoulders instead. The problem was, how could he trust these feelings he had for her when they were together? He could not.

In his boyhood, love was a gift given and taken without rhyme nor reason. His hurt and betrayal haunted him even now. How could he trust that she would not throw his emotions back in his face as she had his marriage proposal?

'Jeb's help is very welcome, Lady Petra. Thank you for your generosity.' Somehow his thanks sounded grudging.

'What are neighbours for, if not to help?' she said lightly.

Inwardly he sighed. Their dealings in future would always be thus. Formal and stiff and uncomfortable.

'Compton's ploughman will come over next week,' he said by way of changing the topic. 'We should be able to plough all of fields we talked about before the onset of winter.'

'That is excellent.' She turned and glanced at the pile of furniture. 'When did you plan setting light to it?'

More trivial conversation. 'As soon as it is all out of the house, I suppose. Shouldn't be more than a couple of days.'

A thoughtful expression filled her face as she gazed up at him. 'Would you mind waiting until next week? I have had an idea.'

'What idea?' Damn, he sounded suspicious.

'I would sooner not say until I am sure it will work. I need to talk to Marguerite.

'I suppose it can wait a few days. It can't do any harm where it is. As long as we don't get a lot of rain, it will just as well light in a few days from now. However, I am due at the opening of Parliament on the fourth and I have to go a few days before then for the fitting of my robe and to allow time for alterations. It is all arranged.'

'Oh, then perhaps my idea will not work. I think you should be here when the fire is lit.'

'I'm sorry, I am confused.'

'Can you be at Longhurst Park on the fifth, the day after Parliament opens?'

'If you want me here, then I will be here. It isn't much of a journey.'

She nodded. 'Very well. As soon as I am sure it can be managed, I will let you know which day your presence is needed.'

He gazed at her, puzzled. 'You have something in mind for this pile of furniture? It cannot be sold. I will not put someone else's property in danger.'

Her smile warmed slightly. 'I know you would not. No, I have an idea about the fire.'

He glanced around. 'It can't do any damage here. It is far away from the house and the trees. You need not fear that.'

'I would expect no less from you, Lord Longhurst.'

Damn it, she was not going to tell him her idea. Because it might not work. And she didn't trust him enough to know that he wouldn't tease her, if it turned out to be without merit.

The thought made him feel unaccountably sad. He nodded briskly. 'Then I shall wait to hear from you before doing anything with it. But I hope we do not get a downpour before I have a chance to light it. The quicker it burns, the better.'

She winced. 'You are right, of course. Perhaps tarpaulins would be the answer. You must have some about somewhere.'

He closed his eyes briefly. 'Of course. I'll see what we can find.'

He handed her up into the trap and watched her drive off.

Tarpaulins. He heaved a sigh and looked at O'Cleary.

'As it happens, Yer Lordship, there be a pile of tarpaulins in the hayloft. I'm guessing they were used to cover the haystacks in inclement weather.'

He should have known about that. He still had so much to learn. 'Right. See if you and Jeb can cover up the damned bonfire with them after all the stuff is out of the house.'

Chapter Fourteen

'Are you sure His Lordship agrees with all this?' Marguerite asked, looking at the list Petra was working on.

'Yes. I wrote to him shortly before he left for London and he agreed to the plan.'

'Well, it is very generous of him.'

'Not that generous. His only outlay is two or three barrels of beer from the Green Man. Jenks is providing them at an excellent price. Everything else, the ladies from the church are providing.'

'I suppose so.' Marguerite looked doubtful.

'The village needs this, Marguerite. Everyone has been at sixes and sevens since the Beckridges left. Quite a few of them still blame His Lordship for letting the gypsies stay on his land as being the reason for the departure of the Vicar. This will help establish some goodwill.'

Marguerite nodded slowly. 'I can see your reasoning. And free beer will go a long way to smoothing any ruffled feathers. But I can't help asking...' She coloured. 'This thing between you and...'

So that was what bothered her sister. 'It is over. We are friends. Nothing more.'

Sympathy filled her sister's face. 'Oh, my dear Petra—'

Petra's heart clenched. 'No. No. You misunderstand. It is ended at my instigation. It was a fling, nothing more. I made it perfectly clear I did not wish for marriage.'

Marguerite looked at her with an expression of wonder. 'If you are sure?'

'I am sure. We get along famously as friends, but the very idea of marrying again gives me nightmares.' Nightmares of Harry being shot alongside her brother and Marguerite's husband. The letter that had come from the military had been a little too graphic in that regard. Red had tried to stop her from reading it, but she had insisted. She did not want to be imagining the same thing about Ethan. Obviously, now he had the money to hire the bailiff he needed to turn the estate around there was no need for him to stay in England and he could be back to the war, exactly as he wanted.

'I see.' Marguerite cocked her head on one side. 'It is good that you are able to be friendly with him. He seems like a very nice man.' Yet there was still some doubt in her voice.

'He is a very nice man and we are friends. That is all there is to it.'

Marguerite recoiled a fraction. Oh, dear, she had spoken with a little too much force.

'The question is,' Petra added hastily, 'can you put this together in time?' She pointed at the rough picture she had drawn. The picture that had started them off on this tangent.

Marguerite gave a rueful little shake of her head. 'Of course I can. It will make a nice break from what I am working on.' She tilted her head back as if easing a crick in her neck.

Petra threw her arms around her sister's shoulders and kissed her on the cheek. 'Thank you, thank you. I knew you would come through for us. Tell me what you need and I'll find it for you.' She pointed to the bag she'd brought from the church. They were clothes donated for the poor. As far as she knew, not one single person had ever taken anything from the bag in all the time she had lived in Westram.

Marguerite rummaged through the bag and set several items on one side. A shirt. An old coat. A pair of workmen's trousers. 'These will be a good start.'

'Wonderful. Let me know when you are finished and I'll have Jeb take it over to Longhurst. Mr O'Cleary knows what to do with it. Now, if you will excuse me, I need to take this list to the church ladies and this advertisement to Mr Barker. He promised to make sure everyone knows about the change in venue.'

'And the free beer.'

The villagers usually had to pay for their beer at this particular annual event. Feeling extremely satisfied with her efforts, Petra grinned. 'And the free beer.'

The ride down from London had been unusually pleasant. Despite the chill in the air, Ethan could only describe it as a perfect autumn day. Beneath a clear blue sky, the trees displayed their reds, yellows and browns, making the rolling countryside come alive with colour and making his travel all the more enjoyable.

Though, to be honest, he was more interested in seeing Petra again and discovering what surprises she had in store for him this time.

He hadn't expected to enjoy being an earl and running an estate, but she had opened his eyes to the bounty and the beauty of the English countryside. Which was why it was a disappointment that she wanted nothing to do with him as a husband. More than a disappointment. It was a cold lump somewhere in the centre of his chest.

He turned Jack into the driveway. The old lad picked up his pace, no doubt thinking of a manger full of hay or a bucket of corn. Ethan could only think of Petra.

Would she be at Longhurst as she had promised?

He hadn't quibbled about any of the things she had requested for her village festival, as she'd called it, even though it had used up all the money from selling his commission. He still could not believe he had sold out from the army without a qualm. His regiment had been his life, yet the thought of leaving England, of leaving his estate in the hands of another now he had the means to do so, had not sat well in his gut.

The house came into view.

Home at last.

He started. When had he come to think of this place as home? He hadn't even known he wanted one. He'd been perfectly happy moving from camp to camp across Europe. It wasn't always comfortable, but he'd enjoyed the comradeship of his fellow officers, leavened by the occasional excitement of battle. Perhaps he was getting old?

His heart lifted at the sight of the diminutive figure on the lawn beside the tottering heap of furniture now more than ten feet high. She lifted a hand to shield her eyes from the glare of the sun as she watched him ride towards her. He sighed. Maybe she was the reason he thought of this place as home.

Except she wasn't part of it.

That icy weight settled on his chest once again, making him struggle to breathe.

He dismounted the moment he came within a few feet of her. 'Lady Petra. Here I am, as requested.'

'Good day, Longhurst.' She smiled brightly enough, but with less warmth than she used to. He ignored the hurt and beamed back.

He liked it better when she called him Ethan. But, of course, that was all over now.

'How was your first taste of the House of Lords?' she asked, tilting her head as if she really cared about the answer.

He forced himself not to respond like an eager schoolboy to that display of interest and reminded himself she was only being polite.

'Not as bad as I thought, to be honest. I took my seat. Asked my question and met the Prince of Wales, who decided to be charming. Of course, he wanted to talk about my treasure trove of paintings. News of that sort travels fast. It appears he is going to be one of those bidding at the auction, but he was angling for a special price. I was able to make a bargain with him.'

'Then I am glad it all went well.'

She sounded happy for him and that pleased him greatly.

'I see you have been busy also,' he said, looking up at the woodpile. At the very top was one of the armchairs that had graced his study and in it was sitting the effigy of a man. He stepped back to get a better look. 'My word, that looks lifelike. Fortunately, it doesn't look like anyone I know.'

Her laugh was full of delight. 'No, indeed. Marguerite was very careful on that score despite that there were a few models she might have liked to use. She used one of the drawings of the original Mr Guy Fawkes as her inspiration.'

'It is splendid. What can I do to help?'

'The funds were all the help we needed. The ladies from the church have the food well in hand, Mr Jenks will deliver the beer barrels in a short while and Mr O'Cleary will set out the benches and the hay bales for people to sit on before everyone arrives.'

'Benches?'

'O'Cleary and Jeb made them up out of odd bits of your furniture. They will go on the fire after everyone has left.'

'Let us hope they do not collapse beneath anyone in the meantime.'

'Even if they do, I doubt anyone will mind, provided they have quaffed a sufficient amount of the beer you have so generously provided.'

He laughed. 'It is my very great pleasure to assist the village in its celebration of the foiling of the plot to blow up the Houses of Parliament, given that I am now one of those sitting above the barrels of gunpowder. Several tuns of beer is a small price to pay for my safety.'

A thought occurred to him. 'When I was a lad we would light squibs and set them off among the folks gathered around the bonfire. I assume that is not the order of the day?'

'No. It is expressly forbidden. Everyone understands that and those with unruly lads are checking their pockets before they leave home.'

'I think I will check O'Cleary's pockets, as well. He is as unruly as any boy I have ever encountered.' He grinned at the thought of the surprise he had brought with him from London. The villagers should enjoy it. He hoped.

She laughed. 'Mr O'Cleary has been a great help. It was he who climbed up and set the chair and Mr Fawkes on top.'

'As I said, a most unruly lad. I wager he enjoyed himself thoroughly.'

'He did. He made sure to do it when I was here showing some of the women from the church what was required. He basked in their admiration.'

'I presume they included one or more of the lasses from the Green Man.' O'Cleary had been spending a good deal of his free time at the inn recently and came home looking very pleased with himself to boot.

'Naturally.'

He wagged a finger at her. 'A man can be convinced to undertake the most dangerous of tasks when watched by one or more pretty ladies.'

They chuckled together, like old friends. Perhaps they could indeed be friends, but he found the idea didn't help with the ever-present chill in his chest.

'I am glad you made it back in such good time,' she said. 'It will help greatly if you are here when the villagers start arriving. I also asked the constable to come and keep an eye on things, and sent a note to Lord Compton inviting him to attend. Unfortunately, he declined. It seems he doesn't like to leave his children.'

'He has several, I believe. All female. I never met them on any of my visits there, but from the noise I heard, they are an unruly lot.'

'Poor man. He lost his wife not long after the birth of his third girl. I am surprised he hasn't married again. He must need an heir.'

Ethan's heart jolted. Was that why she had turned him down? She was thinking of setting her cap at Compton? His earlier regret that Compton would not attend the fire was replaced by a feeling of relief.

'Is there anything you need me to do?' he asked.

'Just play the part of the lord of the manor and make sure no one gets out of order and all will be well.'

'I can do that.' He couldn't wait to see her face when she saw his surprise. And those of the villagers, too, of course.

'I am on my way home,' she said. 'Marguerite and I will come together later. The ladies of the village will arrive shortly to help Mrs Stone in the kitchen. I hope that is all right.'

'Of course. As I said, do whatever you think is best.'

'Thank you. I will be back in plenty of time.'

'Good. I don't want to face the hordes alone.'

She patted his arm and he basked in that little sign of affection. He gritted his teeth against the foolish emotion.

'You know,' she said musingly, 'it is a good thing the Beckridges left when they did or we would be facing a sermon on the evils of popery instead of a cheerful gathering around the bonfire.'

'A blessing indeed.'

Her pretty laugh rang out. He wanted to capture it and put it in a jar. Oh, hell, what had happened to him that he had become so maudlin?

'Make sure you dress warmly when you come back,' he said. 'It will be chilly tonight.'

She gave him an odd look, a measuring glance that he did not understand, but she nodded. 'I'll make sure and remind Marguerite, too.'

He didn't care about her sister. Only her. 'Good idea.'

He watched her hurry towards her waiting trap, her skirts swaying with every step.

What had that expression on her face meant?

Dress warmly. Did he think she was a child? Or was it something else which had prompted his concern? The look on his face when he had said those words had made her really look at him. He looked lonely. When she first met him, he had seemed perfectly happy. Now there was an expression of longing in the depths of his blue eyes.

She shook her head at her wandering thoughts. She had been seeking some sign that he missed her as much as she missed him and that was nonsense. She glanced over at her sister driving the trap. She, too, was bundled up against the evening chill.

'Hopefully, it will be warm by the fire,' Marguerite said as if guessing at her thoughts. Or at least part of them.

They came up on a group of villagers walking down the lane towards Longhurst. They waved cheerfully as the trap passed. 'See you soon, my ladies,' Mr Barker called out.

'Yes, indeed,' Petra replied turning in her seat to wave back. 'All will be ready for your arrival,' she called out.

'Arr,' said another member of the group. 'We seed the beer cart go by. 'Tis all we need.'

The ladies among them giggled.

Petra felt a sense of pride that she had been instrumental in bringing this evening about, though she could not have done it without everyone's help. Especially Ethan's.

Dress warmly.

Did it mean that despite everything he had said, he really did care about her? And if he did, why did it matter? She had ended their affair. They had both agreed it was for the best. The man needed to marry and set about getting an heir.

Her chest squeezed uncomfortably.

No. She did not want to marry again and risk all that heartache.

Only Ethan was not like Harry.

He was honourable and kind.

But he did not love her any more than Harry had.

They turned into Longhurst's drive. A glow in the distance made her frown. 'Have they started the fire already?' Disappointment filled her.

'I don't think so,' Marguerite said. 'No. Look. There are torches set up around the bonfire and partway down the drive. So we can see our way.'

'Oh, yes, I see now.' Ethan must have done that. How clever of him. And it would help keep an eye on the younger revellers, too.

Ethan was waiting to help them down when the trap drew up at the front door. One of the young men from the village leaped forward to take care of Patch and lead him to the stables at the back of the house.

'My,' Petra commented with approval, 'you have been busy in my absence.'

He grinned down at her with his lovely boyish smile. Her heart gave a little jolt. 'And I have found myself a new groom, provided his family agrees.' He gestured to the lad leading their horse away.

She chuckled. 'You are not one to let the grass grow under your feet.'

He glanced down. 'It can't grow under these enormous boots, so I have to keep moving.'

She shook her head at him. 'I'll go and check on things in the kitchen.'

He grasped her arm before she could move. And Marguerite's, too. 'You ladies have done quite enough. Mrs Stone has everything in hand. Leave her to it. Come and take your place by the fire. It will soon be time to light it.'

He led them to a bench. 'Mind how you sit. I cannot promise it won't give way beneath you.'

'I am not that heavy,' Marguerite said with a teasing note in her voice.

'Oh, no, my lady. You are not heavy at all, but those timbers are as weak as water.'

Marguerite sat down with Petra beside her and within a very short space of time all the benches were filled and the men had their mugs of beer and the ladies were quaffing lemonade or the mulled wine set out on a trestle table.

'Light the fire,' someone shouted.

'I'm freezing,' a woman grumbled.

Ethan came forward with a mug of beer in his hand. 'Before we start the festivities, I want to thank you all for coming this evening. We will raise a glass to our King, if you please.'

When the chatter died down, Ethan raised his mug. 'God bless His Majesty, King George. Long may he reign.'

'Even if he is mad,' Marguerite whispered.

'King George,' the villagers shouted, holding up their mugs before drinking.

'God bless His Lordship!' someone else shouted.

Mr Barker, Petra thought.

'His Lordship,' they all cried and drank again.

Ethan looked pleased. 'And here is to the health of Lady Petra, whose idea it was to have this bonfire.'

More cheering and laughing. Then Mr O'Cleary grabbed one of the torches and went around the fire, lighting the strategically placed paper spills. Smoke wafted up and the people on the windward side coughed, fanned their faces and wiped their eyes. Then a chair caught light and flames shot up, and the fire was soon burning merrily.

The women came out of the kitchen and filled the table with trays of food, roasted meat, breads and cheese. 'Help yourselves, everyone,' Ethan said, gesturing to the bounty. A queue formed instantly, with some good-natured pushing and shoving.

'Enough of that now,' O'Cleary said, shouting like a sergeant major. 'There's plenty for all. And I've put some tatties and chestnuts in the ashes to keep your hands warm later.'

Everyone murmured appreciatively and the queue became orderly.

A few minutes later, Ethan arrived at their bench with two plates, one for her and one for Marguerite.

'Don't tell me you used your title to get to the head of the line,' she teased.

'All right, I won't.'

She and Marguerite laughed.

'There have to be some privileges for all this work, you know,' he said cheerfully. 'Besides, the moment I went to the end, they all moved back, to put me at the head, so what else was I to do?'

She laughed at the puzzlement on his face. 'They like and respect you. This is good.'

'I like them, too.' He still sounded puzzled. He handed them cutlery and wandered away. Petra thought he had gone back for food for himself, but then she realised he was moving from group to group around the fire, talking and laughing, and from their beams of delight, clearly charming them.

She had thought Harry charming. But he was not. His charm was shallow and false, used to get what he wanted. Ethan charmed because he was genuinely kind and listened to what each person had to say to him. He had truly found his feet. He would make a wonderful landlord and an excellent lord.

He filled his new shoes as easily as he drew breath. From here on in, he would manage perfectly well without her help.

A lump rose in her throat. A feeling of loss.

Nonsense. They would remain friends.

Not once he was married. They would become nodding acquaintances only. It had to be that way, she could not bear the idea of being the cause of a wife enduring what she had gone through with Harry.

The food on her plate was like cotton wool in her mouth. She ploughed through it determinedly. She did not want Marguerite questioning her appetite or, worse yet, it coming to Ethan's attention.

Who had not as yet eaten anything himself.

She rose and took their dirty plates back to the table, where they were being stacked and from there carried back to the kitchen. She smiled at Mrs Stone, who was presiding over an enormous sponge cake, and was given two napkins and two large slices of the confection. She leaned over the table and murmured, 'I don't believe His Lordship has as yet had any of the food.'

'Ah,' said the cook, nodding in understanding. 'I'll see about that.'

As Petra walked away, Mrs Stone was directing Mr O'Cleary to see to his master's needs.

Petra smiled. His staff loved him almost as much as she did.

She closed her eyes against a sudden burn in their depths. She really had fallen too far and too fast. How could she have done such a foolish thing?

Fallen for a man who frankly admitted he did not love her. At least he had told her the truth. She had to respect him for his honesty.

She went back to her seat beside Marguerite.

'Mmm, this is delicious,' Marguerite said.

'It is, isn't it?' she said cheerfully.

When the food table was empty and everyone had settled down around the fire to keep warm on the outside and quaffed their chosen libations to warm them on the inside, Ethan joined her and Marguerite on their bench.

The warm glow of the fire danced across his face. 'I have a surprise.'

'You do?'

'I do.'

There was a sudden loud bang and the night sky was filled with a million-coloured stars.

'Fireworks,' Petra squeaked. 'Oh, my, how did you manage it?'

'My bargain with the Prince.'

'I love fireworks,' Petra exclaimed and put an arm around his shoulders and gave him a squeeze.

She gazed up in awe, along with everyone else, until she felt the sensation of someone watching her in the flickering firelight. She glanced at Ethan. His gaze was fixed on her face, not the display.

'Is something wrong?'

'No,' he said slowly. 'Nothing at all is wrong.'

Petra looked confused.

'Or maybe there is one thing.' He tipped her chin up and kissed her mouth. 'I have missed this.'

'Ethan! Do not. Someone may notice.'

He straightened. 'No one is looking at us. Watch the fireworks, Petra.' He got up and went to speak with a group of boys who looked like they were about to get up to mischief. He held out his hand and she very nearly laughed when the ringleader dropped what looked like a couple of squibs in his palm.

The man would make a wonderful father.

Her heart felt like it was breaking.

His front was warm from the fire, but his back was freezing. He was used to it from his army days. He glanced at across the circle at Petra. It was probably one of the last times they would be in each other's company. Even if they were sitting far apart.

He had told her to wrap up warm, but the coat she

wore wasn't nearly thick enough. Ladies always preferred fashion over comfort. Although most of the time Petra seemed a great deal more sensible than most women.

He gestured to O'Cleary, who sauntered over, tossing a tattie from one hand to the other. 'Bring out blankets for all the ladies.'

O'Cleary's jaw dropped. 'All the ladies.'

It wouldn't do to single Petra out. Ethan nodded. 'All who want one. There are enough to cover a regiment in the linen cupboard. Take young Jeb with you. He'll help.'

'At once, my lord.'

It wasn't many minutes before he and Jeb returned with armloads of blankets and Petra and her sister were snuggled up warmly. For once he was glad his cousin had hoarded so many items. He didn't even care if the village women took theirs home as long as Petra was warm.

She looked up at his approach. 'Handing out blankets was a wonderful idea,' she said.

He grinned and handed her one of the hot potatoes. 'Eat it or simply use it to keep your hands warm. It's an old army trick.' Not that soldiers ever didn't eat theirs when they could get them. He gave another to her sister, who took it and got to her feet. 'I will go and see if Mrs Stone needs any help.' She wandered off, tossing her potato from hand to hand, her blanket trailing behind her.

'Your sister doesn't look happy,' he remarked.

'No. She's been unhappy since her husband died.' She wrinkled her nose thoughtfully. 'Even before he died. Sometimes I wonder if she lost a child, she seems so sad. But she always denies anything is wrong.'

'There was no issue from the marriage, then?'

'No, and she was married a great deal longer than I.'

'Perhaps that is why she is not happy.'

'Perhaps.' She smiled at him. 'This has been a wonderful celebration, Lord Longhurst.'

A change of topic. He liked that Petra did not gossip about those closest to her. 'Thanks to you.'

She smiled briefly. 'It was my pleasure. I have enjoyed it enormously, but it's probably better if we do not appear to be too cosy together. You know how people gossip.'

The hard, cold lump in his chest expanded until it was once again almost impossible to draw breath. What was the matter with him? He'd faced all kinds of danger in the army and never once felt such a horrible feeling of dread.

He got to his feet and bowed. 'As you wish, Lady Petra.'

He walked away. But he walked away blind. He saw nothing until a young woman stumbled, putting a hand on his chest to save herself. He grabbed her by the elbows.

'Oops, sorry, Your Lordship,' she slurred. She flung her arms around his neck and he barely avoided her planting her lips on his.

'Who are you?' he asked, frowning. She was obviously inebriated. He steadied her, then set her back on her feet a little distance from him.

'I be Kitty, Your Lordship. I work at the Green Man.'

He didn't recognise her, despite the fact he'd called into the tavern for a pint on a couple of occasions, since the one thing his cousin had not collected was good-quality ale. She looked to be about nineteen or so. 'I think you should sit down, Miss Kitty.'

O'Cleary appeared at his elbow, taking charge of the young woman in a most territorial way. 'Feeling a bit under the weather, are you, Miss Kitty?' he said solicitously, putting an arm around her shoulders. 'I think maybe I should see you home.'

Ethan glared at him. 'Not taking advantage of the young lady, are you, O'Cleary?'

'Not at all, me lord.' O'Cleary gave him a cheerful grin. 'I'm making sure those who gave Miss Kitty here too many swigs from their flasks aren't going to take advantage.'

Ethan frowned, then realisation dawned. 'She's the reason you spend so much time at the Green Man.'

O'Cleary winked.

Well, damn. O'Cleary had never been what Ethan would call a lady's man, but judging by his expression when he looked at Miss Kitty, that might well be about to change. 'Well, go on. Get her home safe and sound.'

O'Cleary saluted and put his arms around the girl's waist, whispering something in her ear as he walked away. Apparently, whatever he said found favour with the girl, for she leaned her head against his shoulder.

Ethan had no doubts that Miss Kitty would be safe. In his own rough way, O'Cleary was also a gentleman.

He glanced over to where Petra was seated. All that remained on the bench was a neatly folded blanket. Had she seen what had happened with Kitty and assumed the worst? He did not want her thinking he was the sort of man who would take advantage of a girl out of her wits with drink.

Marguerite was still chatting with the ladies from

the church so Petra could not have gone far. She'd likely be back in a few minutes. He turned at the postmaster's greeting.

'Good evening, Barker. Mrs Barker.'

The lady dipped a curtsy. He supposed he'd get used to all this bowing and scraping one day. 'Thank you for a lovely evening, Your Lordship,' she said. 'It is getting late. Time I took the little one home.' She gestured to the child clinging to her skirts. 'I don't remember when the village had such a good Guy Fawkes Night, truly I do not.'

'I am delighted you think so.'

She beamed. 'So nice not to be forever starting and jumping at the squibs being thrown. And the fireworks were wonderful. I never saw anything so fine, truly I did not. Let us hope we can make it an annual event.'

Good Lord, it seemed he'd started a tradition. Or Petra had. He glanced back to her seat.

Still not there.

His heart gave a horrible lurch. Had something happened to her?

Chapter Fifteen

Petra lay on the grass looking up at the stars. She'd noticed them on her way back from taking care of a call of nature at the conclusion of the fireworks. And as a way to recover from that soft kiss Ethan had pressed on her lips.

It must never happen again. He'd known it, too. The pain of recognising that brief touch of his lips to hers as the end of their relationship had sent her wandering off the moment he left her side. Soon he would marry and rejoin the army. Perhaps once he was out of the country, she would be able to regain some peace. Her heart twisted painfully. How could she ever do that? She would worry about him every single day he was risking his life. Hopefully, in time, she would be able to put him out of her heart, but seeing him tonight, talking with him as if there had never been anything between them, had been difficult to say the least.

She forced her gaze up into the firmament, tried to focus on the vastness above her as a way to redirect her racing mind. She recalled how she and her siblings had crept out on a clear night just like this one when Red had pointed out the constellations with all the authority of an elder brother. She had been very young and she remembered little of his lecture. She did, however, recognise the Milky Way.

Would it appear the same to Ethan in Portugal? How hard he had worked to learn about the estate these past few weeks. And he had an excellent manner with the villagers. Friendly but firm. They would, in time, come to trust him to be fair with them. He would make an excellent earl. If he returned. A hollowness filled her stomach. So many men did not return from the war. She closed her eyes briefly. She would not think of that.

The patch of sky above her went dark.

'Are you all right?' a worried voice asked.

She came up on her elbows. 'Ethan? Oh, you gave me a start.' Dash it all, she should have guessed he would seek her out when he did not see her at the fire. Being alone with him was the last thing she needed right now.

'Did you fall?' he asked. The concern in his voice caused her heart to clench painfully. Why could he not see she came here to be alone? To get her feelings under control. He could not understand, precisely because he did not have those same feelings as she did.

She blinked away the moisture dimming her vision. She would not cry. Their affair was over and that was that.

'I was on my way back to the fire and stopped to look at the stars.'

He sank down beside her and tipped his head back. 'How clear it is. We will have frost tomorrow morning, I fear.'

She forced a laugh. It sounded brittle even to her

own ears. She had to end this and quickly. 'You sound like a proper farmer now.' She sat up, preparing to rise.

He chuckled. 'Soldiers also keep an eye out for the weather, I can assure you.'

'I suppose they must. It is a hard life, yet you miss it.'

'It is all I have known since I was little more than a lad.' He sounded wistful.

She didn't want to talk about his return to the army. She would end up begging him not to go. She did not want him guessing at the depths of her feelings for him. He might feel under some sort of obligation to offer for her again. She really could not bear another of his cool proposals. She pointed upwards and grabbed for a faint memory. 'Isn't that Ursa Minor? I seem to remember it had a bright star at the top.'

'Yes. Polaris.' He pointed and his finger traced a line. 'And there is the Plough.'

She gazed up. 'The vastness makes one feel quite insignificant.'

He lay back. 'Yes, it does.'

Oh, no, him joining her out here was not what she intended at all. 'Oh, my lord, Marguerite. She will be wondering where I am.' She began to rise.

He touched to her shoulder. 'About just now. That girl.'

She froze. 'What girl?'

'You didn't see her?' He hesitated. 'One of the girls from the Green Man threw herself into my arms a few minutes ago beside the fire. I didn't want you to think there was anything untoward going on.'

A chill travelled outwards from her chest. That was just the sort of excuse she always heard from Harry.

Not my fault. I only stopped to help. She kissed me. It meant nothing.

She shook off his hand and scrambled to her feet. 'I have no idea what you are talking about and whatever happened between you and a tavern girl is certainly none of my business.'

He stood up beside her. 'That wasn't why you left the fire and went wandering in the dark?' He sounded confused.

'What you do and who you do it with is none of my concern.'

He stepped back. 'I— No, of course not. I beg your pardon for thinking it might be.'

His cool response stung. But then she had snapped at him the way she never would have dared snapped at Harry, who would have gone off in a sulk for days. Ethan, on the other hand, simply sounded calm and matter-of-fact. Uninterested.

'The fire is dying and people are leaving. It is time I went home.'

He gazed towards the fire, not looking at her. 'Allow me to send you home in my carriage.'

'That will not be necessary.' She did not want to be under any sort of obligation to him. Men. They were all the same. Why had she thought he was any different? She should have known better than to let him worm his way into her heart. Apparently, she had learned nothing from her marriage. Thank heavens she had turned down his proposal. If only it didn't hurt quite so much, then she could be truly grateful.

'Then at least allow me to escort you back to your sister.' The indifference in his voice sent a shiver down her spine.

'As you wish.'

They walked back in a silence so fraught with tension she wanted to scream.

The Guy was nothing but ashes in a fire that had dwindled to a glowing heap of embers. With the food and the beer all gone, the villagers were drifting away in little groups.

'Thank you for a lovely evening, my lord,' Petra said as good manners dictated and honestly, up until the last half an hour, she had enjoyed it immensely. She wasn't one to deny credit where it was due.

He bowed formally and aided them into the trap. The journey home seemed a great deal longer than usual and the wind had the cold bite of looming winter.

Compton's ploughman, Martin Mudge, arrived ready for work the morning after the bonfire. A quiet man with a straw gripped between his teeth, which waggled in front of his face when he spoke. Most distracting as Mudge happily shared his knowledge about ploughs, horses and how to keep a row straight and at the right depth.

For the next two days, Ethan learned all he could. On the third day Mudge let him handle the reins on his own. His back and arms ached from the efforts of the previous two days, when he'd had a hard time controlling both the horses and the plough, but he was determined to continue. Fortunately today, it seemed he had mastered it, somewhat, and with a feeling of satisfaction, he guided the horses across the width of the field, turned them and started back down under Mudge's watchful gaze.

The work did not keep Ethan's mind off the way Petra had turned from warm to frigid in a heartbeat at the bonfire. It had hurt. Perhaps he should not have mentioned the girl, but how could he not? Even if Petra had not seen the way the girl had hung about his neck, she would have learned of it, eventually. Nothing passed unnoticed or uncommented upon by the village gossips. It was the same in the army. The men loved to talk and whisper about anything and everything. When they were in camp for the winter there was little else to do.

Too bad Miss Kitty hadn't fallen into O'Cleary's arms instead of Ethan's. If she had...

Ah, well. There was no point playing what ifs. Petra had assumed the worst of him, the way his father had always assumed the worst. There would be no pleasing a woman like her and it was as well to discover her true nature before he did something stupid like proposing to her again. God help him, she might have accepted, too, if it were not for little Miss Kitty.

He certainly had not expected her to immediately judge him guilty of some wrongdoing. His father always had and his mother had always taken Father's part. Not that Ethan blamed his mother for that. Father had had a wicked temper. For years, Ethan hadn't stood up to him either. Until that last time Father had lashed out.

His father had not realised just how much Ethan had grown that summer. He'd gone from a weedy fourteen-year-old to a strapping lad of fifteen summers in the blink of an eye.

Tired of the bullying, Ethan had lost his temper and struck back. He'd landed a solid blow. Enough to put

Father on his back. Father had at first looked shocked and then furious.

Ungrateful bastard! his father had yelled at him.

The usual feelings of guilt assailed Ethan. And the wish that he could have found a better way of settling his differences with Father. A way that would have brought them closer together. Instead, he'd lost his temper. He had made sure never to do that again. He'd even apologised. But Father had stormed out of the house and Mother had blamed Ethan for the contretemps.

It had struck Ethan then that the only way to get along with his parents was to do his best never to put a foot wrong, never to have opinions of his own or to be anything but perfect. And perfect was something he could never be. Not in his father's eyes anyway.

He'd retreated into silence. Speaking only when spoken to and doing what he was told, no less, no more. He'd been miserable and confused.

A few days later, his uncle came for a visit. His uncle had been a jolly fellow with lots of stories of high jinks from his army days. Ethan expressed interest in the service and his uncle had offered to buy him a cornetcy in the infantry. Ethan had leaped at the chance to leave home.

Much later he had learned that the offer of a commission was his mother's idea. He never knew if it was because she'd wanted to help Ethan or because she simply didn't want Father upset ever again. He'd never cared enough to ask while she was alive and now it was too late.

He shrugged. He doubted he'd like the answer. The army had been the best thing that ever happened to him, despite the risks. And now the army was no longer an option, he was determined to make a go of managing his lands.

He plodded on, up and down, letting his mind go where it would until they reached the other side of the field. It was done.

He dropped the reins and gave the rump of the nearest shire a good solid pat. The rows of heavy soil, curling like ocean waves spread out before him, gave him a feeling of accomplishment. It reminded him of the first time he'd got a company of raw recruits to finally march in unison.

Compton's ploughman grinned at him around his straw. 'We'll make a farmer of you yet, my lord.'

A band seemed to tighten around his chest. Petra had said something similar when they were looking at stars and he had thought about proposing to her again. And then, like an idiot, he had tried to explain what had happened with little Miss Kitty. Just like his parents, Petra had turned on him as if Kitty's actions had been his fault.

Damn it. He should have known better than to attempt to trust anyone, no matter how close they had once been.

He glanced down the rows. No, they were not perfect. Just like him. 'I need a bit more practice.'

'I ain't never seen anyone get the hang of ploughing as fast as you, my lord.'

That was something, he supposed. 'You'll be heading back to the Compton estate this evening, I gather.'

'Yes, my lord. We also has a couple more fields to turn over and they can't wait.'

'I'll send Lord Compton a note of thanks for his

help, if you would be so good as to deliver it. Having you here has been invaluable.' He gave the man a coin.

The old fellow grinned, touched his forelock and was soon on his way. Ethan bade him farewell and led the horses to their stable.

Entering the house through the kitchen door, intending to scrub some of the filth off himself in the scullery, Ethan found O'Cleary dressed, ready to go out.

'It's cook's day off,' O'Cleary announced. 'She left a cold roast in the pantry and there's soup on the hob. I thought I'd go to the pub for a bite to eat, if that suits you, my lord.'

'Very well. I'll help myself.'

'Yes, sir. By the way, the carter arrived with some of the furniture you selected from the town house. I had him put it in the barn. I'll get a couple of lads from the village to help move it inside tomorrow. Meantime, I put your desk and a sofa in the study. Mail is on the desk.' He rattled the information off at great speed.

Ethan nodded.

'Is there anything else I can get for you, my lord?' O'Cleary clearly wanted to be off. 'No, thank you. Give my regards to Miss Kitty.'

His friend grinned shyly. 'That I will.' He shot off.

Oh, good lord, the man was besotted. Well, he wished him good luck. He just hoped he wouldn't lose him. He'd lost too many people in his life and O'Cleary was one of the better ones.

Along with Petra. He stilled. Where had that thought come from? She'd shown herself to be like every other woman in his life, hadn't she? Hot one minute, then cold the next and without a scrap of caring for him as a person. She certainly didn't want him for a husband.

Ethan stripped off, washed in the scullery sink and, after putting on his dressing gown, ate his supper at the kitchen table. He was starving after working all day in the fields. He hacked hunks off the loaf of bread and dipped them in the soup. He even polished off most of the roast beef. Thoroughly replete, he wandered into his study.

A pile of mail sat in the centre of his new desk.

Thank heavens there had been no woodworm at the town house. He'd been able to keep the plainest pieces for his own use and still had plenty left to sell.

He sorted through the mail. The duns he put to one side. He would deal with those in the morning. He was left with two. One from his man of business and the other in a feminine hand that looked vaguely familiar.

He opened it.

The more he read, the heavier the food in his belly seemed to become. At the end of reading the missive from Lady Frances, his elderly cousin removed by several degrees, he closed his eyes and leaned back in his chair.

Damn her.

She complained that he hadn't let her know he was planning a visit to London or she would have cut short her visit to Bath to meet him there. However, now she was back in town, she had arranged a party to introduce him to the family and to present him with several choices for a bride. The woman arrogantly stated she intended to see him wed and with an heir and a spare before she died.

Not content with forcing an earldom on him and

having him sent home from the war, she now planned to organise his life to her satisfaction.

Well, the lady would have to learn he was not a man to be shoved around.

'His Lordship's gone off to London again,' Mr Barker announced, handing Petra the mail for Westram Cottage.

Petra's heart gave a painful little squeeze. She hadn't known he was going. But then why should she?

'Has he?' she said vaguely, sorting through the letters as if interested in what they contained, yet waiting on tenterhooks for him to say more.

'Yes. Poor Miss Kitty, she be weeping fit to bust.'

The pain in her chest grew worse. She knew exactly how poor Miss Kitty felt. 'Really?'

'Oh, yes, he got all his furniture delivered from town and off he went. Visiting a relative, Mr O'Cleary said.'

Mr O'Cleary should know better to gossip about his master. 'How nice.'

'Arr. When he comes back they are getting married.'

She blinked.

He gave her a smug look. 'Thought you'd be surprised. Old Jenks couldn't believe it hisself. It is not like his Kitty's been an angel, though she seems a lot steadier now.'

'They are getting married?' she said faintly. Indeed, perhaps she was going to faint she felt so dizzy. She had never fainted before, but this news...it robbed her of breath. Ethan and Kitty?

'Yes, my lady. As soon as His Lordship returns and the new Vicar arrives to read the banns.'

'How…how delightful.' She turned to leave.

'Whoever would have expected Kitty Jenks to catch as fine a fellow as Mr O'Cleary? You would think he would have more sense. But there's no accounting for love, they says.'

The world that had been spinning around Petra's head came to a sudden stop. She grabbed for the nearest object to steady herself. It proved to be a table full of bolts of cloth and she leaned against it gratefully.

Barker rushed around the end of the counter. 'Are you ill, Lady Petra?' he asked. 'You've gone all pale. Can I get you something? Water? Smelling salts?'

Petra looked at him through watery eyes. Great heavens, was she crying? 'I am perfectly fine, Barker.' Oh, goodness, yes. She was perfectly fine.

It was if the world had shifted on its axis, giving her a whole new perspective on things.

She put the letters in her basket and marched for home.

'I need to go up to town,' Marguerite announced, glancing up from one of the letters that had arrived in the post.

Petra put down her pen. She had been trying to write to Ethan, but she hadn't got past the initial greeting. How did one apologise and ask a gentleman to offer for one again? 'You do?' Her heart leaped with gladness, because London was where Ethan was and it would be far easier to talk to him than write a letter. But there was an odd expression on Marguerite's face. Petra looked at her sister. 'Why do you need to go again so soon? It is barely three weeks since we were there last.'

Colour washed up Marguerite's cheeks. 'I need to

deliver these drawings in person, they took longer than I expected and I need the money owing on them.'

Marguerite looked…uncomfortable.

'You aren't in any sort of trouble, are you?'

The colour seemed to deepen. Poor Marguerite with her colouring, she never could hide her embarrassment. 'No. I am not in any trouble, but it is not something I wish to discuss.'

Marguerite and her secrets. She would tell Petra only what she wanted her to know. Besides, why did she care about Marguerite's reason? She also wanted to go to London.

'When do you wish to leave?'

'First thing in the morning. Can you be ready by then?'

'I can. Will the town house be open?'

'We are not staying at the town house. We will go to a hotel.'

'Is Red not to know that we are going, then?' Petra asked.

'I will write and tell him. I expect we shall be home before he receives the letter.'

'I wouldn't bank on it. You would be better to give Briggs two days' notice so he can put the knocker on the door. Then Red won't be annoyed.' Briggs was the caretaker and also served as butler when the family came to town.

Marguerite frowned. 'You are right, but I don't have time to await Briggs's pleasure. Dash it, he can put the knocker on the door the moment we arrive. It is not as if the place has been closed up for months. I certainly don't want Red hotfooting down to London for no reason.'

'I'll get started on my packing.'

With a hopeful heart. Petra went upstairs and pulled her trunk out from beneath her bed.

Her heart dipped a bit when she stared into the bottom of it. What if Ethan wouldn't see her after she'd been so distant towards him?

Chapter Sixteen

To Petra's pleasant surprise, Red had been invited to meet the new Earl of Longhurst at a ball being given by Lady Frances. The invitation had been waiting on the hall stand when Petra and Marguerite arrived. To Petra's disappointment, she and Marguerite were not included in the invitation.

'But there is no need for us to go in Red's place anyway,' Marguerite said. 'We have met him many times. He is our neighbour.'

'He is also our friend,' Petra argued. 'I am sure he would appreciate the sight of a familiar face or two.'

'Lord Longhurst seems perfectly capable of taking care of himself.'

'I am going regardless.'

Marguerite heaved a sigh. 'You always were a spoiled brat.'

Capitulation. Petra smiled. 'You always were an absolute dear.'

Marguerite laughed and gave her a hug. 'So, what are you up to, Petra? Have you decided you want him after all? If so, I pity the poor fellow. He doesn't stand a chance.'

She did want him. She'd realised that after the storm of emotions she had suffered in the post office. She wanted him so badly it hurt. But she wanted all of him, not just his friendship or his duty. She wanted his love. On reflection, she was almost convinced he felt more for her than mere friendship. Or attraction. If only he would admit it.

The way he looked at her, spoke to her, responded to her, said he did, whether they were making love or simply talking about his fields. Except that every time things got to a point when he should be expressing his feelings for her, he seemed to shy away from doing so. Perhaps there was something in his past holding him back? It had taken her a great deal of thinking to come up with this revelation. She just hoped she wasn't fooling herself.

'I am not yet completely sure he wants me. Not as much as I'm certain I want him.' She noticed she was not using the word *love*. She had flung it about with abandon in regard to Harry, but with Ethan it seemed too precious, too vulnerable, too easily broken to be sprinkled hither and yon. When she spoke of it, he would be the first to hear it from her lips.

Marguerite patted her shoulder. 'Did you argue the night of the bonfire?'

'Oh, dear, was it that obvious?'

'Perhaps not to others. I sensed a coolness when you bid each other farewell.'

Petra sighed. 'It was my fault. I jumped to a wrong conclusion.'

Marguerite's expression filled with sympathy. 'And you wish to apologise.'

'Yes.'

'Then we shall go to his introductory ball. I will reply to Lady Frances that while Red is not in town, you and I will be delighted to attend in his place. I doubt she will have the nerve to refuse us admittance.' She winced. 'I have heard that Lady Frances is doing her best to marry him off to her niece.'

Petra felt the blood drain from her face. 'Don't tell me she is an heiress.'

Marguerite frowned. 'Not that I am aware. But she is from a very good family, just out of the schoolroom and quite lovely.'

Petra's heart sank. Perhaps he'd prefer to marry a fresh young miss than a widow who had not trusted him to behave with honour.

Well, there was only one way to find out.

Introductory ball! Ethan ran a glance over the debutantes arrayed before him in their finest silks. It was more like market day in Oxted. He tried not to show his distaste. The young ladies were only doing their parents' bidding after all.

Lady Frances, the woman he thought of as his nemesis, had turned out to be a feisty elderly lady with dropsy who favoured the enormous wigs of the last century. And he liked her a great deal despite her odd ways. He stood beside her where she presided over the ballroom from a golden chair of state near the fireplace. She hated to be cold. Something she had in common with the Prince Regent.

Lady Frances slammed her stick against the floor. Her way of getting his attention. 'All you have to do is pick one. Do your duty and get an heir. I went to a great deal of trouble to find you. Now repay me by playing your part, young man.'

While the words were harsh, the twinkle in her eye was not unfriendly. He'd crossed swords a few times with her since their first meeting and she had been delighted by his spirit, as she called it. Apparently, she liked a man who could stand up for himself.

Good lord, what sort of men was she used to? 'I do not suppose you care that I would have preferred to remain a simple soldier.'

'Nonsense.'

It hadn't been nonsense. But… While he didn't care much about the title, there was that odd sensation that at Longhurst Park he was finally home. Much as he had tried, he could not shake it loose.

He had decided that having someone to share his home with would be a good thing. Provided it was the right person. He did not want to end up in the sort of marriage his parents had endured.

'Lady Marguerite Saxby and Lady Petra Davenport,' the butler announced.

His heart gave a painful thump.

'Widows,' Lady Frances said, grimacing. 'Their husbands, silly fellows, went off to war because of some foolish wager. Died for it, too. Those two gals went off and buried themselves in the country.'

She'd been editorialising every guest as they entered. 'They are my neighbours at Longhurst.'

'Are they, by God?'

Her salty language kept taking him by surprise and making him want to laugh. 'They are.'

She perched her pince-nez on the end of her nose and leaned forward. 'Handsome pair. The older one had a come out. The younger married straight out of the schoolroom. Married a proper rogue, as I hear it. Had a wandering eye. Never let an opportunity pass when it came to an available female. She is far better off without him in my opinion.'

Ethan froze, recalling his last conversation with Petra. He'd been explaining the Miss Kitty event, as he'd come to think of it. He'd been wounded by her lack of trust, but in light of this information, her reaction made far more sense. Somewhat. He remained troubled by how quickly she'd turned chilly towards him.

'Which one takes your fancy?' the old lady asked.

Damnation, he had been staring at Petra like a love-lorn swain. 'Lady Frances, I would be obliged—'

'Fiddle-faddle. What is a mind for, if it is not to speak it? Why not enjoy yourself with a lovely widow? They are both of an age to choose a lover.'

Anger heated his blood. 'The ladies are friends of mine. You will not speak of them with such disrespect.' He forced a smile that was both pleasant and dangerous. 'And you will listen to me. I am, after all, the head of your house.'

Lady Frances reared back. Ran her gaze up and down his length. A smile appeared on her face. 'Proving your mettle, are you? Have at it, then, sirrah.' She nodded. 'You will do. Yes, indeed, you will. Glad I didn't let that totty-headed Prince of Wales put the title into abeyance. Very glad.'

Strangely, he was glad, too. 'Good. I will bring the ladies to meet you.'

He marched across the ballroom. People moved out of his path and for once he did not mind that his height and his bulk tended to make people give way.

Petra was smiling at him.

And he was grinning back like a fool.

She held out a hand as he reached her and he took it, touching his lips to the back of her glove, though he knew he should not have. He turned and greeted Lady Marguerite.

'I did not know you ladies were coming up to town.'

'We arrived two days ago,' Petra said. 'We are here as representatives of our brother.'

That would account for their presence. Lady Frances had insisted on inviting every member of the *ton* to this ball. And all their daughters and nieces.

'I want you to meet my elderly relative, Lady Frances.'

'Good heavens, must we? The woman terrifies me,' Marguerite muttered.

'You know her?' Petra asked.

'She is one of the denizens. I was warned at my come out to make sure I did not annoy her or I would find myself barred from Almack's and all sorts of other horrid fates.'

'Oh, my goodness,' Petra exclaimed. 'She sounds like a tartar.'

'Her bark is worse than her bite,' Ethan explained. 'She likes people who stand their ground.'

'Tally-ho!' Petra said and laughed.

God, he'd missed her sense of humour. And her laughter. He'd missed all of her. 'Will you save a dance for me?' he asked. 'The supper dance?' That way, he would be able to take her into supper and sit with her while she ate. It would be a chance to talk. He also had reacted badly at the bonfire. He had withdrawn from combat when he should have regrouped and counter-attacked.

His dealings with his parents had taught him that in relationships it was better to leave the field, but Petra was not like his mother or his father. On the other hand, she should have trusted him. Still, he should not have pulled back without giving her his side of the story.

He offered the ladies an arm each and walked them to stand before Lady Frances's chair. Both ladies dipped elegant curtsies.

'Lady Frances, may I introduce Lady Petra Davenport and Lady Marguerite Saxby. As I mentioned, they are neighbours of mine in Kent.'

'I know them,' the lady replied. 'The Westram girls. Where's that brother of yours? Westram. He was the one I invited.'

'Our brother finds himself detained in Gloucestershire, my lady,' Marguerite replied. 'As I wrote to you.'

The old lady waved a dismissive hand. 'My secretary takes care of correspondence.'

'Our brother suggested we come in his stead,' Marguerite said. 'I had no idea you were related to Lord Longhurst, Lady Frances.'

'Nor did he,' the old lady replied drily. 'But I winkled him out in the end.'

'You did indeed, my lady,' Ethan said, keeping a straight face. 'You are a force to be reckoned with. Even Wellington bowed to your wishes.'

Lady Frances beamed. She was not in the least averse to a bit of flattery.

'Perhaps you ladies can help me,' she said, lowering her voice. 'I need to get this rapscallion cousin of mine married off so I can die a happy woman. Which of these lovelies—' she gave an all-encompassing glance around the room '—would you see as being ideal for him?'

Petra's eyes widened and Ethen wanted to put his boot in his cousin's mouth. Gently but firmly.

Marguerite gave one of her cool smiles. 'Regretfully, I doubt we can be of much help, my lady. We have been out of society for some considerable time and know nothing of this Season's crop of debutantes.'

'Then you are of no use to me,' Lady Frances said, waving them away.

They curtsied and left.

'That was rather rude of you,' Ethan said, watching Petra's diminutive figure as she crossed the room.

Lady Frances sniffed. 'It was the truth. No one ever likes to hear the truth.' She beckoned another young lady hovering on the sidelines just out of earshot. 'Let me introduce you to Miss Carver. Her family have ironworks in the North. Related to some of the best families in England.'

'Not even you can spike my guns, Lady Frances,' he murmured as the young lady hesitantly moved closer.

Lady Frances cackled. 'Don't tempt me.'

The girl, executing a perfect curtsy, gazed at her in terror.

'My word, she really *is* terrifying,' Petra said as she and Marguerite wandered the length of the ballroom.

'Longhurst is more than a match for her,' Marguerite replied. 'She can't resist a handsome face.'

Petra sighed. 'He truly is handsome, isn't he? But more than that he is a truly honourable man.'

Marguerite made a face. 'He certainly appears so.'

'You think otherwise?'

She shook her head. 'I have no reason to doubt him. But then I had no reason to doubt Neville either. Before I married him.'

Petra stopped walking to look at her sister. Really look at her and what she saw was worrisome. Marguerite looked weary and desperately unhappy. 'I—I thought you loved Neville.'

'I hated him so much I wished him dead.'

'Oh, my goodness, Marguerite. Truly?'

'Truly. And that is all I am going to say about it. But, Petra, unless you think you have a real chance for happiness with Lord Longhurst, I recommend you think very carefully before you jump in with both feet.'

'As I did with Harry. He was certainly no angel.'

'As I believe Red tried to tell you.'

Petra sighed. 'He did. But I am older now and much wiser. Besides, I know Ethan a great deal better than I ever knew Harry before we wed. In Harry's case, I saw only what I wanted to see.' She gave a little shrug. 'To be honest, I may have burned my bridges with Longhurst. I was awful to him the last time we spoke.'

'Whatever you do, don't rush headlong into things. It may have worked for Carrie, but that does not mean it works for everyone.'

Was she rushing headlong into Ethan's arms? If only that were true!

'Marguerite Saxby!' One of Marguerite's friends from her debutante days sailed towards them. 'It is an age since I saw you. How are you?' The two ladies entered into a deep conversation about everyone they recalled from their come out and Petra let her mind and gaze wander. It didn't take but a moment for her to spot Ethan dancing with a young lady. A very pretty young lady.

A pang of jealousy struck savagely behind her breastbone. She ignored it. He was the honoured guest at this party. He had to dance with as many young ladies as were introduced to him, but he had claimed her for the supper dance, the best dance of all. She clung to the hope that thought engendered deep in her heart.

'Lady Petra, may I have this dance?'

The gentleman standing before her looked familiar. One of Harry's friends.

He grinned. 'Nate Weatherby, you may recall.'

'Mr Weatherby. I'm sorry. I was wool-gathering. I would love to dance.'

It certainly wouldn't do to dance only with Ethan. People would see it as marked behaviour and start to gossip. Not for anything would she spoil his introduction to society or his chances of making an advantageous marriage, if that was what he wanted.

No one in their right mind would consider her a good match for him. A widow with no fortune. What if he once more offered for her out of a sense of duty? Could she accept that, when she loved him so much? Could she pin her hopes on him growing to love her? Harry certainly hadn't.

She should not have come here. She was doing what she had done with Harry. Chasing him until he had no choice but to make an offer. A sense of panic filled her. The urge to run.

'Is everything all right, Lady Petra?' Weatherby asked. 'You look worried.'

She smiled the way one did in company. One did not wear one's heart on one's sleeve. It simply was not done. 'Everything is wonderful, Mr Weatherby.'

They joined a set that was not yet full and she

danced with all the liveliness of a lady enjoying herself, while inside her stomach was churning and her head was aching. But the more she thought about it the more she worried that she might be ruining Ethan's life.

You ruined my life. The last words Harry had flung at her before he went off to war and got himself and two other men killed.

She could not do that to Ethan, too.

Chapter Seventeen

All evening, he'd anticipated this dance with Petra, but something had changed. Earlier she'd seemed pleased to see him, but now her smile was too bright, her laughter too brittle. And a waltz was no place to hold a serious discussion.

As the music drew to a close, she glanced up with another forced smile and dipped a curtsy. 'Thank you, my lord.'

For a moment or two, he considered walking away. It was what he'd always done at home when Father was in one of his moods and Mother began to flutter in distress. But not this time. He was going to get to the bottom of this. If Petra was upset, then he wanted to know the reason.

He escorted her into the supper room, helped her fill her plate and then found them a table in the corner. It was not the best place for a serious conversation either, but it would have to do.

A waiter brought them drinks—wine for him, ratafia for her—and finally they were as alone as they could be in a crowded room.

'What is making you unhappy?' he asked.

'What are you talking about?' She sounded wary.

'I believe we know each other well enough to sense each other's moods. I cannot tell what is wrong, but I know something troubles you.'

A softness filled her expression as if he had said something that touched her heart. Then she straightened her shoulders as if steeling herself to say something unpleasant. These contradictory signals were driving him mad.

'I wanted to apologise for doubting your word at the bonfire, about Kitty. I was wrong to react as I did.'

Now, that, he had not expected. And how did he tell her that he understood perfectly why she'd reacted that way, without revealing his knowledge of how her husband had behaved? 'Don't give it another thought.'

She frowned.

Clearly that was not the right thing to say. Dash it all, most of their dealings had been honest and straightforward. He wasn't a politician to be dancing around the truth. 'To be honest, I thought you knew me to be better than that.'

There it was out in the open, the plain truth.

She was staring at him, open-mouthed.

'Eat your supper,' he said sotto voce.

Mechanically, she lifted her fork to her mouth, chewed and swallowed. She gave him a bright fake smile. 'You are right. I should have known better.' The words were spoken with great seriousness, but something about the way she looked did not bode well.

'We really need to talk where we cannot be overheard,' he murmured.

'I agree.' She glanced around. 'Where?'

'My chamber.'

'You are staying here?'

'Yes. The auctioneers are still preparing the items in my town house for sale and they have bidders coming and going all day long so Lady Frances offered me a place to stay in the meantime. I actually think she wants to keep an eye on me, in case I decide to make good my escape.'

At that he got a genuine laugh. He relaxed. Somewhat.

'Do you feel like escaping?' she asked gently.

'From here? Certainly.'

'I meant from the Earldom?'

'Not in the least. Much as I hate to admit it, I believe General Wellington will deal with Napoleon and his generals without the aid of yours truly, whereas Longhurst needs its Earl.'

And he planned to do the best job he could, whatever the outcome of this evening. It would be far better, though, if he managed to convince her to stand by his side.

'Where is your chamber?' she asked quietly.

'On the second floor. I'll meet you at the top of the stairs in an hour.'

When they'd finished their supper, he escorted her back to her sister, danced with the next young lady presented to him by his cousin and then slipped away.

With her heart pounding in her chest and her stomach in knots, Petra felt like a schoolgirl up to no good. What if someone saw her? Marguerite might forgive her, but Red never would. What if all Ethan was going to tell her was that he had offered for another lady? Or that he had not forgiven her for mistrusting him? Twice she almost turned back.

Once, when she made her excuses to Marguerite and again now when she set foot on the bottom stair. But then she had not come all the way from Kent and arrived at this party without being specifically invited, only to creep away quietly. If she did not meet him, she knew she would regret it for the rest of her life. She glanced around. There wasn't a soul to see her, so she took a deep breath and hurried up to the second floor.

As he had promised, he was waiting at the top.

He kissed her, a brief hard kiss full on the lips that shocked and delighted her by turns, then he hurried her a few yards down the corridor and opened the door into his chamber. Or rather a suite of rooms. This first room was a grand sitting room, with a sofa and armchairs and beautifully polished wood. The muted dark blues and reds made it seem like a very male domain. An interior door led to another room, which she assumed must be the bedroom.

'How very grand,' she remarked, looking around.

'As Earl, I am entitled to the best bedroom in the house.'

She chuckled. 'I can imagine Lady Frances saying those very words.'

He smiled. 'Please. Have a seat.' He poured them both some brandy and handed her a glass and sat beside her on the sofa. 'We might as well be comfortable.'

Always so thoughtful.

She sipped at her drink. It was the very best brandy. She was glad Lady Frances was taking such good care of him.

He gave her a considering glance. 'Do you want to start?'

Did she? Yes, she must. Because if she did not, she might never say what had to be said. 'I am sorry I jumped to such an awful conclusion about you and Kitty Jenks. I value our friendship too much not to attempt an apology. You are right when you said I should have known better. I do hope you will forgive me.' One thing she knew for certain was that she could not bear it if he now hated or despised her.

His mouth tightened a fraction. 'I, too, value our friendship.' He hesitated. 'To be honest, given that you had already declined my offer of marriage, I did not understand why you would react so strongly to a young inebriated wench making improper overtures towards me as if it was all my fault.'

Somehow, he had managed to give her the perfect opening to explain. To reveal her deepest fear. If she dared take it.

She sipped at her drink, whether to grab some courage or time or a bit of both, she wasn't sure. But if she did not take this chance to explain, how could she ever expect him to understand?

'I was very young when I met Harry, my husband,' she said. 'Thirteen. He was only three years older, though it seemed a great deal more at the time. He was charming and fun and he used to talk to me as if I was the most interesting person in the world, unlike my older brothers, who could not wait to get away from me. To them I was nothing but a nuisance.'

'I never had siblings,' he said, 'so it is hard for me to relate, but I can recall friends who had little sisters. They were much the same.'

'Harry was so different from my brothers. So charming. He always took the time to speak to me. I learned later he could not help himself. There was never a female he met that he did not feel obligated to charm. But back then, I thought I was the only one. And I decided he was the man I was going to marry.'

She hung her head in shame when she thought back to how she had plotted and schemed to be in his company every time he visited their home.

'You are a very determined lady,' he said gently. 'It is not a bad trait.'

She forced a smile. 'I am not so sure. I was a spoiled brat, used to getting everything I wanted. Mama died not long after I was born and it so happened I take after her in looks. My older siblings all said I was Papa's favourite and, truth to tell, I knew it. I used his weakness to get what I wanted.'

'And you wanted Harry.'

'Yes. Unfortunately for him, his father also wanted the match. He was in trade and what better way to lift the family up than by marrying into the nobility. He handed over a handsome sum for the privilege of becoming part of our family. Apparently, Harry was pushed into making me an offer.

'I had no idea whatsoever that it was being forced on him. I was full of romantic dreams and proud of being his wife. Until I caught him kissing one of my friends at a party. Another time I found him flirting with my ladies' maid. He laughed it off. Blamed the lady and the maid and said it would not happen again. But it did. Repeatedly.'

Misery filled her heart. She had never been good enough for Harry.

'Finally, I accused him of not loving me or he wouldn't be tempted to stray. He told me he had never loved me and that he wished we had never met. In fact, he said marrying me had ruined his life. The next day he went to join the army on the Peninsula, taking my brother and my brother-in-law with him. They had made some sort of stupid bet about who would make the better soldier. I should never have objected to his dalliances. He was only doing what fashionable men do. All my friends said so.'

Ethan took her hand and stroked it. Even through two layers of gloves it was a lovely sensation. Comforting. Understanding. 'Are you saying because you confronted him with his infidelities, you somehow caused his death?'

'If I had just let him do as he pleased, he would never have gone off to war and Marguerite and Carrie would not have lost their husbands. I swore then that I would never marry again. I was clearly not cut out to be a conformable wife.'

'The man was a fool not to see the treasure he had won.'

Her heart gave a sweetly painful little thump. She swallowed. 'That is the kind of thing my family used to say. But how can I believe it? I chased the man until he had no option but to offer me marriage. I spent hours in his company on our estate, yet I didn't know him at all. He hated the country. He was only happy when in London attending balls and gambling hells.'

'He should have told you this before you wed.' He made a wry face. 'I have met other men like your husband. Men who need to conquer every woman who cross their path. There are also a great many more of us who are true to their wives, you know.'

'I know. There must be something wrong with me, that I could not keep his attention. That is what makes it so hard. Knowing if I had been a better wife, a more interesting woman, Neville Saxby and my other brother might also be alive today.'

'Nonsense. You did everything a wife was supposed to do, not to mention that you are beautiful and clever and sweet. What more could a man want in a wife?'

It wasn't enough. Not without love.

She shook her head miserably. 'I do not know.'

His heart went out to her. Indeed, it was a most painful feeling in his chest now he realised how badly she had been treated, not just by her husband, who was clearly an ass, but also by her family in allowing her to marry at such a young age.

He had learned that all young people go through what was commonly called calf love. He'd experienced it first-hand with one of his superiors' wives when he was about sixteen. He'd made calf's eyes at her for weeks. Fortunately, she'd been kind and motherly and he had recovered very quickly. And later, as he'd matured, he'd recognised it for what it was when other recruits had gone through similar experiences.

Never had any of them married their objects of utter devotion, but then, most of those ladies had been married.

'Petra, I can imagine Harry being flattered by your adoration and letting it go to his head. But he was three years older and three years wiser, and once he agreed to marry you he should have done his duty and been loyal to his wife.'

'His duty.' She sounded appalled.

Damn.

He closed his eyes briefly. 'Ah, yes, my proposal.'

She pulled her hand from his and clasped her hands in her lap. 'Please do not think I am expecting you to offer for me again. I am not. Nor would I accept—'

He touched a finger to her lips. 'I was an ass.'

She kept her gaze fixed on her hands, but he could tell by the slight straightening of her back that she was listening.

He forced himself to continue. 'I waffled on about friendship and duty and companionship when I should have told you instead what was in my heart. Petra, I grew up in a household where my father used love as a weapon. If you did not do exactly what he wanted, praise him to the skies, devote yourself to pleasing him, then you clearly did not love and respect him as you ought. He cared nothing for anyone's accomplishments or successes unless it added something to his own. And when I fell out of favour, which was often, then I fell out of favour with my mother, too. She would whisper that she loved me, but never ever took my side against my father even when she knew I was right. Not that I was the only one to suffer because of his pride. My mother took her fair share of his temper and accusations. When I joined the army, I thought I had found a haven of peace.' He laughed. 'How ironic is that?'

She was gazing at him now. 'It sounds as if you were never sure you were loved.'

'I was not loved in the true sense of the word,' he

said flatly. 'I also learned to distrust the use of that word. It usually followed some sort of punishment.'

'Oh, Ethan, here I am bemoaning that my family loved me far too much for my own good and you were deprived of even a smidgeon of family closeness. What a selfish person I am.'

He retrieved one of her hands and brought it to his lips. He wasn't sure how he'd managed to say all of that, but her response was just what his poor bruised heart needed. 'No. You are a person who gives love as well as receives it. Whereas I have avoided anything closer than distant friendship, or at most companionship. I thought I was happier that way. But when you told me, and rightly so, that what I offered was not enough for you, well, it made me think that perhaps I was missing something important.

'Petra, dearest, I have been drifting through life feeling reasonably contented, satisfied by my work, sure of my honour until I met you. Then I started feeling uneasy to say the least.'

'Oh, Ethan, I am so sorry. I had no idea I made you uncomfortable.'

Hell. That wasn't exactly what he meant. Not at all close.

'What I am trying to say is that, although it has taken me some time to understand what has changed, I now realise that I love you. Indeed, I am in love.' He realised with a wince that he sounded surprised, when he had intended to sound confident and sure of himself.

She gave him a worried look. 'You are?'

'I am.' He threw caution to the wind and went down on one knee. 'Darling, I love you madly. Marry me, please.'

Her pretty face crumpled as if she was going to cry and a chill ran through his blood. She was going to turn him down. Again. He had said too little too late.

'But I am a widow and I have nothing to bring to a marriage. And what if you tire of me and look elsewhere for companionship? I wouldn't be able to bear it.'

He took her in his arms and held her. 'It cannot happen, because I really, truly love you. You have all my heart, my love. There is nothing left for anyone else. I promise.'

He brushed her lips with his and she looked at him shyly. 'I love you so very much, Ethan. Until now, I was afraid to trust what my heart was telling me. It hurt so badly when I thought I had lost you.'

His heart swelled in his chest at her painful admission. He enfolded her in his arms. 'I will trust in that love to see me through all the years of my life. I will never ever give you cause to doubt me, sweetheart, I promise. Shall we go and announce our engagement to the awaiting world?'

'What? Now?'

'Do you still have doubts, then, my sweet?' He held his breath, but, no, he let his breath go. His Petra was as loyal and true as he was himself. And brave, too. She would never back away from a challenge.

'No doubts at all.' She hesitated. 'Oh, dear, but what about Marguerite? I will be leaving her to manage alone.'

'We will invite her to live with us. There is lots of room at Longhurst. She may have a whole wing to herself if she wishes, my love.'

My love. He would never tire of saying it. Until

now, he hadn't realised it was the one thing he didn't have. Had never had. And it was the one thing he really needed.

Her heart was in her eyes when she gazed back at him. 'Oh, Ethan, thank you. I do love you so much. You are the kindest, sweetest...' She flung her arms around his neck and kissed him.

And he would never ever tire of her kisses. When they finally broke apart, they were both grinning like children. He could never remember feeling as happy as he did at this moment.

He squeezed her hard. 'Then let us not delay, please. Let us announce it to the world. Today. Now.'

'I see you have no sympathy for all those debutantes waiting below in hopes of snagging an earl.'

He laughed out loud. 'Not when I can only think of you.'

She sighed. 'That is the most romantic thing I have ever heard. Let's do it.' She swallowed. 'What will Lady Frances say?'

He grinned. 'She will do what any sensible general does when he is faced with defeat. She will withdraw with good grace and say it was part of her strategy all along.'

'Then lay on, Macduff, for tonight will be ours.'

'And all the nights following.'

Arm in arm they went down to the ballroom to make their announcement.

Epilogue

'Let me take a look at you, gal.' Lady Frances rustled into Petra's chamber at the Westram town house, where Marguerite and Carrie were helping her dress for her wedding. Petra had grown fond of Lady Frances, despite her rather dictatorial manner.

Today, the old dear looked magnificent in a striped-black-and-emerald-green silk gown, though her grey-powdered wig with its stiff curls and elaborate decorations made her look eccentric rather than fashionable. When questioned, Lady Frances had explained her hair was far too thin and white to be worn au naturel and, she had added in lowered tones, she felt naked without her wig.

Carrie and Marguerite stepped back out of Lady Frances's way.

Petra twirled to give her about-to-be relative a full view of her wedding gown of rose silk, decorated with Bruges lace and pale cream ribbons. 'Do I meet with your approval, Lady Frances?' she asked in teasing tones.

Lady Frances stared down her nose, but there was a

twinkle in her eyes. 'Pretty enough. I'll say one thing about this modern-day taste for skimpy skirts—looking at your figure, there will be no talk of a babe.'

Marguerite gasped.

Carrie choked on a laugh.

It was also the reason Lady Frances has insisted on a St George's wedding, with the banns being called and the whole of the *ton* invited to witness. There must be nothing havey-cavey or rushed about a Longhurst wedding, she had declared.

While it had been the longest three weeks of Petra's life, she and Ethan had survived the wait and now, today, she was getting married. Her heart picked up speed at the thought of the eyes that would be watching her as she walked down the aisle. But why would she not want to please an old woman who had been nothing but kind, in her own gruff way?

Petra rose up on her toes and kissed the old woman's powdered cheek, inhaling the scent of attar of roses and brandy. 'I am glad you are pleased.'

Lady Frances cackled. 'I liked your spirit the first time I met you, my gal. Now, enough of your titivating, Westram is pacing the floor downstairs.'

'I will be down in a moment.' Petra had quickly realised that while Lady Frances's bark was worse than her bite, the woman was a shocking bully and would ride roughshod over anyone who did not stand up to her. 'But, my dear cousin Frances, you need to leave for St George's right away if you wish to arrive ahead of me.' Lady Frances was renowned for not letting her carriage move faster than a crawl.

The old lady glanced over at her sisters and frowned.

'Who are you?' she asked, pointing a gnarled finger at Carrie.

'That is my sister-in-law, Lady Avery,' Petra said. 'I told you she and Lord Avery were invited to the wedding.'

Lady Frances grunted. 'The other Westram widow.'

Petra winced. None of them liked to be reminded of their disastrous first marriages. Especially Marguerite.

'That's right, my lady,' Carrie said calmly. 'But I'm a married lady now and a Gilmore besides, but I still consider Marguerite and Petra as my sisters, as I hope they consider me.' She opened her arms wide and Petra and Marguerite moved to each side and tucked an arm around her waist.

'Always,' Petra agreed.

'We suffered a great deal together,' Marguerite explained. She gave them both a warm smile. 'It does my heart good to see them happy.'

'Sentimental claptrap,' Lady Frances declared, but she looked pleased. 'All we need now is to see the last of you married and no doubt your brother will be very satisfied. And relieved.'

Marguerite paled.

'Not every widow needs to re-enter the married state,' Petra said firmly, ushering Lady Frances towards the door. 'Why, you yourself never married again after the death of your husband.'

Another cackle greeted this sally. 'I was already an old woman before my Peter died. Well past my child-bearing years and not once did he chide me for not giving him his heir.' She glanced back over her shoulder at Carrie and Marguerite, grinned and winked. 'Not that we didn't give it our best try.'

Carrie giggled. Marguerite looked pained.

'Well, you can be assured Longhurst and I will also give it our very best effort,' Petra said. She opened the door and shooed the old lady out, closing it before the woman could deliver yet another of her shockingly frank remarks.

Carrie collapsed on the bed with a hand over her mouth and her eyes dancing with merriment.

Marguerite lifted her chin. 'It's a good thing she plans to retire back to Bath after the wedding. She is a handful and no mistake.'

'I know,' Petra said. 'But Longhurst seems to manage her very well. She has accepted that he is head of the family.' She chuckled. 'He just has to smile at her and she turns up sweet.'

'He is an extremely charming man, Petra. You have found yourself a gem,' Carrie declared.

'Not charming enough to convince Marguerite to live with us at Longhurst Park,' Petra said. Both she and Ethan had tried to convince Marguerite it was for the best, without success. She was determined to maintain her independence.

'You are planning to get married today, are you not?' Marguerite gave a significant glance at the ormolu clock on the mantel. 'Your poor bridegroom will start to worry that you have changed your mind.'

'Oh,' Petra said, realising how close to the hour it was. 'Let us go.'

They walked down to the carriage arm in arm and climbed in. Red gave the orders to the coachman, who really didn't need any orders. He knew exactly where they were going.

'Next is your wedding, Red,' Marguerite said when he had settled himself beside Carrie.

'It is,' he said, shoulders stiffening as if the reminder was not exactly pleasant. 'The offer still stands for you to come and live with me at Danesbury, you know, Marguerite.'

'Or with us in Wrendean, my dear,' Carrie offered.

'I wouldn't dream of intruding on newly married couples,' Marguerite said firmly. 'It would make none of us happy. I promise I will not be a stranger to your homes and will visit as often as you would care to invite me, but I am happy in Westram with my drawings for company.'

'And she has said the same to me,' Petra added, 'but you may be assured I will be visiting our sister every other day, so you have no need for worry.' Red did worry about her and Marguerite, and Carrie, too, but Petra wanted her sister to lead the life she wanted.

'Not quite every other day, I hope,' Marguerite said drily.

They all laughed and the tension in Red's shoulders eased.

The coach drew up at the door of St George's. On the steps, Lord Avery was waiting for his wife. He looked so handsome in the weak early-December sunlight and the way Carrie's face lit up when he took her arm and gazed down at her was a delight to see. She knew her own face lit up the same way, whenever she looked at Ethan. She just wished Marguerite could find a similar joy.

That wasn't fair. Marguerite was perfectly happy with her independent state and Petra certainly did not want her sister to lose what she considered her precious freedom.

Once the others had entered the church, Red helped her down. He gave her a cheerful brotherly smile, though there were shadows in his eyes. 'It is not too late to change your mind, you know.'

Her jaw dropped. 'W-what?' she spluttered.

He gave her a look askance and shrugged. 'I have been doing some thinking. I do not want you to feel obliged to wed just to please me.'

'I can assure you, I am marrying to please no one but myself.' And Ethan, of course. Dear Ethan.

Red nodded. 'Then on your head be it.'

He had to be jesting, surely. She shook her head at him. 'Really, Red, you do pick the worst of times to tease me. Really, you do.'

His mouth tightened, but he held out his arm to her and together they walked beneath the imposing portico and through the great doors into the church.

Standing at the altar, Ethan turned to watch her walk towards him. For some reason, while this was exactly the way she had pictured this in her mind for the past three weeks, she suddenly felt terribly nervous. Everything inside her fluttered wildly. This was her second time walking down the aisle after all.

Ethan smiled and held out his hand, taking a few steps towards her as she approached. She calmed. This was Ethan. Her beloved, sweet, dear Ethan, who had been deprived of love as a child, yet love for her still shone in his lovely blue eyes and in his expression.

She smiled back and placed her hand in his and together they walked the last few steps to meet their new life. He leaned close. 'You look beautiful. Have I told you recently how much I love you?' he murmured.

'Every day, for the last three weeks,' she whispered back, hugging the memory of their stolen kisses.

'Every day, except today,' he whispered. 'I do love you, my darling Petra.'

'And I love you,' she murmured, leaning into him.

The Vicar gave them a severe look over his glasses.

They released hands and Ethan nodded at him to begin.

'Dearly beloved,' the Vicar said.

Petra had never felt so happy or beloved in her entire life and she knew she would feel like this for ever.

* * * * *

If you enjoyed this story,
be sure to read the first book in
The Widows of Westram miniseries:

A Lord for the Wallflower Widow

And while you're waiting for the next book,
check out these other great reads
by Ann Lethbridge:

Secrets of the Marriage Bed
An Innocent Maid for the Duke
Rescued by the Earl's Vows